The Watcher

By

Lisa Voisin

The Watcher
Copyright © 2013 Lisa Voisin
All rights reserved.

ISBN-13: (Print) 978-0-9856562-2-5

ISBN-13: (ebook) 978-0-9856562-1-8

Inkspell Publishing
5764 Woodbine Ave.
Pinckney, MI 48169

Edited By . Rie Langdon
Cover art By Najla Qamber

Library of Congress Control Number: 2013900872

Praise for The Watcher:

Voisin's story builds in strength, easing readers into Mia's first encounter with another realm and drawing them on, inescapably, to the shocking discovery at the novel's heart. Inventive, romantic, and filled with tension, this is a great start to an intriguing series. --A.M. Dellamonica, author of INDIGO SPRINGS and BLUE MAGIC.—winner of the Sunburst Award for Indigo Springs.

"Perfect for fans of angels and demons, Lisa Voisin has created an uplifting tale of redemption, love, and spirituality that gives hope. Never preachy, The Watcher is the perfect answer to critics who claim Young Adult literature is too dark."--Stephanie Lawton, author of Want and Shrapnel

"Voisin's THE WATCHER blends paranormal mystery and romance into a book that is sure to keep readers turning the pages late into the night."--Eileen Cook, author of THE ALMOST TRUTH

"Filled with forbidden love and a war between good and evil. If you are a fan of the Twilight Saga and The Mortal Instrument series, you will love this book."--Selena Lost in Thought

"This book was amazing and grabbed me from the very first chapter."--Angie Stanton-Johnson at Twinsie Talk Book Reviews

"[A] deliciously captivating story, that definitely earned FIVE STARS! "--Iris, from Booksessions

LISA VOISIN

DEDICATION

For Matthew

Chapter One

I'd never seen a dead body before.

The man lay on the ground near an uprooted tree stump with his face turned away. His tangled gray hair glimmered like ancient pewter in the late summer sun. He wore plaid pants with muddy cuffs and leather shoes split with holes. His tattered brown coat, stained from years of wear, was far too warm for daytime. Had he been here all night?

Was he even breathing? Somebody should check. But since I was alone in the middle of a park, at the intersection of two heavily-wooded trails, "somebody" meant me.

If he were dead, his skin would be cold, but I didn't want to touch him to find out. I couldn't help him if he needed serious medical attention. I couldn't even call 9-1-1. My cell phone was dead on the sofa at home. If only I could call Mom at the hospital. She'd know what to do.

He could be sleeping. I watched for the rise and fall of his chest. Either it wasn't moving or my mind was playing tricks on me. I pulled a tissue from my purse and leaned over to place it in front of his nose. Loud cawing startled me. I vaulted, staggered over the man, and almost fell right on top of him.

Behind me, a crow landed on a high cedar branch and fluffed its shiny black wings.

"Stupid crow." I turned back to the man.

The air chilled. Hoarfrost trickled down my spine, and over the aroma of cedar and damp earth I smelled rotten eggs. Covering my nose, I backed away.

A sharp pain pulsed behind my eyes, followed by a high-pitched hum. Squinting, I saw a hazy shadow appear over the man, the kind you see when clouds pass over the sun.

The shadow started to move, undulating at first, then roiling and twisting into a heavy smoke that grew darker, more substantial. Inky blackness folded in on itself like boiled tar, forming first a head, then a muzzle as the darkness stretched out into a neck...body...four legs.

What kind of shadow does this?

Then it growled.

My stomach clenched into a tiny fist, and a voice inside me shouted: *Run. Now!*

I sprinted down one of the trails, scanning the forest for any sign of shadows. The path narrowed until it was barely a few feet wide, and the gravel beneath me surrendered to dirt. Soon I was dodging serpentine roots and mossy, fallen logs. Low-hanging branches caught in my hair. My pace slowed. In the dense underbrush, looming trees birthed shadows everywhere, none of them like the one I'd just seen.

I stopped. Listened. Heard my own breathing and the whooshing of cars from the main road. In the distance, seagulls screeched at each other. Closer were more crows. Perhaps it was safe.

With a sudden crashing of leaves, the shadowy creature bounded through the underbrush, baring its teeth. Solid now, and huge, it was bigger than any dog, with fur so black as to absorb the light and red eyes that glowed like lasers. I tried to scream, but the air had been sucked from my lungs. I made only a dry rasp.

My heart hammering against my ribs, I pressed through a wall of branches to an open clearing and made a dash for it. The creature was on my heels, but then it flickered and faded back into the shadows like a ghost.

Looking for it, I twisted and tripped, bashing my knee. The creature melted out from the branches. *Would shadow teeth hurt as bad as real ones?*

I tried to get up, but my muscles trembled and refused to work. White static erased my thoughts.

As the creature slowly edged closer, sure of its prey, I closed my eyes, sucked in my breath, and, finally, screamed.

A blinding flash against my eyelids silenced me, so I kept my eyes closed. I heard a strange muttering, a chorus of male and female voices, layers of tones speaking all at once. They were clouded by static.

"Report."

"A breach. I think it's torn."

"Well, seal it."

"There's a girl… No—it can't be!"

"We should go."

The voices stopped. A silent wind rushed over me, like a tickling of feathers against my skin. When I opened my eyes, everything around me had calmed. The sun shone brightly overhead and the park was empty. The shadowy creature was gone.

I gulped air into my aching lungs, waiting.

Across the clearing, at least forty yards away, stood a tall figure in a gray T-shirt and jeans. At that distance, I couldn't tell how old he was. All I could make out was dark hair, a strong jaw, and the fact that he was staring right at me.

I nearly hollered at him, but stopped. For all I knew, he could be some kind of stalker who followed girls into the park. Or worse. Maybe the shadowy dog was his.

Who the hell are you? I thought.

The guy jolted as though I'd startled him.

Had he heard me? I hadn't said a word.

Instead of speaking, he turned and walked away.

As I got up, brushing the wet grass off my sore knee and legs, I realized I was shaking. All I had were questions. The body I'd found—who was that? What had just happened? What was that horrible creature? How did it just disappear?

And most important, what did it want with *me?*

Chapter Two

I arrived at the mall tired and sweaty, with my stomach tangled in knots. The parking lot heaved with shoppers scurrying to take advantage of any last-minute back-to-school sales, while mothers pushed shopping carts filled with screaming kids. Even in public, the slightest shadow creeping along the pavement made me jump.

Inside the mall, my friend Heather lounged by the fountain, checking out the crowds. She waved, and just seeing her sent a flood of relief through me. Dressed in black and white, with her blond hair pulled into a sleek ponytail, everything about her looked crisp and fresh. Unlike me.

"Mia." She rushed to hug me. "It's so good to see you."

I swallowed the lump that formed in my throat. *I will not cry.* "Hi," was all I could say.

"I know we texted and emailed, but…" She paused, her smile fading. I must have looked worse than I thought. "You're flushed. Did you run or something?"

"Uh, yeah." I tried to stay calm, but my voice wavered. "Can I borrow your cell?"

She handed it to me. "Where's yours?"

"It's dead. Can you believe I left my charger in Denver?" My hands trembled as I dialed 9-1-1.

A woman's voice answered, "9-1-1. What is your emergency?"

"I don't know if it's an emergency or not," I began.

"Oh my God." Heather leaned in. "Are you okay?"

"I'm fine. Really," I said to Heather and, covering my ear, spoke into the phone. "There's this old man in the park, and he's just lying there."

"Was he breathing?" the woman asked.

"I don't know."

"Where exactly is he?"

I gave the man's location, adding, "I think he's homeless."

"Okay, we'll send a cruiser," the woman said.

I hung up and handed the phone back to Heather.

"You found a body?" she asked.

Before I could answer, Fiona joined us. "You guys, Dean's here! He just texted, and he wants to hang out." Smiling, she bobbed up and down on her toes, which made her seem even taller.

"Now?" Heather asked.

"Yeah." Fiona's cell phone chirped. She checked it, her smile growing even brighter. "He's nearby."

"Well, it's about time, I guess," Heather said as Fiona typed her response. "You've been dropping hints all summer. If he didn't ask you out, I was going to ask him for you."

"*The* Dean?" I asked. My mind fuzzy, I strained to catch up. "Dean Wilson? The one you've been crazy about all year?"

Fiona turned to me, as though she'd just noticed I was there. "Hey, Mia, how was your summer?" She scanned my sweater and blue sundress. "Cute outfit."

"Thanks," I said, checking it for grass.

"You've got a twig." Fiona motioned to the back of her strawberry-blond mane to show me, but when I touched my hair I didn't feel anything, so she smiled and pulled it out herself. "What happened to you? You look…"

I knew what the next word out of her mouth should have been. She was holding back.

My legs still shook, so I perched on the edge of the fountain and contemplated *how* to explain what had happened. Part of me was screaming not to speak of it. Ever. As though talking about it would make it real. But it couldn't be. *Could it?*

Both my friends were staring at me. My mouth was no doubt hanging open. I needed to say something.

"I–I'm not sure." I hugged my knees into my chest. "I saw this old man and he wasn't moving, and then this dog came at me. At least I think it was a dog."

What *else* could it have been? Remembering its red eyes, the way its form flickered and disappeared, I shuddered.

"Are you okay?" asked Fiona. I'd spaced out again.

I nodded.

"What kind of dog?" Heather asked.

What kind of dog, indeed. "It was huge and black, with a long muzzle, like Anubis." I knew my reference was strange, but Heather had seen enough Egyptian art at my place to know what I meant.

Fiona sat beside me and smoothed the hem of her denim miniskirt. "Maybe it was a bear."

Heather was her usual skeptical self. "A bear? In West Seattle?"

"Yeah. I saw this movie last week. It was set in New York after the apocalypse. A bear took over the city and started to eat people."

"Oh my God, Fiona. *Apocalypse?* You don't *believe* those horror movies you watch, do you?" Heather asked, hands on her hips.

Until this morning, I would have agreed with her. But what I saw could have come from a horror film. Not

11

a bear, though. Something told me this thing was much worse. The memory of it receded, hazy now, as though I were recalling a nightmare.

"Of *course* I don't." Fiona crossed her long, lanky arms, ready to scrap. "How can you be sure it *wasn't* a bear? Wild animals are displaced all the time by deforestation."

"It's probably a stray." Heather turned her attention back to me. "What would make it attack you?"

"I wasn't carrying dog treats, if that's what you mean." I meant it as a joke, but there was an edge to my voice. The entire experience had been surreal. How could I ever explain the way that shadow had formed over the old man? "Can we talk about something else?"

No longer paying attention, Fiona played with her hair and glanced around, no doubt looking for Dean.

Heather pulled a large envelope out of her bag and handed it to me. "Here. I found it at a shop in the U district—welcome back."

"Wow. Thanks," I said. My hands shook as I opened it, but if Heather noticed, she didn't say anything.

Inside, on a piece of thin vellum paper, was a black and white design of angel wings, each feather meticulously outlined and shaded. They would fit perfectly between my shoulder blades.

"It's temporary. Goes on matte, the kind they use in the movies."

"They're amazing, Heather," I said, hugging her. "Thank you." I'd wanted wings tattooed on my back ever since I first dreamt about them in the tenth grade. But my mom wouldn't let me get them, not until I was at least eighteen.

"A real tattoo is so permanent," Heather said.

"That's the whole point," I said, remembering the wings in my dream. Huge and white, they shimmered in the darkness. Someone was always trying to steal them. "They'd become a part of me." *No one could take them away.*

Fiona turned back to me. "How was Denver?" she asked. "Did you have a nice visit with your dad?"

"All right." I shrugged. "He worked a lot, as usual." More like he was avoiding me. I hadn't been back in over a year, since Mom and I moved away. This was *supposed* to be our chance to catch up, but I hardly saw him. He couldn't even make time to drive me to the airport.

"Well, it's good to have you back," Fiona said. Her attention kept shifting to some guy in the food court. He had caramel-colored hair. When he turned around and waved, I realized it was Dean. I didn't remember his hair being so light.

Fiona waved back at him and said, "I should go."

Heather rolled something cherry-scented on her lips. "Text me if you want to meet up later," she said. When she finished glossing, she reached an arm around my back and pulled a dead leaf from my long, tangled brown hair. "I brought a brush. Let's get you tidied up."

Before I could even think about how many strangers had seen me in this state, she had me back on my feet, hurtling into the crowds.

***

Our next stop, the food court, buzzed like an upset hornet's nest. It was even shaped like one: circular with at least a dozen vendors along the outside. Inside, a large seating area wrapped itself around a small cluster of palm trees, and a high, Pantheon-shaped glass dome bled direct sunlight on everyone eating below.

Heather rushed off to get herself a smoothie and find us an empty table, but I had no idea what I wanted. I must have walked the perimeter three times before settling on some onion rings and a cola. After I ordered, the woman working the counter gave me a number and told me to wait, so I searched the rotunda for Heather.

Instead, I spotted a tall, broad-shouldered guy with wavy dark hair standing with his back against one of the palm trees. As he scanned the area with a steady, watchful gaze, I noticed his hair, his size, his gray T-shirt and jeans.

The guy from the park!

Instinctively, I ducked behind the garbage station so he couldn't see me, and wondered what he was doing there. Had he *followed* me? He was younger than I'd thought, around my age, but that didn't mean anything. Stalkers didn't have to be old. In the park, he'd been in shadows. Now, sunlight from the domed ceiling caught the dust particles in the air and bathed him in a golden light—as though he were the Persian sun god Mithra himself—and for a moment, I forgot everything that had happened.

It was one of those rare times where I wished I could paint, just so I could catch the effect of that light playing off his skin. His features belonged in a painting too: straight nose, even jaw, full lips that curled slightly at the edges as though something amused him. Under any other circumstances, I might have found him attractive. That is, if my stomach hadn't kept turning over from the second I recognized him.

"Excuse me," a woman's voice said right behind me. She startled me so badly I jumped. "Number sixty-three?"

I turned. The woman who had taken my order handed me my food on a teal-colored tray.

"I called several times," she scolded, and shaking her head, walked away.

Wondering if this woman had outed me, I turned back, but the guy was gone. Curiosity outweighing fear, I stepped out from my hiding place. He couldn't have gone far. Had he run off? Sat down somewhere? Guys that tall usually stood out in crowds, but he had disappeared.

When I was sure he wasn't going to leap out at me from behind one of the palm trees, I went off in search of Heather. I found her sitting at a small table on the other side of the trees.

"What took you so long?" she demanded.

I raised my tray and made an apologetic face. "Had to wait for the onions to grow."

I was so queasy I didn't know if I could eat at first, but the onion rings and cola slid right down—the miracle of grease and sugar. I kept looking around in case the guy returned. He had to have gone somewhere. He couldn't have just disappeared.

"Is everything okay? You're acting weird," Heather said.

"I don't want you to freak out."

"What do you mean you don't want me to freak out?" she said. "What kind of opening is that?" Realizing how loud she was getting, she put down her drink and leaned across the table, lowering her voice. "Tell me what's going on."

"Well, after the, um, dog chased me…there was this guy staring at me, and I'm not sure, but I think he's here."

"You *think* he's here?"

"I might have seen him," I replied.

She sat up, looking around frantically. "Do you think he's following you?"

"I don't know," I said, wishing I hadn't brought it up. There were plenty of guys my age who wore gray T-shirts and jeans. I could probably count a dozen today in the mall alone. Besides, this guy was taller, well over six feet, and broader in the shoulders.

"What does he look like?" She stood up. "We'll go to security."

"No." Grabbing her arm, I pulled her back down. Now I had her fear to deal with as well as my own. "I can't even be sure it was him. I think I'm just freaking out."

"But—"

"Even if it was him, he hasn't actually *done* anything, has he? So he was in the park and now he's here? That's not a crime," I said, but I wasn't sure which one of us needed convincing: me or her.

Taking a long, loud slurp from her almost-empty smoothie, she studied me, no doubt trying to figure out if I was telling the truth. "Okay, but if you see him again?"

"We'll go right to security," I promised.

Chapter Three

That night, I had the strangest dream.

Two great birds were locked in combat. Talons entwined, they spiraled toward the ground. One of them had blood pooling in holes where its eyes should have been. The other dripped blood from its claws. Behind them, the sky shone a purplish black, the color of bruises, and the air smelled of charcoal. As the birds fell, I kept wishing they would separate, that at least one of them would let go, flap its wings, and fly away.

I even cried out, trying to startle them out of their fight, but their battle seemed endless. And I could do nothing but watch, unable to reach them, unable to stop their fall.

***

It was the first day of school and the grounds hummed with excitement. Students hovered everywhere—some standing, some sitting, some walking and talking—greeting people they hadn't seen in months. Above us, the September sun shone so bright and warm it could have been July. Blue sky reflected off the windows of the school, a tall, modern, wood building. Its three-story glass foyer let in tons of light and made me far too visible. Senior year should have been exciting, but all I wanted was to head inside where the walls could keep me safe.

"Safe" was a relative term. When I got to my locker, I discovered it was next to Elaine Carter's. Apparently I got *her* spot in AP Ancient Civ last year when I'd first arrived at Westmont. She'd never forgiven me. I loved the class, but Elaine's obsession made it like those ruby slippers in the Wizard of Oz—they came with a half-crazed witch chasing after them, too. Before Dorothy could find out what she was in for and say *no thanks*, it was too late. The shoes were already on her feet.

Elaine always wore designer labels, not the knock-offs, and she'd had her red hair cropped short over the summer. If she weren't such a bitch to me, I might have said she looked good. Instead, we gave each other tight-lipped smiles and fake hellos before I opened my locker and unloaded my bag. No point in being rude. Elaine ran a gossip blog so scandalous it would make Perez Hilton blush.

Being her neighbor wasn't only inconvenient, it was dangerous. I'd have to watch everything I said so it couldn't be used against me.

One of Elaine's friends rushed up to her, so I hid behind my locker door, hoping they'd forget I was there. As I put my things away, I could hear the two of them gossiping.

"Congratulations on getting your own column," the friend gushed.

Elaine had a column now? In the school paper? What had the rest of us done to deserve that?

"Thanks, Lor," Elaine replied. "It's about time we put something relevant in there."

Something *relevant?* I had to bite my lip so I wouldn't laugh out loud. With all the things going on in the world, how was gossip relevant?

Lor quickly changed the subject. "That new guy you saw." She chewed a piece of gum loudly as she spoke. "His name's Michael Fontaine, and he transferred from Sealth High."

"Yeah," Elaine said, "but is he newsworthy?"

She cracked her gum. "He had a major accident or something last spring—almost died—and couldn't graduate. So he's repeating senior year."

"You're sure?"

"Uh-huh. I hear he's really different, too."

I wondered what Lor meant by "different," but they changed the subject. Perhaps he had been disfigured, or confined to a wheelchair. Mom had told me all sorts of stories about terrible accidents from her years of working in hospitals, enough to put me off ever becoming a nurse. I was half-tempted to ask, but I made the mistake of asking Elaine a question about a guy last year, out of curiosity, and she posted on her stupid blog that I was interested in him. She hated me that much. So I kept my head down and hurried off to class. It was going to be a long year.

I didn't see my friends until lunchtime. Westmont High's cafeteria consisted of an indoor concession stand and a common area the size of Macy's with a wall of sliding glass windows rolled all the way open to let in the sun. Outside, a patio overlooked our track and football field, and the far edge of the school grounds backed onto a ravine.

Heather dashed for one of the large patio tables. "Let's sit out here."

I hesitated. Out here we'd be unprotected. Any sort of creature could come rushing right at us. "What if it gets cold?"

"Are you kidding? It's practically summer out here."

I nodded and sat with my back to the cafeteria so I could keep watch. Other students had obviously thought it was a good idea to spend lunch outside today, too. Some guys ran around tossing a football on the field, and a group of girls sat on the concrete, their voices a mixture of murmurs and squeals. Beside us, a few kids did their reading assignments in the sun. Everything seemed fine. There was safety in numbers, I hoped.

Fiona soon joined us. As we ate, I told them both about the strange dream I'd had the night before—how real it seemed—expecting I don't know what. Understanding?

"Freud said that flying dreams are really about sex," Heather answered plainly. She was planning to study psychology at college next year and had been reading everything she could get her hands on, from Freud to *Psychology Today*. She especially enjoyed diagnosing her friends. We were test subjects to her, lab bunnies.

"Sex?" Fiona perked up. "Now we're talking!"

"Did you hear *anything* else Mia said?" Heather asked.

"*Sex*? How did you even get sex out of *that*?" I gulped my orange juice and gazed out the window, wondering why I'd bothered saying anything. The dream was vivid and gory. The birds were tragic. Surely I didn't see sex that way. Not that I'd had *that* much experience to base it on. Making out with Paul Mathers at a party last summer didn't count.

"It could represent two sides of your own nature battling things out," Heather said. "You know, a fear of intimacy."

"I don't *fear* intimacy," I said, wondering if anyone else thought that about me. "Granted I don't have a boyfriend, but does that make me frigid or something?"

"Okay, *abandonment* then."

At that exact moment, Heather's boyfriend Jesse came along. He was with Dean, who slid onto the seat beside Fiona.

Jesse hesitated. I wondered how much he'd heard.

"Girl talk?" he asked.

"No," I said, welcoming a change of topic. "Have a seat."

Heather tucked a lock of blond hair behind her ear and grinned at Jesse. They were a blend of opposites. With his shoulder-length dark hair and leather jacket, he looked like a biker, while she was soft and feminine, verging on preppy.

Around Dean, Fiona's smile brightened and her laughter grew louder and more frequent. I couldn't help but think she was compensating for being two inches taller than him, but he ate it up. At least Heather played it a bit cooler with Jesse, so I wouldn't have to be sick.

"Hey, we're going hiking on Saturday—Fiona and I," Heather said. "We've been going all summer. Wanna come?"

"Yeah, we discovered this great trail," Fiona chimed in.

Hiking in the *woods*? Were they kidding me? I could barely stand eating outside on a busy patio.

I hesitated. "You going, Jesse?"

"Nope. Gotta work."

"Come on," Heather insisted. "The weather's supposed to be great."

Maybe I was being silly. It was time to live my life like a normal person again. "Okay," I said slowly. Surely a hike would be fine. I wouldn't be alone.

Jesse motioned to someone behind me. "Hey, Mike. Why don't you join us?"

"Hi, Jesse," said a rich, deep voice. It had just a hint of an accent.

I checked over my shoulder to see who was speaking and froze. *Mike?* It was the guy from the mall!

Fiona and Jesse moved over to make room for him at the table, and he ended up sitting across from me. Not knowing what to say, I studied the remains of my salad. If I recognized him, surely he must recognize me, too.

"Hi," he said. "I'm Michael Fontaine."

This was the new guy? Up close, he was even more attractive, and when his eyes widened for that fraction of a second after meeting mine, I actually thought I saw starlight. *Could he be any more gorgeous?*

"I'm Mia…short for Maria," I offered. My palms began to sweat.

"Hello, Mia short for Maria." His lips curved into a hint of a smile, but his gaze scorched right through me.

"H-hello." I wanted to say something to him about the day before, but didn't know how to start. Demanding to know what he'd been doing in the woods didn't seem the best opening. "W-Where'd you come from?"

He raised a perfectly arched eyebrow at me. "The lunch line?"

"Actually," I said, "I meant your accent."

"We moved here from England when I was ten."

He didn't ask about me. In the background, I could hear Fiona laughing too loudly at something Dean said. The fact that I was having a totally awkward moment made her laughter even more irritating.

"You seem really familiar," I blurted. "Have we met?"

He paled. "I don't think so."

Now what? Obviously he didn't recognize me, and I couldn't trust myself to speak without sounding stupid. *Mia short for Maria* and *have we met? God, I am so useless!*

One of the guys on the playing field shouted "Look out!" as a football hit the wall over my head. It landed on the concrete beside me. Michael got up and tossed the ball back to him.

"Careful," he said.

"Thanks," the guy shouted.

Michael folded his long legs back under our table and took a bite of his cheeseburger.

"Wasn't it you?" I sputtered, wondering why I was going down *that* road again. *What am I thinking?*

A muscle in his jaw twitched. "What?"

Not wanting to draw anyone else's attention to what I was about to say, I lowered my voice. "Weren't you in the park yesterday morning?"

He let out his breath and smiled down at his plate. "*That* was you?"

So it *was* him. Sitting across from me, he didn't seem too dangerous, unless you could kill someone with good looks. In which case he was *lethal*. "Whatever happened to…" I realized I couldn't accurately describe what I'd seen, and there was a look in his eye that I couldn't quite place. "Whatever happened to the weird dog?"

His smile never wavered. "Didn't see any dogs." It made me wonder if I'd noticed anything in his look at all.

"So you didn't see *anything*?" I asked, trying not to show my desperation. I had hoped for a witness, someone to tell me I wasn't crazy, that what I saw was real. But if it *was*, then what?

"Some girl screaming in the park."

The blood rushed to my cheeks as I realized how insane I must have sounded. Not only was I asking about a dog he hadn't seen, but I'd just let him know that the first time he saw me, I'd been screaming like a crazy person. No wonder he stared at me. Maybe I *was* seeing things and I actually *was* crazy.

No. I was sure there was a dog, *or something*. But it wasn't the time to make my point. "What about at the mall? What were you doing there?"

"The mall?"

"Yeah, what were you doing there?"

"Um…" Swallowing another bite, he furrowed his brow as though he were seriously concerned about my mental health. "Shopping. You?"

"Shopping," I said. Here I was thinking this guy was some kind of stalker when it was obvious he didn't recognize me.

He turned his attention to his French fries and ate one. I followed by eating a forkful of salad. Heather and Jesse were telling a story about someone in their drama class, but Michael wasn't listening. With his elbows propped on the table and his hands clasped, he took in his surroundings, sizing everything up. He seemed so observant; how could he not have seen that dog? Had it run away before he got there?

Michael's shoulders stiffened and he inclined his head like he was listening. Even though we had just met, there was something oddly familiar about him doing that, and not from the day before, either. It tugged at my memory like a headache. Had I seen him somewhere else too?

He stood abruptly. "Excuse me," he said.

"Where are you going?" Jesse asked. "We've got another half hour."

"I have to be somewhere," he said. He picked up his tray and left.

Once he was gone, Fiona leaned across the table. "That's the new guy, isn't it?" she asked. "He's really hot!"

"Hey," Dean said. "Should I be jealous?"

Fiona giggled, stroking his arm. "Of course not."

"How do you know him, Jess?" Heather asked.

"I used to go to Sealth too, remember?"

Heather fed Jesse a french fry. "So, dish. What's he like?"

"Decent. He parties a lot, doesn't take himself too seriously, used to ride a Triumph Daytona."

That last point made Jesse's face light up but left us girls unimpressed.

"It's a motorcycle," he explained.

"I heard something about an accident," I said. In spite of myself, I was curious, remembering what Elaine had been gossiping about.

"Yeah, last year." Jesse leaned across the table and checked to make sure we were listening before he continued. "Really bad, too. Totaled his bike."

"I heard that his heart stopped beating, but they revived him," Fiona added, twisting a lock of her hair and smiling at Dean. "He spent almost three weeks in a coma."

"Who told you that?" I asked her.

"Overheard Jen in the bathroom," she said. "Her cousin goes to Sealth. It's big news there."

"He's lucky to be alive," Heather said. She directed her next comment at Jesse. "I don't know how you can ride that bike of yours."

"Do you want to hear this or not?" he asked her, frowning.

"I know, I know," Heather muttered, scrunching her napkin into a ball. The fact that Jesse rode a motorcycle was a constant worry for her. It was the only thing they argued about.

"He got in that accident on the night of Brad Morelli's party," Jesse continued. "Remember that night? Huge storm—roads were terrible. Apparently, a tree fell over right in front of him." He reached for Heather's hand, and she let him hold it. "I'd never ride on a night like that, not after a party."

"A *tree fell over*? Doesn't that sound—I don't know," I said, not sure why the details of Michael's accident bothered me so much. "I mean, don't you think there's something *odd* about him? Why is he here? Why didn't he stay at Sealth?"

I wanted to tell Heather that he was the guy from the mall but something held me back. I didn't want to have to explain it with everyone there, especially when it was probably a coincidence. The mall and the park weren't that far apart. *He has the right to go shopping like everyone else.*

Heather's eyes widened, and a deep voice behind me said, "We moved."

I practically jumped as I spun around. There was no doubt Michael had heard me. It was as if the gods had all conspired for me to say or do the wrong thing around this guy. I wasn't even the gossiping type. What had come over me?

"Oh, hey, Mike," Jesse said, his face opening into an easy smile. If he was nervous about being caught, he covered well. "Speak of the devil."

Michael gave him a nod and motioned to where he'd been sitting. "Forgot my keys."

"Oh." Jesse grabbed them off the seat and tossed them at Michael. "Here."

Michael caught them in mid-air. "Thanks," he said to Jesse, then turned to me. The muscles of his jaw pulsed beneath his skin. "You don't know anything about me."

My face heated like I'd been running a marathon. It was all I could do not to cry, but I refused to let my feelings show. Being called out was embarrassing enough. Tears would only cause a scene.

"What was *that* all about?" Heather asked after he left.

Jesse shrugged. "Never seen him act that way before."

She turned to me. "Just forget about him, Mia."

Forget about him? If only I could

.

Chapter Four

The trailhead didn't seem like much at first—nothing to be frightened of, anyway. Its wooden sign had long since become overgrown by blackberry bushes, obscuring the name, and two giant cedars shrouded a wooden staircase that snaked its way up the hill. At the top of the stairs, the trail opened onto a wide dirt path shaded from the morning sun by a canopy of trees. Their roots, gnarled and knobby, gripped the earth like talons.

As my eyes adjusted to the dim light of the forest, I followed my friends, winding and zig-zagging along a trail that narrowed as the forest thickened. While my friends moved with ease, loose rocks nestled between the roots easily threw me off balance. I had to concentrate on my footing, using their steps as a guide.

Shade loomed everywhere and the threat of shadows lurked behind every tree, but Heather and Fiona didn't seem to notice.

"Did you manage to change your appointment, Fi?" Heather asked. "So we can run the booth at the team and club fair?"

"No," Fiona said. "There's no getting out of it."

"What's that?" I said, checking the bushes around us for movement, for sounds.

"It's new," Heather said. "All the clubs and sports teams have booths." She pulled her hair back into an elastic band. "It's to let everyone know what's available, kind of a job fair. Fiona and I were going to work it together, but she can't make it."

"Wish I could," Fiona said. "I hate going to the dentist."

The air cooled and a strange tickle ran down my spine.

"Did it just get colder?" I asked.

"The sea air's damp. It can seem cold," Heather said. "Or did you forget that in Denver?"

A shudder crawled along my skin. Droplets of sweat chilled on my brow. What was going on?

"Can you help out with the booth, Mia?" Heather said. "Hand out flyers?"

Looking around, I checked for moving branches in case a wind had brought the cold air, but the trees were perfectly still.

"Mia?"

"Uhh…yeah," I said. I hadn't answered her question. "Sure. I'll help."

Fiona's long legs carried her steps ahead of us. She slowed down to let Heather pass, so she could talk to me. "Did you meet any interesting guys in Denver?"

"What?"

"Guys. In Denver," she repeated slowly, as though I were dense. Her fair skin, also unaffected by the chill, glowed pink with exertion. *Was I imagining things?*

I stifled a shiver. "Nope. No guys." Maybe it was nothing.

"That's too bad."

Fiona made it sound tragic. Did she think I was pathetic or something? I tried to shrug it off, digging my hands in my pockets to warm them. "I was with Bill a lot," I said. Bill, my brother, was in his third year at Berkeley. He had come back to work for Dad over the summer, and if it weren't for him my summer would have completely sucked.

"How 'bout his friends?" Fiona grinned at me suggestively.

"Eww. No. *Not* computer geeks." I grimaced.

"You're never gonna get a boyfriend with that attitude," said Fiona. "You gotta be open to it."

I wanted to retaliate and say *Does being open mean I have to throw myself at guys the way you do?* But I held my tongue. It wasn't worth fighting over. Besides, after my encounter with Michael in the cafeteria last week, he wouldn't even look at me. So much for being "open." It was pointless.

As we continued along the path, the chill subsided. Fiona steered the conversation to the topic of Dean. I resigned myself to listen, all the while staying alert to any more strange sensations. There were none. I must have been freaking out over nothing.

***

The Peak, as they called it, had an unobstructed view of Puget Sound that was worth the climb. Below us, the mid-day sun glinted off the water surrounded by giant evergreens lining the cove. Dozens of boats cruised the harbor and a cool breeze blew in from the ocean, but it was nowhere near the same chill as before.

The hike back was mostly downhill, and the steep declines challenged my balance and coordination. The less experienced one of the group—half-sliding, half-hiking—I soon lagged behind my friends, who chatted happily, not noticing I'd slowed down.

The trickling sounds of the creek grew louder as we approached. The bridge was closed and cordoned off with yellow tape, but ten feet away spanning the creek was an old moss-covered fallen log, its soft bark crumbled with decay. Fiona and Heather practically skipped across it to the other side. I slowed down.

"Hey, guys. Wait up!" I called as they rounded the corner, but they didn't look back.

Icy prickles spread along my skin like frost forming on glass. *I can do this*, I thought, until I saw the eight-foot drop to the shallow streambed below. How had Heather and Fiona gotten across so easily? Knowing that thinking about it would only make it worse, I focused on the log, placing one foot carefully in front of the other.

I was halfway across when a crashing of branches rustled the trees in front of me. From behind me came a growl. *That dog again—two of them!* My back tensed and I almost lost my balance. I had just righted myself when a smoky black canine with glowing red eyes came charging out of the bushes right at me.

I turned on my heel to get back to the other side. But the log shifted and sent me flying. With a scream, I plummeted, landing first on my ankle, then on my tailbone.

Icy cold water soaked my clothes as a white, searing pain shot up my leg. Gasping, I scanned the steep wall of rock and dirt for any signs of danger, expecting to be overrun with snarling, horrible dogs. What were they doing *here*?

Grabbing a rock from the riverbed, I waited. Listening.

Nothing.

I was alone. My friends hadn't even noticed I was gone. How long before they came back for me? My ankle throbbed painfully, even in the cold water. I didn't want to move it but had to. How else would I get out on my own?

I was bracing myself to get up when a tall dark-haired figure approached. As he descended the embankment with giant, graceful strides, I couldn't believe who it was.

"Are you okay?" Michael asked.

Part of me wondered what he was doing there, on this obscure hiking trail across town, or why he was helping when he'd ignored me at school. But another part, the part that was probably in shock, considered it perfectly normal, as if I'd seen him here every day.

"Something black…" I muttered, in case he saw whatever came at me. I didn't want to bring up the dog again. What if I'd imagined it?

"Did you hit your head?" he asked, crouching before me.

Of course he didn't see it, Mia. Black things don't just come at you. He thinks you're delusional.

I blinked and shook my head. He seemed to be talking to me through a long dark tunnel. Everything— even the pain—was dim and distant. "My ankle took most of it."

He knelt in the water, facing me, and said, "I'm going to check it, okay?"

I nodded blankly at the water soaking his jeans. *He must be cold.* I could no longer feel it myself. I knew on some level that something was wrong in my body, but the messaging was numbed somehow. All I felt was static, like my circuits had overloaded.

Holding my heel, he untied my shoelace and removed my boot. I bit my tongue to avoid crying out. It tasted metallic. When he touched my ankle, pain exploded up my leg.

"Oww!"

"Sorry." He frowned. "I really do have to check it."

"I know."

I braced myself for pain, but his touch was light, gentle, as though he were examining a wounded bird.

"I'm going to check your spine," he said. The tunnel sensation gone, I could sense how close he was, smell the mint on his breath. "Okay?"

"Okay."

He leaned toward me and reached around my back to gently feel my bones. As he touched me, he searched my face for any sign of pain, and the tenderness in his eyes made me warm all over.

A few moments later he helped me to my feet, offering me his arm for balance. I gripped it so hard my knuckles turned white, and I could feel the cords of muscles beneath his shirt. But I could stand as long as I put no pressure on my foot. The pain was fierce, and my balance so terrible I teetered on the rocks.

"You'll never make it up to the trail on your own," he said. "It's steep."

Well, that much was obvious. What was he going to do? Leave me there?

He stepped in closer, and I had that feeling again, like I recognized him from somewhere. It wasn't from that morning in the park either. I wracked my brain, trying to place him. Had we been to the same party? Hung out in the same café? Perhaps I'd seen his picture somewhere.

"Trust me, okay? I won't hurt you," he said, and his voice sounded strange, almost musical, a chord rather than a single note.

Before I could reply, he placed one of my arms around his shoulders, scooped an arm under my legs, and picked me up as though I were weightless. As he carried me up the steep hill, he didn't seem to notice how close we were, his face inches from mine—too close and yet not close enough.

Not knowing where to look, I gazed over his shoulder and noticed a strange light flickering behind him. Tinged with blue, it flashed and rippled in a flowing motion. What the heck was it? Was I in shock?

When I looked back at Michael's face, it was alight, as though a beam of sunlight bathed both of us, especially him, in a warm golden hue. Like that day I saw him in the mall, only more brilliant. I gasped.

"Pain?" he asked.

I nodded, not wanting to admit I was hallucinating. He'd think I was crazy. *Again.*

A warm tingle filled me all the way to my toes. It made me feel open and exposed, as though a million eyes were watching me. Something inside told me to relax, and when I did, it eased not only my fright from earlier but all the pain I didn't know I had, as if all of my struggles had been seen: the difficulties our family had through the divorce, the strange distance between Dad and me, even my awkwardness around Michael.

My chest tightened and, as I exhaled, the tension released. Everything became warm and floaty and I felt completely accepted and at peace. An image of a lush garden on a hot sunny day flashed in my mind, as vivid as the inside of a dream. It surrounded a primitive house made of mud-brick and plaster. Inside was an open fire pit with a hole in the roof for smoke to escape. The bed, made of straw, was draped in furs. In the corner stood a simple loom, strung with hundreds of cream-colored threads that formed a half-woven cloth. This place, these things, seemed so familiar, as though I was the person who had been working this loom, and I wasn't alone. Someone else had been there with me.

But as quickly as the images came, they were gone, and I didn't have a clue what they meant.

Chapter Five

My friends were waiting for me at the crest of the trail, their mouths agape as Michael set me down on a nearby log.

Heather rushed over and threw her arms around my neck. "Oh my God, Mia. Are you okay? We turned around and you were gone."

Michael stepped back to let her get closer, but his tall frame hovered as though he could lend me his strength by proximity.

She turned to him almost accusingly. "Where did you come from?"

He cleared his throat. "I—"

Gushing, Fiona cut him off. "Michael, that was so awesome! Carrying her up that hill. It was crazy-steep. Your feet barely touched the ground."

"It was nothing," he scoffed, and I could feel his attention on me again. "How is it?"

How's what? I thought, blinking at him, still marveling at what I'd seen. Had I just remembered a dream? It seemed so familiar, so *real*.

Heather touched my shoulder, but asked Michael, "How's *what*?"

He focused on me. "Your ankle?"

I checked it. I could point my toe now without cringing. "It's okay. Much better."

"What happened?" Heather asked. "Can you walk?"

"Sure." I stood, but when I took a step, pain burned the length of my leg. I flinched before I could stop myself and nearly fell over.

Michael grabbed my elbow to steady me. "Maybe you shouldn't walk yet."

"It's not nearly as bad as I thought," I said, sitting back down.

"Uh huh," he said. "That's probably shock."

An indescribable emotion welled inside me, catching in my throat. I felt frail and drawn, like something made out of tissue paper. Fighting a strange urge to cry, I swallowed hard and took deep breaths.

"I'm such a klutz," I said to Heather and Fiona. "Sorry. I didn't mean to—"

"Shh!" Sitting beside me, Heather put an arm around my shoulder. "Don't even think that way, Mia."

Michael spoke to Heather and Fiona this time. "We should get her to the hospital so she can get checked out."

"I'll be fine," I said.

"We can help you get back," Heather said, standing. "You can lean on me. We'll make it back okay."

I tried another step on my own. It hurt but seemed easier than the last one. Heather, who was closest to my height, encouraged me to lean on her and we took slow, careful steps down the dusty trail together, with Fiona leading the way. It was slow going. We had to stop often so I could rest. Michael took up the rear, but when we stopped he was so preoccupied with the forest that he hardly spoke.

On our third stop, Heather sat beside me on an old stump. "We're almost halfway," she said, trying to encourage me. "We're making good time."

Finding a patch of sunlight, Fiona lunged into a yoga stretch that showed off her long, elegant limbs. Tossing her hair, she grinned up at Michael and my stomach hitched. She could be such a flirt.

To my relief, he didn't notice her. His attention was on the golf-ball-sized rock he was rolling beneath his foot.

A chill ran through me again, and I got the feeling that someone, or something, was staring at me. One of the bushes around us seemed darker than normal, shadowy, and I thought I saw a glimmer of red. A jolt of fear seized my chest. If one of those dogs came after me, I'd never be able to outrun it. I could barely walk.

Heather followed my gaze, but obviously didn't see anything. "You okay? You've gone really pale."

"I thought…" I began, but when Michael glanced at me, I stopped. I didn't want to bring up the shadowy dog again, not when he and I were starting to get along. "It's nothing."

Beside me, he kicked the rock into the bush and it landed with a satisfying crash of branches and leaves. When I looked back at the bushes, the darkness was gone.

I stared at him, amazed, wondering if he'd seen it too. He had been in the woods that morning when I was chased. Maybe he'd seen that dog after all.

He cocked an eyebrow at me. "What?"

"Nothing," I said, chickening out.

Slouching, he shoved his hands into his pockets. "This isn't working."

"What isn't?"

He tilted his chin to look up at me through his long, dark lashes and there was something so intense, so intimate, about his gaze that my breath froze in my chest. "If you keep walking on that foot, you'll hurt it more."

"She's not walking. She's hobbling," said Heather, drawing her arm across her brow. Helping me was making her sweat. "We're taking it nice and slow."

Fiona stepped in a little closer. "I can take a shift," she said.

"It would be better if I carried you," Michael interjected.

Fiona's jaw dropped, unable to contain her surprise. Was he serious? He seemed genuine enough—sincere, like he was living some code of chivalry, the kind you read about in medieval history. I remembered the feel of his hand on my back, his arm under my legs, and my heart sped up. When he first carried me, it was so intimate, so peaceful, it awakened a craving in me that I didn't even know I had. I would have given anything to feel that way again, and that's what made it seem wrong somehow, *illicit* even.

Heather grinned at me, as though she could sense what I was feeling.

"Thanks, but I think I can handle it," I said.

Fiona wore a stunned expression. Obviously *she* would have accepted his offer.

Michael rolled another rock beneath his foot. "No need to be stubborn. You'll only make it harder on yourself."

I raised my chin defiantly. "Stubborn? I'm not—"

"Yeah, okay." He laughed under his breath.

So maybe I was a bit stubborn, but what was so wrong with that?

There was a noise in the forest behind us. We both looked. Then he turned back to me. "Why don't I piggy-back you?" he said. The smile he gave me could have melted gold.

If it were anyone else, I might have said piggy-back rides were for kids, but really it was a good suggestion. It wasn't nearly as intimate, and it gave me the option to hold on, some semblance of control, instead of the helplessness of being carried. But when he crouched down so I could get on his back, the heat and closeness of his body permeated the dampness of my clothes. I stopped.

"Everything okay?" he asked.

"Uh-huh." Biting my lip, I eased onto his back. His hands held my bare legs like they would sear me. The sides of his waist were warm and solid against my thighs, and that *illicit* feeling came back. Trying to focus, I clung to him with my remaining strength.

He shifted, readjusting his grip. "Relax. I got you."

"I am relaxed," I squeaked.

"Then why are your knuckles turning white?"

I could hear the smile in his voice. Could he tell how I felt?

"Oh, sorry!" I willed the fists clutching his black T-shirt to loosen until I felt the tautness of his muscles under my fingers and the steady beat of his heart. Which was better, I guess, but also worse.

Being the one with the cargo—meaning me—on his back, Michael set a quick pace that Heather and Fiona could barely match. Fiona talked about an upcoming horror movie she was excited about. Heather was against it. I could hear the exertion in their voices as they climbed up and down hills. In contrast, Michael was silent and his breathing even, as though carrying me was hardly any difficulty at all.

Soon we were back at Fiona's old Honda Civic, parked in the shade of a huge maple, and Michael lowered me onto the car's hood. The cold metal pulled the skin on my legs into goose bumps, and I was suddenly aware of how warm I'd been pressed against him. Then, holding my hips, he gently guided me down to my feet. Our eyes locked–there was such light in his – and the air grew warm between us. In that moment, nothing else existed: just that light in his eyes and the touch of his hands on my hips. If I were more experienced with guys, I might have known how to flirt with him. But I didn't. All I could do was hold my breath and lean in ever so slightly, willing him to come closer.

It didn't work. Letting out his own breath, Michael dropped his hands and swept his gaze to my feet.

"How's your ankle?" He took half a step back.

My foot was swelling inside my boot, but the pain was completely manageable. I put weight on it and didn't cringe. Not having to walk back must have helped. "It's good. Thank you—for everything."

"You don't have to—"

"Michael, that was awesome of you!" Fiona cut in, still a little short of breath from the hike.

Oblivious to the moment we'd just had, she praised and thanked Michael a few times, and then reassured him that she and Heather would take me to the hospital to get checked. I thanked him again too, but only once. Fiona's profuse attention made me uncomfortable for all three of us.

Once we were inside the car and Michael was well out of earshot, Fiona gushed, "Oh my God, he's *so hot—celestial* hot. You're so lucky!" She sighed for emphasis, putting the car into drive. "He didn't even break a sweat when he carried you. And did you *see* that body? Like an Olympic swimmer."

Heather made a face. "Fiona, Mia had a serious fall and may have broken her foot. That's hardly lucky."

Fiona backpedaled. "Of course not lucky to have fallen…but lucky he was there."

"It was nice of him to stay," Heather said, studying me for a reaction.

I schooled my expression to a neutral one so she wouldn't notice my rush of excitement from thinking about him. With my luck, she'd analyze my feelings, try to set me up on a date, and I'd embarrassed myself around this guy enough already, thanks. Whatever I felt would be best kept secret for now. "Yeah, it was nice, I guess."

"You *guess*?" Fiona turned her head to look at me in the back seat. Then remembering she was driving, she turned back to the road. "The way he carried you was so romantic. If he'd carried me like that—"

Heather began to laugh. "I think we have a pretty good picture of what you'd do, Fiona."

I laughed too, grateful for Heather's injection of humor. The strange sensations and pain coursing through my body after the fall were overwhelming enough, not to mention all the strong feelings I'd had around Michael, or the strange things I'd seen. I didn't need to add Fiona's fantasies about him to the mix.

***

Luckily for us, the Emergency Room wasn't too busy. Heather walked me in while Fiona went foraging for something to eat.

The nurse at the administration desk paged my mom and asked me to take a seat in the waiting area. Mom came down a few minutes later wearing the lilac-colored nurse's uniform we'd picked out together last spring. It brought out her green eyes and softened the gray streak in her hair. After greeting Heather, she drilled me about the accident. Between her crazy hospital schedule and my starting the school year, I hadn't had much time to spend with her since I'd returned from Denver. I had to admit, getting injured was a strange way to do it.

I told her about the log bridge and that some noise had startled me, for lack of a better explanation. I didn't want to talk about the likelihood of seeing the same dog again, not with Heather present. If it were real, *surely* someone else would have seen it.

"Eight feet," she said coolly. She was never one for big emotional scenes, not when it came to injuries. "It could have been a lot worse. How did you get back?"

Mom was far too smart sometimes.

This was where Heather chimed in. "A boy from school came by. He knew some first aid and helped us get Mia out."

Mom squinted at me suspiciously. "Were there boys on this hike?"

"No, Mom." It was silly to have to apologize for a boy helping us out. Mom could be so overprotective.

"It's a popular trail," Heather added.

Fiona joined us, carrying a large box of pizza in one hand and the slice she was eating in the other. She greeted my mom and plunked herself into the empty seat beside us.

"Hi, Fiona. Heather and Mia were just telling me about the accident."

I tensed. This was not a time for Fiona to talk about the glorious attributes of Michael Fontaine—or his swimmer's body. I didn't need my mom prying about him, or worse trying to play matchmaker.

Fortunately, all she said was, "Yeah, it was really scary."

The topic of Michael didn't come up again. Instead, Mom shared a pizza slice with us and asked about our first week of school. I settled in with my pizza, hungrier than I expected, and let my mind wander.

Behind the administration desk, the paramedics rolled in a girl on a stretcher with tubes in her arms. A poppy-red blood stain pooled through the blanket on her chest. Doctors and triage nurses swarmed her, and the previously quiet ER erupted like an upturned anthill. As they wheeled the patient behind a room divider for privacy, I noticed a tall figure standing in the doorway bathed in a soft golden light. Michael. What was he doing here?

I raised a hand to wave at him as a nurse in surgical scrubs walked by, but by the time she passed, he was gone. Why didn't he stay? Staring at the empty doorway, I wondered if my eyes had deceived me. I wished I could get up and follow him, to find out if he was real, but with my ankle not working right, he'd be a block away by the time I hobbled to the door.

A few moments later, Heather and Fiona left and I was led into a semi-private examination room with pale yellow curtains for walls. After checking me for injuries and applying a tensor bandage, the doctor said I had a mild sprain and recommended ice, over-the-counter painkillers, and rest.

Mom drove me home and set me up on the couch with a cold pack and some movies before she went back to finish her shift. I couldn't focus on them. My mind kept wandering back to that house I'd imagined. Thinking I might have seen it in a book somewhere, I hobbled to my room and rifled through my books on ancient civilizations.

Sitting on my bed, I scanned for pictures and descriptions to see if anything jogged my memory. As I worked through ancient Greece, my mind played over the morning's events. Had I been imagining the dreamlike images, the strange flashing lights, the shadows in the bushes? None of these things made any sense, no matter how much I wanted them to. Perhaps I had a concussion.

But the doctor had checked me for any head injuries. I was, by all accounts, perfectly fine.

Chapter Six

Tuesday morning before English class, a copy of the *Westmont High School Gazette* landed on my desk, startling me.

"What's this?" Michael demanded.

I marveled at how he could still be gorgeous when he was scowling. His lips tightened into a hard line, he pointed to an article at the top of the page. The headline read: *Local Girl Makes a Big Splash*.

"Oh no!" I read the first few lines, which gave some vague details about my fall into the creek and then expounded on Michael's prowess in rescuing me. The article made me out to be some kind of loser while he looked like a superhero. "Who wrote it?"

He pointed to the byline. "Elaine."

Of course! "How did *she* hear about it?" I asked quietly.

"She wouldn't say—something about journalistic ethics."

"There's irony for you." Had Elaine overhead Fiona gushing about it somewhere? It was entirely possible. I'd have to watch what I said around Fiona, too.

He sighed, tore the paper in half, and tossed it into the recycling bin. I heard him mutter "Just what I need" before sitting down and ignoring me for the rest of class. As if it was *my* fault. On Monday he had almost been friendly. Now I was some sort of pariah he couldn't be seen talking to—never mind helping. Several rows back, Elaine watched our interaction with a smug look on her face.

In class, we were reading Act 1 Scene 2 of *Hamlet* and Michael was asked to read the lead part. With his slight accent, the lines rolled off his tongue naturally. He was the perfect Hamlet. Judging from the faces of all the girls in class—even Heather's—I wasn't the only one affected by the sound of his voice. Hamlet's grief-stricken first soliloquy—*O, that this too too sullied flesh would melt*—blazed through the room, melting a few of us in its wake. As he breathed new life into my favorite Shakespearean character, I felt like he was reading the words right to me.

The rest of the week, the teachers doubled everyone's homework. I was assigned a six-page Gov/Econ report, pages and pages of math problems, and a quiz for Latin. Elaine had a permanent smirk, no doubt pleased by how much her article had humiliated me. Kids I barely knew whispered in the halls and gave each other looks as I walked by. Some of them asked me if the story in the *Gazette* was true, and a few junior girls asked me about being carried by Michael Fontaine—as if I needed reminding!

In class, Michael kept to himself. By the end of the week, it was like the incident in the forest had never happened. I wanted to ask him if he'd been at the hospital that Saturday, but he was even less approachable than usual. I'd hoped to see him at lunch or catch him alone in the halls, but outside of class he practically disappeared.

***

On the weekend, my brother Bill came up for a short visit. Mom took Saturday off and the three of us went sightseeing around the waterfront and Pike Place Market. My ankle was almost healed, so I could walk normally again. We even had a mini heat wave.

Sunday afternoon, Bill took me to the University of Washington's Burke Museum of Natural History, so we could see an exhibit on ancient Egypt. He and I had been talking about it all summer and he'd promised to go with me. Though I'd first heard of ancient civilizations in grade school, Bill got me a book on Mesopotamia for my fourteenth birthday. I'd thought it was a joke at first, because it had *mia*—my name—in it. But since then, I'd been fascinated by the prehistoric civilizations, especially around the Mediterranean and Fertile Crescent.

The entrance to the exhibit was designed to resemble the temple at Luxor, with its high columns and hieroglyph-inscribed stone. If I squinted, I could pretend I was actually there. The main room opened up to be much larger than I expected, big enough to accommodate the crowd. The walls surrounding the glass cases were painted faux sandstone, and each case was labeled with the era it came from—Pre-Dynastic and Early Dynastic, and the Old, Middle, and New Kingdoms. Inside the glass cases were artifacts ranging from bronze and iron weapons to jewelry, hand mirrors, and cosmetics cases. On one side of the exhibit were replicas of paintings from inside a step-shaped pyramid; on the other side were mummies, mummy cases, and tombs. Bill and I saw a few items together, some scarabs and clay pots, but when I took my time reading everything, soaking it all in, Bill wandered off to look at things on his own.

I was inside a full-sized stone replica of the tomb of Kitines, examining an ornately painted mummy case, when Bill sneaked up behind me and grabbed my shoulders.

"Ahh!" I shrieked and stumbled backward into him.

Laughing, he caught me. "Gotcha."

"Jerk!"

I punched his arm but he dodged it, heading toward the tomb's exit. "You gotta admit this stuff is pretty creepy."

"It's not. It's cool how advanced they were."

LISA VOISIN

Outside the tomb was a case of mummified animals that had served as pets in ancient times, mostly cats, but there was also a hawk and a tiny crocodile.

"Still want to be an archaeologist when you grow up?" Bill asked.

"When I *grow up*? I'm not five!"

"You know what I mean. You're going to study this stuff next year, right?"

"I hope so."

I stopped to admire a reproduction of a painting from the tomb of Menna, a man spear fishing in the Nile with his wife and family. The animals and marshes were captured in meticulous albeit stylistic detail, and the caption explained that the painting's fertile environment symbolized the Egyptian belief in rejuvenation and eternal life.

"Any idea where?" Bill persisted.

"Not yet." It depended on what Mom and I could afford, because I sure as hell wasn't going to ask Dad for the money. But I didn't want to get into that with Bill. Dad had paid for his education. I seriously doubted he'd pay for mine.

Near the end of the exhibit was a section on weaving. The caption outlined the evolution of fabric and Egypt's history of working with linen and flax. When I saw it, some invisible string tugged at my insides, pulling me there.

"Saw that already," Bill said behind me. "I'll meet you outside."

I nodded, my attention fixed on the display. Beside a case of fabric fragments, heddle jacks, and loom weights was a small replica of a loom that took up to four women to operate. I'd hoped something might click, but I'd seen these things in books before. They were nothing like what had come to me that day in the woods.

After the museum, Bill and I decided to go for coffee in the nearby U District. We found a small bohemian-style café with comfortable-looking chairs and dark wood walls. The place was surprisingly crowded for such a nice day, so I pounced on some red velvet armchairs and saved us a spot while Bill stood in line.

No sooner had Bill brought me a vanilla latté than something caught his attention; he did a double-take and almost spilled his cappuccino. A girl with honey-blond hair walked into the café. With her striking golden eyes and long legs, she belonged on a runway.

She walked up to the counter and ordered herself a mocha. As she did, the lights in the café dimmed and then flared. I turned back to Bill, whose gaze flicked in her direction despite his attempts to keep them focused on his drink.

"Did you see that?" I asked.

"Hmm?"

"The thing with the lights."

"What thing?" he asked. Usually guys could be pretty annoying when they checked out a girl, but Bill was careful with me around. I could tell he was trying not to look. Having sat in class with Michael for the past two weeks, I could relate.

"Just flickering. It's nothing."

Bill changed the subject. "Dad's seeing someone new."

I nearly choked on my coffee. "Since this summer?"

"Yeah, before you left. They met through an online dating site."

"Wow" was all I could think to say. I couldn't imagine Dad meeting anyone online, but I wasn't surprised he didn't tell me, given how little we spoke. "How old is this one?"

"Closer to his age." Dad's last girlfriend had been only a few years older than Bill. Talk about awkward. "It's still new, so don't tell Mom yet, okay?

"Absolutely not. I'm not going to be the bearer of that news!" I remembered the first time Mom learned that Dad had been with another woman. I'd come home from school to find her crying on the sofa and Dad gone. It happened right after Bill went to Berkeley, so he didn't know what we went through, how hurt she was. Even if Mom was over it now, she didn't need to hear about Dad's affairs.

"Well, he says to say 'hi.'"

"Oh." I bristled. I didn't want to talk about dad or get any messages from him. Things were awkward enough—like he and I weren't even family anymore. It would have bothered me that he and Bill got along, but Bill got along with everyone. His skills were wasted on computers. He should have joined the UN. Maybe he'd invent an app for world peace.

Avoiding the awkward silence that always followed the subject of Dad, I got up. "Want some water?"

Bill shook his head and I went to the counter to pour myself a glass. When I was there, I noticed the lights flicker again and checked the overhead halogens in case one was burning out. They were fine.

"Looking for something?" It was the pretty girl Bill liked.

"The lights are flickering," I said, surprised I was telling her.

She smiled at me, putting a lid on her mocha. "Maybe it's not the lights."

"What do you mean?"

Still smiling, she shrugged and walked out the door.

When I returned to my chair, Bill asked, "Did you get her name before she left?"

Before I could answer, the lights flashed again and the power went out in the café. The cash register shut off and the espresso machine went down, inciting more than a few grumbles from both the staff and the people in line. Outside, two shadowy black blurs dashed across the street, too fast and too small to be cars.

They were more like dogs.

The skin on my neck tightened into tiny bumps. *Could it be those shadows again?*

Then there was a bright flash of light and the shadows were gone.

I turned to Bill. "What just happened?"

"A power outage."

"That bright flash?"

"What flash?" Bill said.

Maybe it's not the lights. The girl's comment stuck in my head. If it wasn't the lights, then what was it? Was I seeing things? *Really?*

The power returned to the building. If anyone else noticed those black blurs outside, they didn't react. Surely they weren't the same dogs, not in the middle of the city. They belonged in the woods. What were they doing *here*? Had they seen me? Heart galloping, I sank deeper into my seat, trying to hide.

Bill pulled a cloth from his pocket and started cleaning his glasses. With them off, you could see we were related. We had the same nose and high cheekbones, but his eyes were hazel like Dad's. Mine were green, the same as Mom's. "You know, you used to see things when you were little," he said.

"No, I didn't."

"You did! Saw a woman flying across the sky when you were four."

I couldn't remember any of it. If I was some kind of freak with an overactive imagination, shouldn't I be the first to know? "No fair. I was a kid."

"Swore it was an angel watching over us," Bill said with a chuckle. "Mom took you in for tests, and not eye tests, either."

I remembered being taken to a brightly-lit office full of furniture that was as small as me. Mom talked with a gray-haired man while I explored a box full of dolls and toy cars, waiting. Eventually, I sat at a table covered in big sheets of colored paper. The man came over and sat on the carpet beside me and told me he was a special kind of doctor. He handed me the biggest box of crayons I'd ever seen and invited me to draw pictures for him. I don't think I ever went back.

I contemplated telling Bill about the strange shadows, the flashes of light, the image of the loom—everything. Maybe I was seeing things again. But I changed my mind when he said, "Turns out you were fine. Well, fine enough for a freak."

"I'm not a freak. Take that back!"

Bill laughed. I kicked him, but not nearly as hard as I wanted to.

"How about you?" he asked. "Any guys on the horizon?"

My thoughts jumped to Michael, the way he'd turned up to help me in the woods and then gave me the brush-off later, acting like a total stranger. Bill might have had some great advice to offer, but we didn't have that kind of relationship and I wasn't about to start one with him. "If there are, I can't see them."

He shrugged, adjusting his glasses. "Several guys have checked you out since we got here. They think you're with me, though, so they leave you alone. And from the looks of them, that's a good thing."

LISA VOISIN

"Eww! You're my brother."

"You let me know if you need me to take care of them for you."

"*Take care of them*? You're a comp-sci geek, Bill, not a mercenary."

"You'd be surprised what a good hacker can do."

Bill's weekend visit ended much sooner than I would've liked. For a few brief days, we were a family again, and it wasn't just Mom and me. After dinner that night, Mom and I drove him to the airport and I found myself missing him before he even left. By the time we said goodbye at the airport gate, both Mom and I were in tears.

***

On Wednesday afternoon, we had the team and club fair, so our afternoon classes were cut. Though it wasn't mandatory, Mr. Bidwell, head of the Language Club, suggested so strongly that we be there that I half-expected him to take attendance, but he didn't. When the bell rang, I noticed Michael slip out to the parking lot and drive away in a shiny new white Volkswagen GTI. It was a rainy day, so instead of being outside, all the booths lined the cafeteria. Each club—sports teams, multicultural clubs, and cancer awareness groups, to name a few—had its own table. In the middle of it all was the Environment Club, where Heather was working. She had an extra seat beside her so I sat down, propping my almost-healed foot on a box under the table.

"You're helping?" Heather asked cheerfully.

"I said I would."

"Right. I forgot with—you know," she said and gestured at my ankle.

"Hello, Mia."

I looked up at Heather's math tutor smiling at me. A year younger than us, he'd skipped a grade and was at the top of our class.

"Hi," I said, wishing I could remember his name. The caption on his black T-shirt read *This is my clone.*

Heather tucked a strand of hair behind her ear. "Hey, Farouk."

Farouk. That was it. He leaned on the table in front of us and his dark, curly hair fell into his eyes. I remembered him being a lot shorter last year.

Farouk signed one of our petitions for using recyclable containers in the cafeteria, then turned to me. "How'd you hurt your ankle?"

"You didn't read the gossip column?" Heather asked. I hoped she was joking.

He shook his head.

I didn't want to relive the drama of it, so I let Heather tell the story. Fortunately, she didn't play Michael up too much—unlike the article itself.

Farouk picked up a flyer for the city's recycling program and curled it around his fingers. "Michael Fontaine. I heard he had an accident or something," he said.

"We heard that too," Heather chimed in.

"He nearly died," I said a little too defensively.

"Hmm, a near-death experience?" When I nodded, his face lit up. "I saw that in a movie once. This girl dies and when she comes back, she's all weird and different."

"What movie?" I asked.

He put down the mangled flyer. "I don't remember. It was old. I saw it on TV a few months ago."

"You don't believe movies are real, too, do you?" Heather asked, crinkling her nose.

"No," he said, "but some people who have near-death experiences *do* change."

"Change how?" I asked, leaning forward. Catching myself, I pulled back, embarrassed by how much the subject of Michael Fontaine interested me, especially since it was so one-sided.

"Sometimes the person is so different when they come back that other people think they're possessed."

"Possessed?" Heather leaned back and crossed her arms. Math genius or not, Farouk's credibility was at stake if he believed in anything too "out there." "You mean by a ghost or something?"

Before we could talk further, a crowd of freshmen swarmed our booth and asked us a bunch of questions. Farouk helped us hand out flyers while Heather chatted and I passed around the petition. Who knew we'd be so popular?

I tried to keep my thoughts from wandering, but failed. *Was he saying that Michael had been possessed?* It was almost too strange to consider. Everyone said he was different now, and there *was* something about him that was almost otherworldly, something you'd expect from a person who'd cheated death. But possessed? Maybe not.

When the crowd finally thinned out, Farouk was gone but I did see Michael down the hall whispering in Fiona's ear. A shot of jealousy coursed through my veins. Of course he'd be into her. She was tall, willowy, pretty, and she knew how to get a guy's attention. But before I could see any more, someone asked me a question about recycling for a second time, distracting me. When I looked again, Michael was gone.

As Fiona visited a few tables, I wondered what she was doing here. Didn't she have a dentist appointment? Wasn't that why she couldn't work the booth? Or did she have something set up with Michael instead? Eventually, she came over.

"Hey, guys," she said.

"I thought you had a dentist appointment," I blurted.

"I'm heading out now," she replied. "Believe me, I'd rather be here."

"I bet," I said, my voice dripping sarcasm.

"What's with you?" Heather asked me. "If you don't want to be here, I can handle it on my own."

"I saw you talking to Michael," I said to Fiona, ignoring Heather.

"What? When?" She did a great job of looking puzzled. Obviously she was up to something.

"Don't pretend to deny it. I saw him talking to you at your locker not two minutes ago."

Heather was calm. "Mia, I saw her too. She was alone."

"Seriously, Mia. What's gotten into you?" asked Fiona. "I haven't seen him all day."

"Really?"

"Yeah."

There was nothing else to say, other than "Sorry." I didn't get the sense she was lying to me, and yet I was sure I saw him. If she was telling the truth, perhaps I *was* imagining things. It wasn't the first time I saw things that nobody else did: shadows, flashes of light, images of a strange primitive place. Maybe something was really wrong with me.

Chapter Seven

About a week or so later, on a perfectly ordinary cloudy day, another new guy arrived at our school. Heather, Fiona, Jesse, and I were hanging around outside before our first class when a loud, vintage-looking motorbike pulled into the school parking lot.

"Who's that?" Fiona asked, perking up at the sight of its leather-clad rider.

"Is that...?" Jesse sat up, surprisingly animated for first thing in the morning. "Oh my God, it is!"

"You know him, Jess?" Heather asked. Sipping her coffee from a travel mug, she linked her arm through his.

"No, but he's riding a 1988 Norton Rotary Classic." When we weren't impressed, he added, "It's a collector's bike. They only made 100 of them. You know how *hard* they are to get?"

"I think Fiona was asking who, not what," said Heather.

By the time he parked and dismounted his bike, a few of us had stopped to see who the new guy was: teacher, student, or substitute? When he took off his helmet, I guessed him to be about our age. Everything about this guy exuded sexy, from his long lean body decked out in tight leather riding gear to his almost-shoulder-length brown hair and twinkling brown eyes.

A few sophomore girls stood closest to him in the parking lot and he gave them a perfect smile, flustering them into an eruption of giggles and blushes. Everyone was looking at him and he didn't seem to care. In fact, he smiled at all of us equally, as though he enjoyed the attention.

As he walked toward our group, Jesse called out to him. "Dude, that's an awesome ride."

He scanned each of us, but when his gaze landed on me, the corners of his mouth turned into a half-grin. "Thanks." His voice was deep and a little gravelly, appealingly so.

"You gotta tell me how you got it."

He motioned to his leather riding gear and winked. "It came with the outfit."

He then entered the school, leaving an awestruck Jesse and a practically drooling Fiona in his wake.

His arrival set the school on fire. By mid-day, we all knew his name: Damiel Lucas. Everyone was talking about him.

Damiel was in my English class, and it was intense to watch him and Michael interact, or rather *not* interact. They never spoke, but Michael's back went up the second Damiel entered the room, his eyes tightening like fists. But Damiel just gave him a wolfish grin as though it were a game of some sort—one I didn't understand the rules of but really wanted to.

By the end of the day, practically everyone at school had flocked to Damiel at some point. He was dark and interesting and, unlike Michael, he had no past. Try as they might, no one could dig up any gossip about him. We didn't even know where he came from, and people seemed to like it that way. He brought a sense of mystery and adventure that was sorely missing to the senior class, not to mention the school itself.

"He's so *hawt*," I heard one girl say to two of her closest friends in the hall.

***

Those same girls, juniors, stood in a cluster outside their classroom before the bell rang the next morning.

"Bet he's a great kisser," said one of the girls with a little sigh. The three of them giggled.

"So totally badass," said another, flipping her pale blond hair. She had porcelain skin and eyes that were almost cobalt blue. I couldn't help but think she and Damiel would look good together. "Think he's seeing anyone?"

"Hey, Tricia, get in line!" said the first girl. "He's mine."

I walked past them on my way to class. Was I the only girl in school who didn't swoon at the thought of

Damiel? Girls flocked to him. Every day he had a different one on his arm. Blonde, brunette, tall or short, it didn't matter. He petted and charmed each of them, working one girl into a frenzy before moving on to the next. He had a certain appeal, I guess, but all I could think about was Michael.

I still couldn't figure out what happened between him and me the day of the hike. I thought we'd connected, that he cared—until he read Elaine's article. We hadn't spoken since. Occasionally he would give me a look I didn't understand. Deep and intense, as though he really knew me. Sometimes I even thought he might come over so we could talk, but then he'd hesitate and walk away.

I hadn't seen any other strange anomalies lately— no shadowy dogs or flickering lights. But whatever it was that I'd seen nagged at the back of my mind like a chore I'd forgotten to do. I had to know if there was some kind of explanation, and asking Michael *wasn't* an option. So, during a free period after lunch on Friday, I decided to do some research. Not knowing where to begin, I tried the school library. But it didn't exactly have books on the subjects of shadowy dogs or flashing lights, and I was hardly going to ask the librarian for help.

I didn't even know how to describe what I saw. It might have been easier if I could name them, or if there were a pattern to what I was seeing. At first the lights appeared when Michael was carrying me, but it wasn't consistent. The other day, when I was out with Bill, the lights flickered at the café.

I decided to try the Internet and did a search for "seeing flashing lights," which actually produced results. I found lots of information on eye problems and detached retinas. All of it was too scary to consider. I vowed if I started seeing the lights again, I would go to the doctor.

I was in the middle of looking up "seeing shadows" when Damiel slid up behind me.

"Homework?" he said.

Startled, I instinctively closed the web page I was looking at.

If he'd seen what I'd been reading, he didn't let on. His voice was as smooth and rich as black satin. "You're Mia, aren't you?"

I nodded, flattered he knew my name.

"I'm Damiel. I don't think we've formally met." He offered me his hand with an elaborate flourish. I shook it. "What do you normally do for fun around here on a Friday night?"

"Nothing," I said, then cringed inwardly. With both Heather and Fiona dating, my social life was pretty much non-existent these days. But that wasn't something he needed to know.

He pulled up a chair beside me and leaned in close. "How about we make our own fun then? Go for a ride?"

I looked down at the keyboard. Having him so close made me hold my breath, a little freaked out. "I don't know."

He leaned back but reached his hand out on the desk so it rested hardly an inch from mine. Eyebrows raised, mouth open, he paused dramatically before he spoke, as though making sure he had my attention. "You know, I once heard this myth about the afterlife..."

"The afterlife?" I shifted in my seat and pulled my hand away, not wanting to give him the wrong idea.

"Yeah. You believe in one, don't you? Heaven? Hell? Reincarnation? Or do you think when you die it's all over?"

"I–I don't know," I stammered. Many ancient cultures did believe in an afterlife, but I wasn't sure what I believed. "I wasn't raised religious or anything." My mind flashed back to Farouk's comment about Michael's near-death experience, the idea of Michael coming back different. What did it mean?

"Well, some cultures used to believe, at the time of death, that instead of being judged on how well you abstained from the pleasures of life…" He leaned in closer. "…you would be judged by how well you *enjoyed* them." With a smile that could boil glaciers, he ran a finger up my arm from elbow to shoulder. It left a path that tingled all the way down to my toes.

"Interesting," I said, surprised by how fast this was going. No one had ever touched me that way before. All the blood rushed from my head, leaving me dizzy and more than a little scared of him. "W–where did you hear this?"

"Read it somewhere." He shrugged. "In order to honor the gods, they believed you should live your life to the fullest."

"They did?" I asked, trying to recover from the swooning his touch had brought in me, the way it clouded my thoughts. I was reminded of a show I'd seen on TV about sharks. There's a way of hypnotizing them called "tonic immobility." Some sharks use it for mating, where the male would roll the female onto her back and she would be paralyzed in a serotonin-induced euphoric state. On the show, when people learned how to do it to them, the sharks would seek them out so that they could experience this bliss, sinking deep into the water until the human could hold on no longer.

In that moment, I knew exactly how those sharks felt.

"So how about you, Mia?" he asked, a slow, seductive smile forming on his lips. "Do you live your life to the fullest?"

I thought of Michael, how much I'd hoped he'd talk to me, and now here was Damiel offering me pleasures I'd only fantasized about. Despite my feelings for Michael, a voice in my head said *Of course not. Show me how!* All hotness aside, ten minutes ago he was just another guy at school, and now that he was asking me out I was enthralled by him. How did he do it?

Across the library, Michael was leaning against one of the stacks with his arms crossed, as beautiful and unattainable as ever, his mouth set into a hard line. Why was he watching me now when he seemed to care too little on regular days? Was he judging me for flirting with Damiel when he hardly spoke to me himself?

My mouth dried up and I swallowed hard, not sure what to say next.

"Relax," Damiel said, startling me. "I won't do anything unless you want me to."

I laughed. It was more of a nervous trill that rang out through the quiet library. The librarian at the desk put her finger to her lips in admonishment.

When I looked back to where Michael had been standing, he was gone. I was so flustered I hadn't seen him leave.

Despite the fact that Damiel seemed interested in me, I wished Michael was the one asking me out. But that would never happen. My attraction for Michael was pathetically one-sided. It took a crisis for him to even come near me and I half wanted to put myself into some kind of crisis to be near him again.

"Tell me something?" I asked, keeping my voice low.

Damiel gave me a suggestive smile that made my face heat up. "Sure."

"What's with you and Michael?"

His smile wavered slightly. "Why do you ask?"

"Something about the way the two of you look at each other—"

"That makes you think Hallmark card?"

I stifled a grin. "Not exactly."

He chuckled, a low throaty sound. "I can't help it if he acts like he's in a spaghetti western."

"A what?" I gave him a puzzled look.

"You know. Clint Eastwood. *The Good, the Bad, and the Ugly.* You've heard of it, haven't you?"

"Sure." A memory of Bill watching old Clint Eastwood movies with Dad when we were kids clutched at my throat. I swallowed. "Which one are you?"

He leaned in to me and said in a low, sexy voice, "Definitely *not* the ugly."

I had to agree with him, but his ego didn't need the boost. I focused on the computer screen, logged myself out, then asked, "So you two know each other?"

"We met last year in the hospital."

He lifted his booted foot up to his chair and pulled up the leg of his jeans. My attention was drawn immediately to a large serpent tattooed on the back of his calf.

"Did that hurt?" I said, taking a closer look. The serpent was highly detailed, its scales shades of black and gray against his olive skin.

"Wasn't bad at all compared to this." He pointed to the six-inch scar that ran from his shin all the way past his knee.

"Oh." I blushed again when I realized the scar was what he'd meant to show me. His tattoos were none of my business. "How'd you get that?"

"Had an accident this past spring. Michael and I shared a room, became friends even."

"What happened?"

He shrugged and covered his leg. "He doesn't want to remember it, so he avoids me."

"That's strange."

"It is what it is." Leaning in toward me again, he whispered in my ear, "Want to come out tonight?"

I took a deep breath, bracing myself against the onslaught of his charm. "I really can't."

He wore an astonished expression, as though surprised I could resist. Considering how many other girls were all over him, I guess he had reason. Out of the corner of my eye, I noticed a haze around him, as though he were bathed in a faint smoke, but when I blinked and refocused it was gone.

Leaning forward, Damiel touched my hand, then my hair, all the while smiling at me like he was sharing a secret. It would have been so easy to lean into that smile, let it take me places. How could I be so crazy about one guy and so affected by another?

"You're sure?" he asked.

"I'm sure," I said, getting up. I couldn't get Michael's expression out of my head.

When I returned to my locker, Michael was waiting for me. His jeans fit him perfectly, and the red sweater he wore showed off his broad shoulders and the line of his chest—muscular but lean. Standing there, he did more for me than Damiel's touch. He cast his gaze down as I approached, as though he couldn't even bear to look at me.

"How was your little chat with Damiel?"

"How is it your business?" I asked, wishing this wasn't the first thing he'd said to me in weeks.

His scrutinizing glare was as cold as the morning sky. "This isn't a game."

"What isn't?" I flicked my hair over my shoulder, trying to act casual. "Talking?"

He leaned in until his face was inches from mine, and my heartbeat went off the scale like a Geiger counter measuring a solar flare. It was all I could do to breathe. I didn't want him to be angry. I wanted that moment we'd had at Fiona's car after he helped me out of the woods. Staring into his eyes, I held onto the memory of that side of him. The gentle, caring side that I knew was in there.

Even if he hadn't shown it to me since, I still remembered.

All the color left his face and he backed away. When he spoke, there was no anger left. "You have no idea what you're dealing with."

Before I could respond, he turned on his heel and left.

My frustration burned. I wanted to yell after him down the crowded hall but didn't want to cause a scene. Instead, I threw my books into my locker. The force of them collapsed one of the shelves, making a mess of the inside.

What was this—this *thing* between us? Just when I thought he was going to let his guard down, he bailed. I didn't even know what he was talking about. What *was* I dealing with? How was I supposed to know if he wouldn't tell me? Letting out a heavy sigh, I searched among the rubble for the notebook I needed for my next class. I didn't notice Elaine approach.

"Trouble in paradise?" she said, her expression far too smug.

Making no attempt to mask the anger on my face, I returned my attention to my locker. "Everything's fine."

"Michael Fontaine *and* Damiel Lucas in one day." She made a disapproving clicking sound with her tongue. "Do you need to make a play for every hot guy in school?"

The smart thing to do would be to ignore her, but then she'd have the last word. Refusing to back down, I stared into her sparkly brown eyes; they were filled with spite. "Jealous much?"

Immediately, I regretted what I'd said. She was baiting the hook, fishing for something to write about, and the last thing I needed was my name smeared in the paper again. We could fight, but it would be picking a fight with someone carrying a loaded weapon, and she was the one with the gun.

"Me? Jealous of the likes of you?" She let out a dry little laugh. "Hardly."

Grabbing my bag, I proceeded to ignore her.

"You think you're all that, don't you? Believe me, they only notice one thing about you—or is that *two*?" She sneered and motioned to her chest disapprovingly.

She was practically calling me a whore, and on some level it really hurt. On another, I was so angry I wanted to hit her. A few scenarios played out in my mind, the most satisfying of which was smacking the door of my locker into her pointy turned-up nose. But I couldn't afford the repercussions, and I didn't want to hurt anyone, not even her. All I could do was walk away.

"Thanks," I said, smiling at my fantasy of her with a bloody nose. "I'll keep that in mind."

"You'll never get him," she called to me when my back was turned.

As I wandered to my last class, I wondered whom she meant: Damiel or Michael. Perhaps she meant both.

Chapter Eight

I awoke before my alarm Monday morning to the sound of dogs barking and got up to see what it was about. Drawing the curtains aside, I noticed a couple of terriers had chased the neighbor's cat up a tree. They barked at each other and then ganged up on the cat. I rooted for the cat. On the horizon, the sun tried to pierce the dark clouds that loomed threateningly above, exposing a cold blue sky, so I dressed for more rain.

In English class, Mr. Bidwell had me read Ophelia to Michael's Hamlet. We were reading Act III Scene I, and the class started with Hamlet's famous "to be or not to be" speech which Michael read perfectly, his clear and exquisite voice mesmerizing the room. In the scene, Ophelia returns Hamlet's tokens of love to him. It was the perfect scene to let out some of my frustration. I'd read the play enough times now that I was even getting comfortable with the wording.

Hamlet's soliloquy ended with *Nymph, in thy orisons be all my sins remember'd*. When Michael said it, his eyes were hooded and soft. Even though I couldn't understand exactly what Hamlet meant by that line, I knew it had something to do with regret. I found myself wondering what Michael could possibly regret. Or was he *that* good an actor?

In my mind's eye, a scrambled image of blood and shadow flashed before me. Trying to focus on the image made me dizzy. It took a moment for the words on the page to stop moving so I could read my next line.

"My lord, I have remembrances of yours that I have longed long to re-deliver," I read. "I pray you, now receive them."

"No, not I!" Michael said, "I never gave you aught." Again, such remorse emanated from him, as though what he was saying was in fact real and not a play.

My anger returned as I continued to read, losing myself in the script. Like Hamlet, he had been sweet to me and then turned into a jerk. But it was more than that, as though we had a connection that went really deep, and that's what made it hurt. I used to think Ophelia was weak, but now I could relate to her. Her brother was away, her father was a total ass, and she was in love with a guy who was nice to her one minute, cold the next. Everyone had abandoned her.

We continued bantering as Hamlet and Ophelia. As we argued our lines about the role of beauty to deceive, Michael read pointedly and seemed to be enjoying himself. I don't know what he thought was so funny about beauty being deceptive. He was the beautiful one.

"I did love you once," he read. Hearing those words from him caught me off guard, most of all because they sounded so true. My mind blanked. He eyed me expectantly.

I flushed, suddenly remembering my line. "Indeed, my lord, you made me believe so." *This isn't real; it's a play.*

"You should not have believ'd me; for virtue cannot so inoculate our old stock but we shall relish of it. I loved you not." He read the words sharply, coldly.

Ophelia never had a chance! "I was the more deceived," I read, more bitterly than Ophelia might have ever been.

Michael read Hamlet's famous "get thee to a nunnery" speech angrily, as though he really meant it. And when he said the line "Why wouldst thou be a breeder of sinners?" his voice did that strange thing I'd heard before, where it sounded like a chorus rather than a single voice. As he spoke, I saw a flash of two red lights amidst blackness. *Eyes!* I stopped breathing as I remembered that shadowy dog.

Completely assuming the role of Hamlet, he continued mercilessly through the speech, each word slicing into me. When he had finished, I had to bite my lip to keep it from quivering so I could continue with my lines. How could this play seem so real?

We ended the reading with Ophelia's "O, what a noble mind is here o'erthrown!" speech, and I couldn't stop my voice from trembling as I read. I wasn't acting, but it seemed the class thought I was.

"Well done. Both of you." Mr. Bidwell praised us when we were done, encouraging everyone to clap. He went on about our acting abilities and how much passion we brought to reading our parts. If he only knew.

The class discussed what had happened in the scene, but I barely listened. It was strangely personal, as though they were talking about *my* feelings and not Ophelia's. While Michael focused on the discussion, seemingly unperturbed, I stared down at my open textbook, smoothing its worn edges with my fingertip. This used to be one of my favorite scenes in the play. Now Ophelia's words taunted me from the page, "Like sweet bells jangled, out of tune and harsh."

Mr. Bidwell asked the class, "What does Hamlet mean when he says 'for the power of beauty will sooner transform honesty from what it is'?"

Everyone gave him blank looks. It was Michael who raised his hand.

"It means beauty makes men lie," he said.

Readjusting his glasses, Mr. Bidwell repeated what Michael said thoughtfully.

"Isn't that sort of misogynistic?" Elaine asked, leaning forward in her seat as though she were preparing for a debate. "Blaming the woman for being beautiful and using it as an excuse for men's lies?" Mr. Bidwell smiled and leaned on his desk. "Good question, Elaine, but we have to take Shakespeare's time into consideration, and the fact that Hamlet is angry and possibly playing crazy at this point. How about if we rephrase it to 'men choose to lie when presented with beauty'? How's that?"

"Better," she said smugly.

"I don't think we should whitewash it," I interjected, refusing to let Elaine win. "Maybe Hamlet really thinks that way. Maybe he is a misogynist. I mean, look at the way he treats Ophelia, kind to her one minute, cold the next." Michael shifted in his seat and glared at me, obviously catching my insinuation. "Then there's the way he feels about his mother."

Mr. Bidwell took the opportunity to guide us into a discussion about Hamlet's alleged oedipal complex. I only half-listened and was glad when class was over. It wasn't until then that I noticed Damiel hadn't been there at all.

I didn't see him until lunch, and even then it was only briefly. I was eating with Heather as usual, and Fiona, Dean, Jesse, and Farouk all joined us. We were a full table, and everyone was discussing a new action movie that was coming out on the weekend.

"The previews look amazing!" Fiona exclaimed. "Even the critics gave it four stars."

"I think we should go this Friday," Heather said, turning to Jesse. "You in?"

"All in," he said, grinning at her.

None of us thought he meant for the movie. Heather blushed and leaned back in her chair so she could prod him under the table with her foot. Jesse made a face. They were being too cute. Seeing them that way made me wish I had someone to banter with, someone I could be close to. It made me feel even more alone.

"How about you, Mia?" Fiona asked, biting into a carrot stick.

"Sure," I said, and turned to Dean and Farouk. "Are we all going?"

Outside, it started to rain, hard enough that I could hear the raindrops slapping the pavement. Damiel and Michael stood in the wet field, facing off. They exchanged loud words I couldn't hear, clouds of breath escaping their mouths. Usually this kind of argument would draw a crowd, but around the cafeteria people were focused on their own conversations—some laughing, some playing. Nobody noticed the scene outside.

Even angry, Michael was stunning to look at: intimidating, but stunning. Cultures dating back as far as Ancient Egypt and Mesopotamia used lions to represent warrior-hood. Male lions fight to the death to protect their pride from intruders. When these guys faced off, it was that intense; the air itself crackled between them. The wind picked up, blowing wet, dying leaves off the bending branches. After a few moments, Michael stormed across the field to the trails behind the school grounds. Damiel followed and I wondered what would happen next, what they were fighting about. Was it about me?

Don't be ridiculous, Mia!

"Mia?" Heather's voice called me back to reality.

"Mm-hmm," I replied absently.

"Farouk was offering you a ride," she whispered. "He lives the closest."

"Oh." Composing myself, I turned to Farouk. "Do you mean Friday?"

"Yes," he replied.

"Uh, sure. What time?"

"We're going to meet at the coffee shop by the theater at six-fifteen." Heather filled me in on what I'd missed. I was too embarrassed to admit I had been staring at the two most attractive guys I'd ever seen and wishing they were fighting over me.

"How's six?" he asked.

"Good."

Curious about the argument between Damiel and Michael, I kept an eye out for them all afternoon but I didn't see them again. By the end of the day, I began to worry. What if Michael had been hurt? The fact that I was concerned only for Michael was telling. I didn't expect things to happen with Damiel, and when he wasn't around I found myself completely un-attracted to him. It seemed whatever I felt resulted from being in his presence, like he had some kind of vortex of charm everyone got sucked into—including me.

Not being around Michael filled me with a kind of longing I'd never felt before. He made me angry, he made me happy, and I would endure anything to spend a few moments with him.

The rest of my classes dragged and the teachers piled on the assignments, trying to prepare us for mid-terms. By the end of the day, I carried the burden of a full workload to my locker. I was packing for the bus ride home when a warm hand touched the base of my spine, sending a tingle right up to my neck.

I whirled around and saw Damiel smiling wickedly beside me. "Got enough books?"

"Uh, yeah," I stammered, shouldering my bag.

"What do they say about all work and no play?" His dark eyes twinkled, but I noticed for the first time they weren't warm. He stroked his hand up my spine to my shoulder, and another tingle ran through me. "Maybe it's time you played a little. How about it? You game?"

I wondered what *kind* of game he meant. He stood so close it was almost dizzying.

"You should see the homework they've given me this week." I wasn't sure how to say *no* to him, or even if I wanted to, now that he was near me again.

He lifted his hand from my shoulder to brush my cheek, and I noticed small cuts on his knuckles that appeared to be mostly healed. When I looked into his eyes, my reserve buckled, like I was forgetting where I was—who I was—and the pull of his presence drew over my skin. He was bewitching, and I was being reeled in.

Then something broke the fixation, a sound perhaps, or a rush of cool air. Suddenly remembering where I was, I looked away. A few students milled around, talking at their lockers, filling their backpacks, and readying themselves for the trip home.

At the end of the hall, Michael focused on the two of us, singling me out. My spine stiffened. I'd done nothing wrong. Was I supposed to be some kind of nun? *A vestal virgin?* I swallowed the lump forming in my throat and wished he'd stop looking at me like that, as though I'd disappointed him.

Damiel glared at Michael and the air snapped between them, sending a ripple right through me. Touching my chin, Damiel turned me to face him. His smile spoke of pleasures promised. Pleasures I wasn't sure I was ready for yet, but I found myself yearning for them nevertheless. Bringing his lips to my ear, he whispered, "Think about it," before he turned and walked away.

I blinked in the direction where Michael stood and shook the feeling off. He was gone, too. Sadness settled into the base of my stomach. Why couldn't we *talk*? Wasn't that what normal people did?

I grabbed my bag and rushed down the hall to where I'd seen him. He wasn't there, so I ran outside and found him striding toward his car.

It was pouring out but I didn't care. My umbrella was at the bottom of my bag and fishing it out would take too long. I didn't want to stop for fear I'd miss him.

"Hey!" I shouted after him.

When he stopped and turned back to me, my breath caught. He could be such an impressive figure. Tall and strong, he wasn't afraid of his anger; it seemed to be a force that welled up inside him, one he could completely control. While he didn't throw it around, I sure didn't want to cross him.

"What?" he said hotly as I approached his car.

On the road behind him, deep puddles formed into gray pools. Michael stood, his car door open. Rain soaked his already damp hair as tiny streams of water poured down the sides of his face. Even his eyelashes were wet.

My step faltered. My own anger cooled.

"What's going on?" I asked.

He shrugged. "You tell me."

"I don't get you. Why do you seem to be watching me all the time?"

He mumbled something under his breath that I couldn't hear. At least he didn't deny it.

I tried a different approach. "Did I do something wrong?"

"How do you feel right now?" he asked, as though that answered my question.

"Fine," I said, though it wasn't entirely true. I was confused, exhausted, sad, and ashamed of myself for that look of disappointment on his face when he saw me talking to Damiel. More than anything, I wanted him to touch me as Damiel had.

He sighed and pressed the remote on his keychain. I heard the passenger doors unlock. "Get in."

I looked at him, hesitating. Did he mean it? He gave me a nod and motioned inside. Gathering my dignity, I got in and closed the door.

"Fasten your seatbelt," he said, shifting the car into gear. It still smelled new inside.

Rain had already soaked through my shirt; it clung cold against my skin. I wished I'd worn Gore-Tex. I tried to wipe the water off my face with wet hands, for all the good it did me. "Where are we going?"

"I'm taking you home."

A ride home. That meant I had five minutes with him, tops. I was going to ask my questions even though I didn't expect to get any answers.

"Why does it bother you when Damiel speaks to me?" I blurted out, telling myself I wanted things, Michael, to make sense.

His expression was intense but completely unreadable. I had to remember to breathe. He returned his focus to the road. "He's taking from you."

"What does that mean?" I wondered if *taking* meant flirting. "What is he taking?"

"How do you feel when you're with him?"

How did I feel when I was with Damiel? Flattered, as though I was someone attractive and interesting. It was never about Damiel. It was about me. Being alone with Michael in his car was different. It wasn't about how attractive I felt, it was a deep longing that I could hardly put into words. In that moment my whole body thrummed with it, and I found myself wishing Michael would notice me the way Damiel did, even once.

I could sense his attention on me as he waited for an answer, but I couldn't face him. I focused on my school bag, playing with its stuck zipper.

"Wishing I was with you," I whispered.

All the color left his face and it was his turn to look away. I realized that for as much as I'd listened to Heather advise Fiona about guys, I didn't know a thing.

He pulled the car over to the side of the road and parked it. A heavy silence grew between us. The rain thrummed against the roof of his car and my heart stuttered anxiously against my ribs, like a hummingbird flapping its tiny wings.

He took a deep breath and his voice was thick when he said, "If I misled you…"

My heart stopped, and I blinked at him as heat filled my face. He hadn't misled me. The feelings I had for him were one hundred percent my own doing. I should have known better.

"I'm not available," he continued, "the way you want me to be."

What did he mean, the way I wanted him to be? Any way I could be with him would be fine. Anything was better than not speaking at all. And then the pieces came together: gorgeous and unavailable. He had a girlfriend. Oh God! Why hadn't I seen the signs before?

He didn't flirt with anyone because he was *in love with someone else.*

Not caring about the rain, I opened the door and dashed out of the car.

Michael caught up with me and grabbed my arm. I pulled it away.

"It's wet," he said. "I'll take you home."

Tears burned my eyes, making me grateful for the heavy rain that washed them away, cooling my skin. "I'll walk."

"Come on," he said, "don't be foolish. You'll catch a cold." A wet strand of hair clung to my face. He brushed it aside, so gently, and a deep current trembled through me, compelling me toward him. It was all I could do to hold my ground. His eyes widened and he stepped back. In that moment, I knew he felt it too.

I glared at him. How *dare* he touch me? Why did he care? Why did he pay attention to me at all?

He shook his head sadly. "Mia, I'm…"

Taken. I know. I shook my head, not wanting to hear any more, and there was this look he gave me, a mixture of pain and something else—something forbidden—that made me want to kiss the rain from his lips.

The sky was filled with black clouds that made it seem more dusk than afternoon. Small rivers formed on the side of the road and dead leaves floated downstream to the gutters, filling the grates. If the rain didn't let up soon, it would flood.

I couldn't be alone with him now. It was too humiliating. So I turned and walked off. After a minute, I heard his footsteps on the wet pavement, his car door open and close. I wanted to look back but didn't. I could tell he was still watching me. But as to why, I figured I'd never know.

Chapter Nine

I skipped school on Tuesday. Mom was at work, so I called in sick. Even after fifteen hours of sleep, I had to drag my heavy limbs out of bed. Black stains circled my eyes, and my nose was so stuffy from crying the night before that it was easy to pass for having a cold. With all the pandemic viruses going around these past few years, the school's policy was to stay home until you could get your symptoms checked. This rule was working to my advantage today.

But really I couldn't face Michael. Not after telling him how I felt. Not when he was seeing someone else.

I was lying on the sofa watching an old black and white movie on TV when Heather called. I checked my watch; her lunch break was nearly over.

"Will you live?" she asked.

I couldn't help but smile. "I'll live."

"Do you need anything? I know your mom works late. Chicken soup?"

I wished I could talk about what I was going through, but I'd never find the words without bursting into tears. I swallowed back the tightness in my throat. "Can you let me know what the math assignment is?"

"Sure," she said. "By the way, Damiel was asking about you today."

Right. Damiel. At least *someone* thought I was attractive. "Oh? What did he want to know?"

"Where you were, of course. I thought Fiona was going to fall over when he came by, she was practically swooning. He *is* really hot."

"Is he?" I tried to sound nonchalant. She didn't know he'd asked me out on Friday.

"Girl, are you dead? Half the school is talking about him. The entire female population, even a few of the guys."

"What did you tell him?" I asked, flattered he let his interest show to my friends.

"That you were home today."

"What did he say?"

"Not much. Michael came by to have lunch with Jesse, and Damiel was there. Talk about a weird vibe." Her statement hung in the air. She was fishing for information.

Even hearing Michael's name was hard. Thinking about him having lunch with my friends when I wasn't there stung. Had he been waiting for me not to be around so he could visit with Jesse?

"Yeah, they have some kind of past." I figured it was safe to share a little of what I'd heard.

"Oh." I could practically hear the wheels turning in her head. I was pretty sure she wanted to know how I knew that, but I wasn't ready to tell. "He seems into you, Mia. You should go for it."

"Who?" I asked, my mind still faltering back to thoughts of Michael.

"Damiel, of course." She quipped, "Are you on cold medication or something?"

I laughed. "Kind of."

"Michael asked about you, too." Had she read my mind? Known who I was really thinking about?

"Oh," I said, trying to mask the sinking in my chest, the strange blend of hope and despair that Michael brought up in me. "What did he want?"

"To know where you were," she said. "That's all he said."

I could have taken his asking about me to mean he cared a little, but really I wished he would forget about me. Or at least forget everything I said in the car yesterday. How could I face him after that?

When I didn't say anything, Heather added, "Hey, lunch is over. I gotta go to class. I'll e-mail the math homework to you."

I thanked her and hung up. I'd been sitting around in my pajamas all day and needed to wash up, so I ran myself a bath. I couldn't help but remember Heather's praise of Damiel. He *was* hot. The situation with Michael may have been bleak, but at least I still had hope of a social life.

I lay in the tub trying to visualize Damiel's features, not Michael's, nor those blue eyes that had burned themselves into my thoughts. I focused on Damiel, the way he looked at me like I was the only girl in the room. It wasn't as easy as I'd hoped. Thoughts of Michael would soon interrupt and I would be looking at his face, not Damiel's. But I was determined to commit Damiel's features to memory. The bath water cooled, so I refilled the tub several times. Once my skin had completely wrinkled, I got out.

After this exercise, though, I was sure Michael wouldn't be able to faze me again.

***

The next day, Damiel found me at my locker before math class. His black cashmere sweater looked so soft I wanted to curl up in it.

"Feeling better?" he asked, sidling up to me.

"I am now." I dared myself to meet his gaze.

He moved in a little closer and placed his hand on the top of my hip. Reflexively, I held my breath. I'd forgotten how disarming he could be. Behind him, two sophomore girls glanced at us, whispering to each other. Wherever he went attention would follow, and I wasn't sure what to do about that part. I only hoped it stayed out of print.

"It wasn't serious?" he asked, smiling.

"Not deadly, anyway."

He looked me up and down with such heat it warmed my skin. "Oh, I'm sure you could be deadly if you wanted to." Leaning in closer, he whispered, "Wanna do something later?"

I didn't know how to react. I was flailing in an ocean, learning to swim, and had just been hit by my first big wave.

"I–I'm still catching up on what I missed yesterday. Lots of homework."

As though sensing my apprehension, he took a step back and grabbed my hand, half-pleading, half-teasing. "Have lunch with me then?"

That I could do. Besides, if Michael was having lunch with Jesse and Heather, who was I to cramp his style by having lunch with my *own* friends? It also helped to know that in a public place Damiel wouldn't move things along too quickly. After all, he was a difficult person to say no to. "Sure," I said. "See you in the cafeteria?"

He squeezed my hand. "See you then."

At lunch, Damiel held a table for us near the middle of the room. The three girls I'd seen talking about him the other day stood by his table with their lunch trays as though they wanted to join him. When he saw me and waved, they shot me dirty looks. That alone was intimidating. He already had his lunch with him, so I pointed to the concession stand, where I needed to get mine, and he gave me a nod.

Hurrying, I grabbed a panini sandwich and an iced tea. Heather caught up with me in line. Her hair in a messy ponytail, she wore a baggy sweatshirt and jeans, not her usual stylish gear. Grayish rings circled her eyes.

"What's with the outfit?" I asked.

She flushed and said apologetically, "It's Jesse's. I was up most of the night studying for a huge Spanish test and I'm a bit shaky. Spilled coffee all over my shirt."

"How was the test?"

"Okay I guess." For Heather, "okay" was at least an A. I wasn't far behind, but I didn't stress about things the way she did.

"I'm having lunch with Damiel today and he's got us another table."

"You won't sit with us? Is it the sweatshirt?" she teased. "No, seriously. That's great. I'm happy for you. I didn't know you were into the bad-boy type."

Was that what Damiel was, a bad boy? Come to think of it, who was I kidding? "He's nice to me." I had always figured "bad boys" didn't treat girls very well.

"That's the best kind," she said. "Remember the movie on Friday? Dean already got tickets online. Do you want him to get one more?"

"Um, not sure yet."

"Good. You want to make him work for it. But from the way he looks at you—"

"What do you mean?"

Heather raised her eyebrows suggestively. "I think you know."

I blushed. There was something in the way he looked at me that was all-consuming. I wondered what exactly that was as I paid for my lunch and went to join Damiel. The cafeteria was getting crowded and I noticed a few people eyeing our large table enviously.

He was looking at me that way again, and I realized it would be so easy to get pulled right into him, as though his world was all that mattered.

"Wow," I said. "You got us a private table?"

"I do what I can," he said with a flourish.

I sat beside him and opened the can of iced tea, trying to act casual. "So, how've you been?"

"Good," he said with a slow, sultry smile. "Better now."

A fluttering in my stomach made me not want to eat. Unwrapping my sandwich, I hoped my appetite would return once I had actual food in front of me. It didn't.

The lasagna on Damiel's plate must have been the special, but I hadn't even seen it on the menu. As he cut a forkful and put it into his mouth, I noticed he was staring at me. He didn't even try to hide it.

Then again, why would he? With Damiel, I always knew where I stood, but what surprised me was that I couldn't help but stare back. When he smiled at me, his eyes weren't just brown, they had shimmering bronze flecks that caught the light. As I gazed into them, the rest of the cafeteria faded and blurred into the background.

"You should eat something," he said after swallowing a few bites.

Suddenly realizing I'd been staring way too long, I focused on my dry, unappealing sandwich.

"Here," he said, holding up a forkful of lasagna for me to taste. "Try this. It's the food of the gods. I swear."

Was he seriously offering to feed me in the school cafeteria? Out of the corner of my eye, I noticed a few girls glaring at me. Good thing I didn't know any of them.

He leaned in closer, raised his fork slightly, and nodded. A voice in my head said *C'mon, live a little*.

Slowly, I inclined toward him and opened my mouth. It was the most perfect lasagna I'd ever tasted.

"You weren't kidding, were you? That's a drug," I said. "I didn't think the staff here could actually cook."

The corners of his mouth curled into a grin. "They can't cook a damn thing. I got this at a restaurant last night and they just heated it up."

My sandwich was now seriously outclassed, but I took a bite anyway. The lasagna had sparked my appetite. The butterflies in my stomach had subsided, too.

He offered me another forkful of food. I accepted readily, not caring as much this time about what people were thinking, because he was looking at me even more intensely than he had before. He practically smoldered, and I suddenly got how intimate this gesture of sharing food was meant to be. I could feel it all the way to my toes.

"It goes better with a bit of Chianti." He took a swig from a stainless steel water bottle, then held it up for me. "Want some?"

I didn't accept it and lowered my voice. "You brought *wine* to school?"

"They had it at the restaurant, too. It's great what you can get at a restaurant. You should try one sometime." He took another bite of his food, savoring it. "It's even better fresh out of the oven. How about it?"

As I leaned back in my seat to finish eating, I wondered exactly what he was offering: dinner out? Or something more?

"I can get reservations for Friday," he continued.

"I already have plans on Friday."

"How about Saturday?"

Could I actually go out with Damiel? He was charming enough, but he wasn't exactly the type I'd bring home to Mom. I tried to recall her work schedule. If she was working, I wouldn't have to introduce them. She'd never let me get on the back of that motorcycle. "What time?"

"Seven?" he asked. I winced slightly. If my calculations proved correct, she'd be working until seven. "What's wrong?"

"My mom should be coming home from work around then, and she hates bikes…"

"I have a car, too." He motioned to the rain outside. "It's not bike season anymore."

I relaxed a little. "Then seven would be great."

Lunch was almost over. Back at the table where my friends sat, Heather had already left but Jesse and Michael lounged on the benches, talking. Michael glanced over at me and I felt a twinge in my chest. I turned to see Damiel smile at him with such malice it startled me. Michael's expression hardened, and I could swear the energy crackled between the two of them. In my mind's eye, everything went black, followed by a blinding flash of light. It made me dizzy. Damiel put his hands on my shoulders, steadying me, and a shudder ran up my spine. It *was* pleasure, wasn't it? It had to be.

Smiling down at me, he said, "Let's get you to class."

"I can get myself there," I said, guilt sweeping over me. It was difficult enough to get over Michael, but doing that with someone he despised made me seem petty. It wasn't my fault that Damiel liked me and Michael didn't, or that the two of them had some weird bad blood between them. But it had been harder to see

Michael than I thought, and I'd soon have to sit through English with both of them.

"Besides," I added, "I need to freshen up."

I'd read once that the antidote to some venoms is to inject small doses of the venom and let the body develop its own antivenin. They do this with farm animals, horses, sheep, and goats. I would have to do this to myself with Michael. See him in small doses at school every day until seeing him no longer made me suffer. I couldn't expect Damiel to understand, but I needed some time alone to prepare myself for a class with Michael. I needed to let the small dose of him I'd just seen in the cafeteria prepare me for the larger dose.

Damiel squeezed my shoulders gently a few times, and I sighed. I was so tired all of a sudden, I could have taken a nap right then and there. He dropped his hands and whispered in my ear, his breath almost tickling my skin. "See you in class, beautiful." I drank it in and walked away, not looking at anyone on my way out.

Perhaps Damiel was an antidote all by himself.

Chapter Ten

I slept so deeply that night I almost missed my alarm. I awoke Thursday morning feeling jarred, and while I managed to pull myself together for school, I couldn't shake the damp cloak of sleepiness that hung over me. Before my first class, I saw Damiel talking to Fiona at her locker. For some reason she wasn't responding to him, not even flirting. Her normally straight shoulders curled in toward her chest, and she dragged books out of her bag as though each one weighed fifty pounds. Damiel was focused intently on her, and when he touched her arm, my stomach flinched in response.

Farouk joined me in the hallway, his gaze following mine. "Is Fiona okay?"

"I don't know. She looks pretty sad." I made a mental note to check in with her later. "What could Damiel be saying to her?"

He gave me a puzzled look. "Damiel?"

I motioned over my shoulder. "Yeah. Talking to Fiona."

"I see Fiona, but Damiel's not with her."

I looked back in their direction and Damiel was gone. "That's so odd," I said, "he was just there. Didn't you see him?"

Farouk was contemplative. "You know, my sister Fatima sees things."

"I'm *not* seeing things!"

Unfazed by my reaction, he continued, "She had a vision about our uncle when we were ten."

I thought about asking if Fatima ever saw shadows or strange flashing lights or even people who weren't actually there, but decided against it. "What was it about?"

"She saw him in a car crash with a drunk driver on his way home. She was so upset, my mother convinced him to stay in the guest room that night. The next day, we heard about someone else getting killed in an accident on the same road. That's when we knew it saved his life."

I shivered. Did he think I was seeing things the way his sister did? "This is nothing like that. I'm sure he was just there." I inclined my head in Fiona's direction and bit my lip. The last thing I needed was to be having visions. First Michael, then Damiel? Was I incapable of talking to a gorgeous guy without hallucinating about him? Motioning in the direction of my class, I waved as Farouk and I parted ways.

Damiel kept to himself in English. He sat at the back of the room, and after smiling and winking at me he focused mostly on the lecture. Michael's blue eyes were even more intense against the blue shirt he wore, and he even smiled a hello to me before he sat down. I was beginning to think that Damiel wasn't working as an antidote to him anymore. I was going to have to be a big girl and suffer through this crush.

I became increasingly curious about Damiel's conversation with Fiona because, surely, I couldn't have made it up. He could have been interested in her too, though from how sad she looked it seemed more like he'd rejected her. I kept an eye out for him at lunch, but neither he nor Michael was around.

I did spend a fun lunch break with Heather, Farouk, Jesse, and Dean in the cafeteria, where we finalized our movie plans for the next night.

"Where's Fiona?" I asked.

"She had to go to the library," Dean replied. "Something about a history test."

Heather had begun treating the movie outing like some kind of team building exercise. She'd expertly planned the night, giving everyone specific roles. Dean and Fiona would meet us there with tickets, Farouk and I would line up for popcorn, and she and Jesse would stand in line for seats. We planned to get there at least an hour early to allow for all this. If we ran into any difficulty, we would text each other, staying in constant communication. All in all, it was a plan worthy of international espionage, which was perfect considering we were seeing a spy movie.

Farouk eyed me a few times during lunch, but thankfully didn't say anything about our earlier conversation in front of the others. He seemed to have something on his mind, so I wasn't surprised when he walked me back to my locker after lunch. I thought he was going to bring up his sister's vision again, but instead he asked me a question.

"Are you seeing Damiel?"

Caught off guard, I stammered, "I–I wouldn't say I'm seeing him, but he asked me out."

He frowned and leaned on the locker beside mine. "Why go out with him?"

It took me a moment to realize what Farouk was asking. Was I leading him on by accepting a ride to the movie? Was it a *date*? Come to think of it, the others had paired off into couples. It was best to clear up any relationship confusion as soon as possible.

"Farouk, the movie is just a movie, isn't it?"

"Well, it's supposed to be quite *good*."

I tried again. "I mean, you're a sweet guy, and any girl would be lucky to date you—"

"I didn't mean…" His brown skin flushed slightly red.

"Oh!" I said, embarrassed all of a sudden. *God, did I sound full of myself!*

"I saw you and Michael the other day and I thought…"

I heard a siren and ignored it at first, but its wails grew louder as it approached the school.

"No. No," I said, "he's seeing someone."

The siren stopped, and flashing colored lights filled the halls. Everyone stopped walking to class as two paramedics rushed through with a stretcher. They hurried past us to the office, then toward the girls' changing room.

Farouk and I joined the other kids who were following the paramedics, trying to figure out what was going on. A buzz of panic filled the halls as teachers tried to usher us into classrooms, but we wouldn't move. We gathered, waiting to find out what had happened and who had been hurt.

A few minutes later they rolled the stretcher out, with a girl on it. I couldn't see her face because the EMTs blocked my view, but one of her wrists was bandaged. Ms. Callou, the guidance counselor, followed behind them, her lips pressed firmly together, her T-shirt stained with blood.

"It was a suicide attempt," I heard someone whisper. As everyone asked each other what was going on, I heard the whispered words "suicide attempt" echo through the halls.

As they passed, I saw a mass of strawberry blond hair and my heart caught in my throat. Her hands were over her face, but I recognized Fiona immediately. I took a step toward her, but one of the paramedics, a tall woman with graying blond hair, held up a hand to stop me.

"Make room," she said.

"She's my friend," I explained.

"You can see her later."

A hot rush of fluid hit the base of my throat. I swallowed hard and took a step back. Farouk touched my arm, and I turned to him. There was nothing to say. The combination of shock and surprise on his face told me we were both thinking the same thing. Why would bright, vivacious Fiona want to kill herself?

They'd closed the school after the ambulance left, as if sending us home would stanch the flow of rumors. Heather and I rushed to the hospital and spent most of the late afternoon in the waiting room. We hoped someone would let us see our friend or help us make sense of what had happened, but only her immediate family was allowed to see her. My mom wasn't at work, so even she couldn't help. After a nurse told Fiona's parents that her condition was stable, her mother broke down and cried. Her father shook as he held her, his face gray and tight. He spoke to her in hushed tones. I'd never felt so useless, not even the day my parents split up.

Rather than burdening Fiona's mom and dad further by hanging around, Heather and I decided to go downstairs. We wandered aimlessly, not sure where to go. Neither of us ready to go home yet, we ordered some flowers from the gift shop and headed to the cafeteria.

I picked at my beef vegetable soup, but Heather couldn't eat at all. Her coffee sat on the table in front of her getting cold. She'd crumpled a paper napkin between her fingers, the edges twisted into points, and her eyes were red and splotchy from crying.

"Why didn't I see the signs?" she asked.

"What signs?"

"That Fiona was depressed." Heather blew her nose into the napkin, then left it in a heap on the table. "She's always so upbeat."

"She didn't have any signs," I said. Then I remembered how unhappy Fiona had seemed talking to Damiel that morning. My eyes stung. I didn't even go talk to her. What kind of friend did that make *me*?

"I guess she didn't," she said, pulling another napkin out of the dispenser and worrying it with her fingers. "I know it's *terrible* to think of myself in a moment like this, but what kind of psychotherapist will I be if I can't even help my own friends?"

I grabbed one of Heather's hands and squeezed it. "You're going to be a *great* therapist one day, and Fiona is going to be fine."

"How do you know?" Heather asked, blinking back more tears.

"I just do," I said, and in that moment I did.

"You mean some kind of sixth sense?" She smoothed the crumpled napkin onto the table and refolded it. "You know I don't believe in that."

"I know," I said. "But that doesn't mean you're right."

***

Friday was mild and sunny. It hadn't rained for a couple of days and the fallen leaves had a chance to dry out in the sun. As I walked to school, I received another text from someone I barely knew asking about Fiona. That made a dozen since yesterday. I ignored it. I'd avoided the Internet too, not wanting to think what Elaine must have said, for surely she'd capitalize on someone else's pain for her own popularity. It was all a horrible mess.

What would make Fiona want to leave us like that? Without even saying goodbye? She had a great family, friends who cared about her. She got along with everyone. Why would she ever want to kill herself?

I was so caught up in my own thoughts that I didn't notice the white VW pull up beside me. Immediately recognizing the car, I tensed.

Michael rolled down the passenger window.

"Get in," he said. "I'll drive you."

I shook my head, keeping my tone icy. "I'm almost there."

I kept walking. He pulled the car over to the side of the road and parked it, grabbing his bag on the way out. I didn't wait for him, but with his long legs it only took seconds for him to catch up with me.

"We need to talk," he said. "Please?"

His voice was as soft as a caress, and it was sad what the sound of it could do to me, how *much* I wanted to be close to him.

"This isn't about Damiel again, is it?" I said. "Because I don't think it's any of your business."

"Probably not," he said. "But won't you hear me out?"

I sighed. "We'll just argue again."

I'd packed too many books into my school bag that morning. It was heavy, so I took it off my right shoulder and was switching to my left when Michael caught it.

"I got it," he said, slinging it over his shoulder as though it were weightless.

My bag now his hostage, I followed him down the tree-lined street. At least he didn't take off with it the way my brother used to. Instead he stayed close, so close that when a breeze hit, I could smell the shampoo from his freshly washed hair, combed back to dry in waves. If this had happened a week ago, I would have been thrilled to just hang out with him. But now, knowing he was going to talk about Damiel again made me increasingly nervous. Damiel seemed like my chance to get over him once and for all, but with Michael coming around all the time, *that* wasn't working. Not at all.

We walked almost a block before Michael took a deep breath and said, "I'm not trying to make things difficult."

"No?"

"You think I *want* to do this?" He shoved his hands into his pockets, but he was close enough that his arm grazed mine, sending tingles all the way up my neck.

Damn, why do I have to like him so much?

"Do what exactly?" I bristled, struggling to focus. "Meddle in my life?"

I hoped what I said would make him angry, because I wanted him to get so angry with me he'd leave me alone. But instead he was calm. "I'm trying to help you."

"You're trying to *help* me? Maybe you should help *yourself*. You're the one who pushed Damiel away because you don't want to remember that part of your life—"

"What?" He turned on his heel to face me, and I could have sworn the air snapped. "What are you talking about?"

"He said you two were in the hospital together, that seeing him brought up bad memories for you."

"That's a load of…" Shaking his head, he stopped himself, took a breath. "You don't believe that, do you? You're smarter than that."

"Oh, really? I'm supposed to be some kind of mind-reader? Why don't you tell me what's going on?"

He led us across an empty baseball diamond near our school, walking so quickly I had to hurry to keep up. "Haven't you noticed it's hard to say no to him?"

"I can say no." I spat the words at him. Was he implying I was some kind of slut or something? Was I, as the girl, supposed to say *no* because it was what *good* girls did? "Why the hell should I? What if I don't *want* to?"

He took a step toward me, his eyes blazing and yet not with anger. There was tenderness there, and sadness, and I wasn't sure what else. I wanted to commit that look to memory. But then some kind of wall came up inside him, cold and solid as iron, blocking his true self in. Or was it blocking me out?

"That's your choice to make," he said.

I recoiled. "I haven't chosen anything yet."

"Even not choosing is a choice."

I swallowed hard, fighting the sting of tears. He couldn't be giving up on me, could he? "What am I choosing *between*?"

He led us around the corner, down the back road leading to the school. "Don't you find yourself tired around him, drained even?"

When he mentioned it, I realized it was true. I'd been very tired lately. But how did he know that, anyway? I stopped walking and crossed my arms over my chest.

Turning, he stopped too, his hand clutching the strap of my bag. A lawnmower engine droned in the distance. "What if that was by design?"

"I don't understand. Why are you being so cryptic?"

"Are you going to see him again?" he asked. "I mean, outside of school?"

Not wanting to answer *that* question, I started walking again. "Just dinner tomorrow."

He fell in step beside me. "Don't go out with him." His voice was soft, almost pleading, with that strange musical quality I'd heard before.

I didn't have it in me to be angry with him. "I really don't get it. You don't want me, yet you come around like some kind of knight in shining armor and now you're trying to warn me about some guy. Why do you even care?"

"Don't underestimate him. He's not just 'some guy,'" he warned. "He's dangerous."

My throat clenched. "Dangerous? What do you mean? What aren't you telling me?"

He made an exasperated sound. "Can't you just take my word for it?"

I fought back the urge to argue with him, the need to know more. He could be so infuriating, but something in me knew he was telling the truth, or part of it. He and Damiel shared a past, but beyond implying that Damiel was lying Michael didn't say anything. He was hiding something. If he was trying to protect me, what was he trying to protect me *from*?

"You know my friend Fiona?" I asked, changing the subject.

"Yeah?"

"You were talking to her a few weeks ago but she didn't see you, and Damiel was talking to her in the hallway yesterday before she—"

"Look, I'm sorry about your friend," he interrupted, handing me my bag. We'd arrived at the back doors of the school. "What you do is your choice. I'll see you in class."

I was being dismissed.

As I headed inside, I wondered if there really was something about Damiel talking to Fiona. Perhaps he was dangerous. *But they were just talking, weren't they?* This thing with Fiona, could it be a coincidence? If so, *how*? And why wouldn't Michael talk about it?

I went to my locker before class. When I opened it, a small brown paper bag fell out. My name was written on it in tidy cursive script. Inside was a delicate silver pendant, an ornate upside-down hand with a blue glass eye in the middle. Clear gemstones bordered the outside.

I was examining the bag for a clue as to whom it might be from when Heather approached. Her eyes were puffy and ringed with gray, this time not from studying.

"We're still going to the movie tonight, right?" she said.

With all that had happened I'd totally forgotten about the movie. I didn't think anyone would want to go. "Is it still on?"

"Yeah. We don't want Dean to be alone tonight. Though he won't admit it, he's pretty shaken. He can't see Fiona yet either."

"Have you heard anything?" I asked.

"Her mom called and told me she's awake now and going through some tests. She'll be home tomorrow. I'm gonna go see her then."

"Can I come?"

"Of course!" she replied, then noticed the necklace in my hands. "Oh! Where'd you get that?"

"I don't know. It was in my locker. There's no note."

"Maybe it's from Damiel." Heather handled the necklace carefully, admiring it. "For your date tomorrow night."

She handed it back just as Elaine came down the hall, and I quickly slid it into my school bag. I didn't need to give Elaine a reason for more gossip. If Damiel was giving me gifts, he could be more serious than I thought. I should give it back to him and break off the date so I wouldn't lead him on.

As if on cue, Damiel came to see me before English class to confirm our plans. It was the perfect opportunity to cancel our plans and return the necklace, but I hesitated. I could hear my name being whispered in the back of the room; I'm pretty sure it was Elaine. Michael nodded at me encouragingly, as if he knew what I was about to do. Damiel turned to him and wordlessly touched my hand. A rush of heat shot through me so fast it made me queasy, and the smile Damiel gave me melted my worries.

It was dinner. That was all. What was the big deal in that? Sure, Michael had warned me, but how bad could it be? Standing there in jeans and a T-shirt, Damiel looked dangerous all right, but in a different kind of way—a good way. *Definitely not the Ugly.*

"You still want to come, don't you?" he asked. "It'll cheer you up." When I nodded my assent, his smile grew even bigger and he went back to his desk.

Out of the corner of my eye, I saw disappointment on Michael's face as he sat in the row adjacent to mine. I didn't want to disappoint him, but I also hadn't agreed to anything. I'd been warned, though, whatever that meant. But why had it been so hard to say no to Damiel in the first place? Michael had said it would be. I was so embarrassed I couldn't bring myself to look at either of them for the rest of the class.

***

As soon as I got home from school, I sent Bill an e-mail asking him if he could look up Damiel online to see what he could find out. If he had a criminal record or a dangerous past, surely there would be some clues out there. I gave Bill all the information I had on Damiel: his approximate age, a physical description, and the fact that he had recently enrolled at Westmont High. I wasn't surprised to find Bill online. He messaged me immediately, asking *Who is this guy?* and *Is he a new boyfriend?*

Recalling how he'd offered to "take care of" any guy who hurt me, I reassured him not to worry, that this was just someone at school. He didn't need to know I had an actual date, but I wanted to find out what I could. Damiel seemed so open, and yet his side of the story was so different from Michael's. Could he have been lying, as Michael had said?

My online chat with Bill took longer than I expected, so I had to rush to get ready for the movie. Mom and I had such opposite schedules lately that we had taken to leaving each other notes on the fridge. I quickly wrote her one. If she was worried, she could always text me.

Since I was planning to have a lot of popcorn, I had only a snack for dinner: a couple of slices of cheese and an apple. Deciding to dress up, I wore a skirt and tights and kept my hair down. On a whim, I put on the necklace. If it was from Damiel, I would give it back to him the next night. But that didn't mean I couldn't wear it first.

Farouk picked me up at six, and I was surprised to see that he'd dressed up too. It made him look a lot more grown-up than usual. I also liked how at ease he was. All the weirdness from earlier was gone. We were just friends, hanging out.

The movie theater was noisy and dimly lit, with bright flashing lights around the concession stand. The line-up wasn't long, but the short, freckled girl working there had trouble with our three separate orders. She jumbled them up and got flustered. As the line grew quickly behind us, she got even more nervous.

While Farouk helped her figure out the change, Michael walked into the theater. At first I was so captivated by him that I didn't notice he was with someone: a tall, gorgeous girl with honey-colored hair. She seemed strangely familiar. A sharp pain seized my chest. This had to be Michael's girlfriend.

"Mia?" Farouk asked.

Realizing I'd been staring, I spun back to face him.

I'm pretty sure my emotions were clearly visible on my face, because he stiffened and muttered something in Farsi under his breath; I don't think it was complimentary. "We should go find Heather," he suggested.

I nodded and was about to leave, but it was too late.

"Mia," Michael said, approaching us. When he smiled at me, his entire face lit up. You'd never know we'd had an almost argument earlier that morning, or that I'd disappointed him by not breaking off my date with Damiel.

"You know Farouk," I said, afraid my sadness over his being there with his girlfriend might show.

Michael gave him a nod. "I do. Hi."

Farouk held up the bags of popcorn he was carrying and said flatly, "I'd shake your hand, but…"

"Quite a lot of popcorn," he said. If he noticed Farouk's snub, he was ignoring it.

"We're here with the rest of the gang," I said, raising my drinks awkwardly.

The girl Michael was with gave me a beautiful, warm smile, and I realized where I'd seen her before. She was the girl I'd talked to at the café that day I'd gone there with Bill.

"That's a pretty necklace," she said.

"Thanks." I touched it self-consciously, not wanting her calling too much attention to it. The fact it probably came from Damiel would only cause another argument between Michael and me.

"Yeah." Michael leaned in to take a closer look. "It looks Turkish."

"It's *Persian*," Farouk said, edging closer, until he practically stood between us. "My sister Fatima gave it to her."

"Fatima?" I asked. When he nodded, I tried to hide my sudden relief.

"Well, it's very nice," the girl said, then turned to Michael. "Aren't you going to introduce us?"

I wasn't sure if I should say anything about how we'd sort of met before when she spoke to me in the café. Obviously she didn't recognize me. Why should she? She was the one who looked like a Victoria's Secret model. People probably noticed her all the time.

"Of course," Michael said. A flattering shade of pink touched his cheeks as he turned to me. "Mia, this is Arielle, and Arielle, this is Mia and Farouk."

We exchanged polite hellos. Then Arielle said to me, "Michael's told me about you."

I instantly tensed, almost spilling the drinks I was carrying. Surely he hadn't told her about the ridiculous crush I had on him, or that I was going on a date with his arch-enemy. Michael kept his relaxed smile, his face unreadable.

"Oh," I said.

"Yeah, he mentioned you'd had a nasty fall in the woods, I guess it was a few weeks ago now," she said. "How are you healing up?"

"Quickly," I replied, relieved he hadn't mentioned anything else, then added as if I was his PR person, "Michael was really helpful. I don't know how I would have gotten out of that creek without him."

She smiled sweetly at him. "That's our Michael."

Was it me, or was he uncomfortable receiving the praise? He crossed his arms over his chest, looking positively gorgeous. "You would have done the same thing," he said to her.

"We should probably get inside," I suggested to Farouk, "before the movie starts."

We exchanged polite goodbyes and went off to find our seats. Heather waved when she saw us, happy that her night out was going so well—considering. Even Dean, playing a pre-movie trivia game with Jesse, seemed cheerful. As for me, I had a 400-pound sumo wrestler sitting on my chest. It wasn't until after the opening credits, when we were well into the movie's first scene, that I let myself cry. Fortunately, the movie grabbed everyone's attention and whisked them away, so I had time to pull myself together before they noticed.

On the ride home, Farouk played the movie highlights over in conversation, and I was grateful for the recap. I hadn't been paying attention. Neither of us mentioned Michael, or Fiona for that matter.

When we pulled up in front of my house, Farouk said, "I'm glad you wore the necklace. It suits you."

"It's beautiful! I love it," I exclaimed. "It's really sweet that she thought of me."

"It's a Hamsa—a ward against the evil eye."

"What's that?"

"It's a type of protection from people sending you bad thoughts. You know, when people are jealous or wish you harm."

"I could sure use that," I said, thinking first of Elaine, then Fiona. Had someone been sending her bad vibes?

"We sell them at my father's store. They've even been blessed by an imam—a Muslim priest." He gave me a shy grin. "I guess that must sound odd to you."

I shook my head. Who was I to judge his beliefs?

"You know how I told you about her gift the other day?"

"Yeah," I said, remembering how he thought I was seeing things. I still didn't want to talk about it.

"She thinks that someone means to harm you, and that wearing the necklace will protect you."

Invisible, icy cold fingers danced up my spine. "Oh."

"I hope it brings you luck."

Chapter Eleven

In my dream, Michael and I walked hand in hand up an arid, grassy hill. Sheep grazed in the meadows, and gardens stretched out like patchwork blankets below. Heat waves shimmered in the air around us, and the sky shone a crystalline shade of blue. Halfway up the hill, Michael stopped. Wrapping his arms around me, he pulled me close until our bodies grazed each other's—not quite touching. I pressed myself into him. At first his kiss was gentle. Then those kisses became hungry, intense.

A voice in my dream said: *Open your eyes*.

When I did, I was surrounded by darkness, and I wasn't with Michael anymore. I was with Damiel. Startled, I tried to back away, but he was so strong I couldn't move. His smile sharpened, the corners of his mouth pulling fiendishly tight, and his brown eyes glowed red. I got the sense his hunger had nothing to do with kissing. He put his hand over my heart and it lurched, as though it would rip out of my chest. I gasped, pushing away from him with all my strength, but I was starting to weaken…

***

As she pulled her mom's minivan into Fiona's driveway, Heather cleared her throat so loud it made me jump. I'd spaced out.

Fiona lived with her mom and dad in a big, modern house with huge windows overlooking Puget Sound, and the view from their living room was incredible, especially today. The sun peeked through the clouds and beamed rays of light onto the water below like something from an inspirational greeting card. Fiona sat on her bed, fully dressed, reading a horror novel. A large gauze bandage was taped to her left wrist; she must have gotten stitches.

When she saw us, she sprang off the bed, her arms outstretched to hug both of us at once.

166

"So good to see you guys!" Fiona said.

"You too." I hugged her.

Heather backed away first. "I'm so sorry," she said. I wondered where she was going with this. "You're my friend. I should have—"

Fiona cut her off. "I'm the one who's sorry. I didn't mean to put everyone through this. I don't know what I was thinking. I just…" She sat back down on the bed. When she looked up at us, her eyes were shining and wet. "Don't know what happened. I really don't."

Heather sat on the bed and put an arm around Fiona. I grabbed the chair near the vanity table. "It's okay," she said. "We're going to get through this together."

Fiona shook her off. "You don't get it. I've been sad in my life, sure, but I've *never* been depressed. Over the last few days, I've been examined by doctors, psychiatrists, psycho-*everything* and all they could say is I didn't fit the profile for a suicide attempt. My mom was ready to think I did it for attention." She choked out a sob. "But I didn't."

I'd never seen Fiona so emotional before, and it worried me. Was she denying what happened? "Hey," I said. "It's okay. We don't have to talk about it. We can just hang out."

"No, I want you guys to believe me. Nobody believes me! I'm not crazy, okay? I know it sounds nuts, but when I was in the changing room... You *know* me— I'm afraid of kitchen knives. I don't even know where it came from. It may have been my hand holding the knife, but it wasn't me in there." She took in a deep breath and let it out, shaking her head. "Then, as soon as I...cut myself...it's like I came around. I tried to stop the bleeding and couldn't. I called out and Ms. Callou came to help."

"Dissociation," Heather muttered under her breath.

"Heather," I said. "Now isn't the time for psychoanalysis!"

My mind flashed back to that morning when Damiel spoke to Fiona in the hall. He was so intense, and she didn't seem herself.

"I believe you," I said to Fiona. "I saw you that morning. You looked sad."

"I *was* sad that morning. All I could think was what a loser I am, and how no guy could ever want me. Not Dean. Not anyone."

"You're a total babe, Fi! Don't you ever forget it." Heather put an arm around Fiona's shoulder and gave it a little squeeze. "Have you talked to Dean?"

"Yeah. We're good, I think," she said. Grinning, she grabbed a tissue and blew her nose. "He's coming over later."

I couldn't shake the image of Damiel whispering in Fiona's ear. I wasn't sure if now was the right time to bring it up but I had to know. "Did Damiel say something to you?"

"Damiel? No. He's never really spoken to me other than to say hi." Fiona leaned forward tapping her foot. "Why? Did he say something?"

"No. Not at all." I wasn't quite sure what to say next. Hadn't she *seen* him?

Heather cut in. "Mia's got a date with him tonight."

"*Oh my God!* Really? You lucky—"

"About that…" I began. I couldn't go out with Damiel, not if he'd said something that hurt my friend. But if he did, she didn't seem to remember it. While I thought I saw him talking to her, I could be wrong. Maybe it was just my imagination. Was I the one going insane?

"Don't you *dare* cancel that date," Fiona said. "I want to hear all about it."

While the idea of going out with Damiel felt far from right, I agreed to go. My gut was telling me there had to be some kind of link between Fiona's suicide attempt and what I saw that day. Even if he hadn't been in the hallway talking to her, I must have seen something. Farouk had said his sister had visions of future events. Maybe I was having them, too. What if he was *going* to talk to her later and *that* was what I saw? Some possible future event. It was almost too strange to consider. The only way to know for sure was to ask Damiel. He had answers, and I wanted to know what they were.

If he was as dangerous as Michael said, I needed some kind of backup plan, someone who could come and help if I needed it.

"Can I ask you a favor?" I said to Heather when we were on the ride home.

She turned down the car stereo and checked the rear-view mirror. "You know you can."

"Can you call me tonight at eight, just to check in?" I asked. I didn't want to worry Heather with the reason why, not without proof, but I figured if she called me I could make up an excuse to get out of there.

"You mean a bail-out call?" she said, her attention focused on the road. "I doubt you'll be bored."

"Probably not," I said. Being bored was the least of my worries. "You will call, though? At exactly eight o'clock."

"Of course."

After she dropped me off at home and I was alone, I tried to convince myself that the sweaty palms and tightness in my chest were just nerves, but I knew it wasn't true. Something about going out with Damiel, alone, seemed really *wrong*. It was misleading, and I didn't want to do that. What I wanted were answers, but I didn't know how else to get them.

To bolster myself, I decided to wear the temporary tattoo Heather had given me. I'd been saving it for a special occasion, and for some reason tonight felt like I needed to have wings. Wearing my hair up would even show them off. I was so curious about how they'd look, I applied them right away. It took a little while to center them between my shoulder blades and the nape of my neck, but when I was done, they looked amazing.

I put on a little black dress. It was cut low in the front and back, so you could see the tattoo, but not too low. Soft and comfortable, it hugged my curves without being too clingy and looked good with my high black boots. My hair was tied up, and I was putting on eye shadow when the doorbell rang. Startled, I checked my watch; it was only 6:55. Was Damiel early? I double-checked myself in the mirror. I still needed mascara at the very least. He would simply have to wait on the sofa while I finished.

The knock on the door came again. Determined to not let the idea of seeing Damiel intimidate me, I flung the door open.

"Michael." I almost fell back on my heels. "What are you doing here?"

He scanned my outfit with a quiet intensity that made the skin on my neck flush. Catching himself, he focused on my boots and let out his breath. "I've been sent."

"What do you mean you've been sent?" I demanded. "Who sent you?"

He raised his hands as though I held him at gunpoint. "I've come to talk. May I come in?"

I'd forgotten how tall he was. He towered over me, and I couldn't help but notice how clear his eyes were, how even the dim porch light played off his skin, making it glow. His hair shone almost black.

"I'm still getting ready," I said, moving out of the doorway and leaving him to close the door while I put on a light.

He cleared his throat. "Nice tattoo."

"It's not real," I said, turning back to face him. "I can't get a real one 'til I'm eighteen."

"Wings, huh?"

"Yeah. I had this dream about them once. It meant a lot to me." It seemed natural to tell him, as though he'd understand. But when he looked away with a wry grin, I regretted saying anything. "Why are you here?"

"Look, I know Damiel will be here soon..." He ran his hand through his hair. "But—"

"I know. I know," I cut him off. "You don't want me to go out with him. He's dangerous."

If he was upset, he didn't show it. Shoving his hands into the pockets of his jeans, he gave me a shrug that said he didn't care either way. "Why are you going?"

"Because." I sighed. His lack of reaction made me feel all the more foolish. "I need to know what's going on."

"You think he's gonna *tell* you?"

I hadn't thought of that. Here I was about to go all Nancy Drew on Damiel's ass, and my big plan was to lay my cards on the table and *ask* him what he'd said to

Fiona. Maybe I'd dance around it a bit, but I was relying on him to tell me. Michael had all but called him a liar the day before. Why would Damiel say anything resembling the truth?

"Okay," Michael continued. "Say he did tell you. What then?"

"I've got a safety plan," I said defiantly, trying to hide how foolish I felt. "Heather's going to check in, come get me if necessary. I won't be alone." I wasn't sure about the Heather coming to get me part, but I figured she would. I would do the same for her.

"He's a predator, Mia. He could hurt both of you."

The word *predator* caught me off guard. I remembered my dream that morning where Damiel kissed me and it felt like he was draining me dry. I wanted to argue, but I knew deep down that Michael was telling the truth. I'd never wanted to go out with Damiel. I'd been pulled into it right from the beginning, like watching a train wreck. Only the train wreck was me.

Michael took a step closer until I had to crane my neck to see his face. "Tell him you don't want to go."

His eyes met mine and they were filled with genuine concern, same as that day I'd fallen in the woods. I wanted him to come even closer.

"Okay," I said. "You've got to give me some answers, though."

Clearly amused, he raised his eyebrows and said, "I don't *have to*, but I will—once he leaves."

"Once he leaves?" I confirmed, before he could change his mind. "You promise?"

He tensed, as though a jolt of electricity had shot through him, and spun around to face the door. "He's here."

Chapter Twelve

The sound of the doorbell should not have startled me but it did. Michael's presence on the sofa was reassuring, but only to a point. What was I going to say? Swallowing my fright, I opened the door.

"Hello, gorgeous," Damiel said, unabashedly checking me out. His black leather jacket and crisp white shirt accentuated the hard and soft elements of his face: angular nose and cheekbones and plump, full lips. For the first time, I noticed a shiny haze around him—shadows so black they glistened and shone in the porch light.

Heat rose to my cheeks and a queasy sensation wrestled with my stomach. He seemed creepy to me now.

How could I have even thought about going out with him?

"I was going to call you earlier." I said, "but realized I don't have your number…"

There was a sudden pulsing at my throat that made me jump. Thinking a fly had landed on me, I raised my hand to feel what it was. The necklace from Fatima had started to vibrate.

"What's the problem?" he asked, reaching for my hand. "Your skin is like ice." The shadows around him darkened as his hand clasped mine. I'd never seen them so clearly before—maybe that was the necklace too, protecting me. A tingle of heat shivered the length of my arm, and then a wave of dizziness came over me as the strange haze that surrounded Damiel flowed toward me.

"I'm sorry." My eyes started to burn. I scrunched them, trying to concentrate. "I can't go to dinner with you tonight."

The angles of his face hardened and his eyes turned as cold and black as a crow's. "What's going on?" he demanded.

The gleaming haze around him grew, getting darker and fuller. I couldn't find my voice to speak.

"She's double-booked. Sorry," Michael said. His hand on my shoulder steadied me, as a warm golden glow surrounded us. The blackness dissipated the way shadows escape the morning light.

"Well, well. Michael." Damiel released my hand. "Should've known you'd go for the girl...given your history." He turned his attention to me, smiling menacingly. "Mia, you're making the wrong choice. Michael will only hurt you." A dark wave came at me again, in ripples this time like tattered black streamers.

Michael flanked my left side, tense as a bow ready to spring. "Leave her out of it," he said. "It's me you want."

In that moment I knew he might have to fight to protect me, and if he did he would think nothing of it—even if he got hurt. And as much as I was scared for him, I was twice as grateful he was there.

Light grew around Michael as darkness built around Damiel, and the energy between them pulsed and throbbed as though the two forces had a life of their own.

The dark smoke reached toward the light and then pulled back, reverberating—gaining in mass—until it arced back and slammed into the light with all the violence of waves against rock. While the rock would hold, with enough time and pressure it could also be eroded. Could darkness erode light?

"It's *her* that I want," Damiel said, and his eyes flashed a terrifying shade of red, the same as in my dream. I inhaled sharply and the red was gone. His tone changed to one of mocking. "Besides, how can I leave her out of it when you can't? She's always been a part of it—thanks to you."

Before I could ask what Damiel meant, who Michael might be to me, the dark smoke drew closer, swirling around me, forming spikes like an iron maiden. The scents of creosote and sulfur filled my nose.

I coughed. "Michael, what's happening?"

Damiel's smile broadened, chilling me. "See? You can't stop me. She's a weakness to you now as she's always been. She'll take you down again, Michael."

Again?

The darkness encased me. Spiraling tendrils drilled the light around us and inched toward my skin, piercing and burning with a mixture of pleasure and pain—both captivating and revolting. The evil eye necklace quickened at my throat.

Michael whispered in my ear, his voice taking on that musical quality I'd heard before. "Trust me. It's okay. Don't worry." His fingers against my collarbone sent a rush of light and heat through me like sunlight, reminding me how cold I was. I leaned into him as though I were drowning and he was dry land.

"You have no idea what *he's* capable of," Damiel said. "The things he's done." There was a force behind his words that made the necklace thrum like a tiny, terrified heartbeat. Darkness amassed behind him, and the light from Michael faded.

I needed to do something.

"Leave, Damiel," I said. "Leave now!"

A jolt of energy pulsed through me, thrusting against the darkness. Damiel staggered from the force of it. Anger and revulsion crossed his face.

"Good," Michael said. "Use your free will."

"I think it's time you remembered," Damiel said. With one hand he covered my face, and the force of blackness around him enveloped me again. Before I could blink, a flurry of images poured into my mind— senseless scenes of darkness and fear.

"Don't touch her!" Michael erupted and charged Damiel, heaving him down the front steps. Damiel laughed as he regained his balance with an unnatural grace, and his features creased and darkened, making him look more monster than human. With a snap of his fingers, the streetlights extinguished and blackness enveloped the area. All that remained was a dim porch light. He swung wildly at Michael.

As Michael dodged and parried his blows, the light around him grew. It glowed brighter and stronger, until a transparent blue shimmer formed like gossamer behind him into an outline of wings.

Damiel noticed it too and it seemed to compound his fury. Quickening his attack, he landed a fist on Michael's temple and Michael staggered, blinking sweat from his eyes. Damiel lunged at him again but Michael recovered quickly, leaping up onto Damiel's black Maserati, his boots denting the hood.

Pulling a weapon from behind his back, Michael swung a sword around himself that flamed a brilliant blue. Damiel ducked and backed away, but the sword made contact, slicing his cheek. I gasped. Although it visibly weakened him, it didn't leave a mark.

I saw Michael in that other time and place as if it were a dream. He was still beautiful, but more severe, pained, like he lived his life in shadows. In the background stood someone equally beautiful: Damiel. How was it possible? Could all three of us have existed both then and now?

"See the way she's looking at you?" Back in the present, Damiel goaded Michael. "It's just a matter of time before she knows what you are—Brother." His words had the same effect as Michael's sword, cutting him down without leaving a mark. He stepped in, grabbing Michael's arm above the wrist, trying to take his weapon. "That is, if she doesn't go insane first."

The images flooded in faster than I could make sense of them, leaving me dizzy and sick from the recollection. I leaned into the doorway for support.

A cold rage came over Michael. With his left hand he threw a solid jab that connected with Damiel's chin, throwing him backward and downing him. Raising his sword, Michael stood over him, ready to strike. He looked at me briefly and there was a note of sadness between us as he drove the sword right through Damiel's heart. Damiel let out an inhuman shriek and the black mass that hovered around his body disappeared, as though the air around him had just opened and swallowed it up.

A scream caught in my chest, unable to escape. I could hardly breathe. The necklace, which had vibrated since Damiel's arrival, stilled.

Crouching beside the limp body, Michael placed his hands over its heart and pressed his lips to its forehead. The boy opened his eyes.

"W–where am I?" the boy stammered, sitting up. His voice, smooth and pleasant, held traces of an Italian accent. Even his features were different from Damiel's now: coarser, more masculine, less otherworldly in their beauty—more human.

"What's your name?" Michael asked, offering him his hand. "Can you stand up?"

The boy accepted and stood groggily. "Giulio."

"You should go home. Your family's been worried about you." Michael placed a hand on his shoulder to steady him. "Do you know where you live?"

Giulio nodded and Michael helped him into his car.

After Giulio left, Michael turned back to me and let out his breath. The fight with Damiel had popped a few buttons on his shirt. It gaped open, exposing a tightly muscled chest. The flashes of memory I'd seen in that other reality were fading as disbelief took hold of my thoughts. Even this battle with Damiel seemed unreal.

But what did seem inescapably real was Mom's Toyota pulling up the road and Michael quickly zipping up his sweatshirt to cover his torn shirt. In all the evening's tension, I'd forgotten she would be home so soon. It was barely seven-thirty. How had so much transpired in so little time? As Mom's car pulled into the driveway, Michael strode up the drive.

"He'll be back. That boy Giulio has no defenses against him," he said. "If not him, he'll find someone else to possess."

My knees slackened. Luckily I was still leaning against the doorjamb for support. I really needed to sit down. "He was possessed?"

"It's what demons do."

What? Surely I'd heard him wrong. "You mean Damiel is a…"

In the doorway, Michael stood so close that the heat of his body sheltered me from the cold night air. All I could think about was the dream I'd had the night before, the good part where he'd kissed me. I wished it were real.

"We've got a lot to talk about," he said quietly and stepped inside.

Mom eased out of her car as though tired from a long day at the hospital. When she came in, I greeted her with a hug, glad for the sense of normality her presence brought. I tried not to think about what had just happened so the shock and horror of it wouldn't show on my face. But I could already see her curious expression when she registered my behavior, my new outfit, and then Michael standing by the sofa. We looked more like we were going on a date than friends hanging out, which was the story I'd told her last night.

"Mom, this is my friend Michael," I said, introducing him.

Mom smiled, her eyes sparkling. *God, please don't let her say anything embarrassing.* "Hi, Michael," she said, holding out her hand.

"Hello, Mrs. Crawford," he responded, shaking her hand. He was so steady, as though this was *normal* for him. Did he battle demons all the time?

"Shelly, please," my mother corrected. "Mrs. Crawford is my ex-husband's mother."

I tried not to gawk. None of my friends *ever* called her by her first name.

She turned to me. "What's the scoop? I thought you said you were going out with your friends."

I didn't know what to say. So much had happened tonight I was afraid to speak for fear that everything I'd seen and heard would pour out of me in one big purge.

"There was a change of plans," Michael chimed in. "We're going to hang out a bit, maybe get something to eat."

Mom looked at me to verify he was telling the truth. I nodded dumbly, grateful for his quick thinking. He hadn't even lied.

"I'm going to take a long, hot bath." She fussed with my jacket collar and smoothed a lock of my hair back into place. "The living room's all yours if you want it."

"Thanks."

"I should…" She motioned to her room and grinned. Then she whispered in my ear encouragingly, "He's cute."

"Mom!" I whispered, glancing at Michael to make sure he hadn't heard her. Even with his hair messy from fighting, he looked more like a movie star at a photo shoot than someone who had just fought off a demon.

Fought a *demon!* We had a lot to talk about indeed.

Chapter Thirteen

Michael went outside to split some logs while I paced the living room, trying to collect my thoughts. Damiel was a *demon*. If I hadn't seen that black smoke around him attack me like something out of a horror movie, I never would have believed it. And what were those weird images? They came in too quickly to make any sense.

Fiona used to say that she would love it if a guy fought for her, but having just been in that position, I could honestly say it was terrifying. Michael could have been hurt. He tried to warn me, but I didn't listen.

Michael came in with an armful of logs and placed them in front of our old brick fireplace. Crouching on the floor beside them, he grabbed a piece of newspaper and crumpled it in his smooth, strong hands.

I knew his hands when they were callused. How could I know that? Mom told me once that people who experienced psychotic breaks saw things that weren't really there. Was that what was happening to me?

The light was suddenly too bright. I rubbed my eyes, pressing with my fingers. I didn't even know where to begin. "This is crazy. Am I hallucinating?" I asked.

"No," he said.

I kept pacing, the heels of my boots noisy on the oak parquet floors. My thoughts—like a tongue to a broken tooth—kept returning to that small mud-plaster house. Pinkish yellow morning sun filtered through the open doorway. Michael was outside, wearing robes of some kind. He was so tall he had to stoop to come in.

"Why do I keep seeing things? It feels as if I *know* you, but not from now. Everything's…" I realized I couldn't bring myself to explain the way things looked. Nothing made sense. "Different."

Raking a hand through his hair, he glanced down the hallway to see if my mother was within earshot. Her door was closed, but I could hear the water running for her bath.

"Those are memories," he said.

Memories? It was one thing to have hallucinations, but to have them confirmed was something else. Visions of him flashed before me, too numerous to track. Darkness and light. Some were present-day—fighting with Damiel. Others seemed to come from another time.

I shook my head, as if I could shake them away. "It's too unreal."

His back toward me, he stacked small logs around the paper in the fireplace, making a teepee. "Reality isn't what you think."

"I don't know what to believe. It seems like a different life."

"It was a long time ago," he said.

"What do you mean a long time ago? *How* long?" I pressed.

Michael struck a match and held it to the paper. Flames licked yesterday's front-page news, consuming a scrunched color photo of the Space Needle. "You tell me."

I closed my eyes to hold onto what I was seeing. It was *before* the Roman Empire, *before* the Chinese Dynasties, even *before* Mesopotamia, but try as I might I couldn't register how long ago it was. My mind spun. I'd been fascinated with ancient cultures most of my life, only to find out that I'd lived in one. I had *been* there.

Buzzing like I'd had too much coffee, I collapsed on the couch. "How can that be? Both of us remembering that far back? It's impossible."

"No, not impossible," he said. "Improbable. There's nothing left of that time, no artifacts, no written records. Everything it once was has washed into the sea. People can't remember their past lives that far back. If Damiel hadn't tried to dislodge your memory from this life and *throw* it back into that one—"

"Damiel did *what*?" I scowled at him.

"I stopped him."

"Michael. Tell me what's going on!"

Sighing, he blew the flames until one of the logs caught. The light from the fire cast an orange shine in his hair. "I've been given another chance."

"Another chance for what?"

The air around us grew still and cold and the fire gave off too little heat. I shivered.

Michael got up and sat on the couch beside me. Resting his elbows on his knees, he tented his fingertips together; they were gray from the newsprint.

"I'd been sent to watch," he said. "I saw many things over the years and at first I thought all there was to this world was sickness, brutality, and death."

His skin drew a little tighter to the bone and filled with golden light, as though he shone from within. "But one day I saw you...and you were the most beautiful thing..." Heat rushed through my chest: he'd called me *beautiful*. "I became obsessed, neglecting my duties to watch you each day...preparing food, gathering flowers to make dyes for the fabric you wove."

Goose bumps formed on my arms and tickled the back of my neck as he spoke. What he was saying had to be true. I'd never told him about the loom. How else could he have known?

"I wanted to be with you. Wanted you to see me," he continued. "Even though so many of the others had fallen before me, I thought this was different, that *I* was different. That letting you see me would be enough…"

An image of a meadow came to me. Yellow sunlight streamed through bright spring leaves, bathing everything in dappled light. Michael stood there, wearing the robes I'd seen him in before.

"One day, I appeared. You weren't much older than you are now."

I stayed with the image. Behind Michael were wings—actual wings—the same ones I'd dreamt of. Had I been dreaming of *him?* As the goose bumps on my arms spread all the way down to my feet, I remembered how peaceful, how good being near him felt—much as it did now.

"You had wings."

"Your mother had died. You asked me to stay in the meadow to keep you company. An angel's duties."

"You're an…" I couldn't say the word. But it explained so many things: the flashes of light that day in the woods, the way he seemed to glow, his unearthly beauty.

"It was forbidden for us to mate with humans."

A tendril of sadness wove itself around my heart. *What we felt was forbidden?*

"Other Watchers started to see I was in trouble, told me to get reassigned. I should have left you alone… Instead, I came to you often."

I remembered returning to the meadow to wait for him, the late afternoon sun dancing through the leaves.

"Even this lifetime, when I first saw you…It's like I'm being forced to choose again, between Heaven and being with you."

"I'm sorry," I said.

"Don't be," he snapped, then quickly composed himself. "Being with you back then made this world bearable for me."

I could hardly believe what I was hearing. Happy tears welled behind my eyes. I blinked them back, smiling at him.

"Don't look at me that way," he said, frowning at me. "You wanted an angel's presence. I was consumed by lust. What I became, what I did…"

Memories sped through my mind faster than I could catch them, dizzying me—one of Michael kneeling on the sun-baked grass, holding and kissing my hands. I gasped from the force of the memory. "You loved me."

He took both my hands in his now, gripping them as a palpable anger flashed through him. "No, I became obsessed. What I did was wrong." Sighing, his grip lightened as he let my hands go. "But you loved me anyway, believing for the rest of your life that you had seduced an angel. When it was all along the angel who had seduced you."

Not sure what to say, I didn't speak, taking it all in. All I could remember was the love.

"I can't do that again," he said, standing.

"You won't."

He knelt in front of the fireplace. One of the logs had fallen in the fire he'd built, its embers glowing beneath the flames. Poker in hand, he stabbed at it and clusters of hot, angry sparks gasped up the chimney. "You don't know—"

"You *asked* me to trust you." I couldn't understand why he was warning me against him, after everything he'd done to help. "And I do."

"That's different."

Was it? I didn't see how. As crazy as it all sounded, I believed everything he was telling me. I even remembered some of it, and the memories I had were good ones. Though I was curious about *everything*—how we lived, what it was like, and especially what he'd done—I couldn't bring myself to ask. Not yet. It didn't seem right to mistrust him for something he did thousands of years ago, in a different life. Something I didn't even remember. How was it relevant?

"It was a long time ago," I said.

Putting down the fire poker, he closed the screen. "I hurt you."

I joined him by the spitting fire and knelt beside him. "That doesn't mean you will again."

Exhaling sharply, he leaned his head into one of his hands and covered his eyes. As I watched him struggle with his conscience over his past, a tightness gripped my chest. Without thinking, I touched the back of his head, stroking his hair, and it felt natural, as though I'd done it many times before. He sighed as his shoulders visibly relaxed. Squeezing my hand, he moved it to his lips and kissed it, palm up, before taking it in his.

The heat of his mouth lingered on my hand. When he looked up at me, his eyes were soft and unfocused.

"Thank you," he said, and a sense of peace washed over the room.

Chapter Fourteen

Once the fire died down, Michael admitted he was starving and we headed out in his car for a bite. When he turned on the ignition, a loud, moody guitar riff blared through the speakers. I recognized the melody, the steady beat. It was by a local indie band, but their name escaped me. The song itself was about love.

Noticing my smirk, he asked, "What?"

"This is the kind of music angels listen to? I always wondered."

He laughed, a warm inviting sound that curled itself around my insides. "Expecting harp music? No, wait. Gregorian chants."

"Yeah. Something like that." I laughed too, happy for the distraction. "But this is way better."

I leaned back and let the music flow through me as he drove along the tree-lined side streets. Lights from the houses and streetlamps flickered through the leaves, so bright they hurt my eyes. I took a deep breath to relax, but my mind was sprinting. Even as a kid, I'd wanted to become an archaeologist so I could discover ancient civilizations, and here I was *remembering* one. Instead of artifacts, I had memories, fragments of a story. I could have just as easily been remembering a dream.

"Have you been alive all this time? You know, since…?" I tried to fathom the idea of being immortal.

He glanced at me before returning his attention to the road. "No. I was born into this body, but it wasn't until the accident that I got a chance to come back."

"How does that work? Is it like being possessed?"

"Possession implies there's no choice, an invasion by something evil." He pulled the car onto the West Seattle Bridge, overlooking downtown and the Port of Seattle where cranes, lit like sentinels, watched over shipyards below. "This is different. When I came into this life, I thought I was human. The best way to describe it would be to say my soul was some kind of sleeper soul. It wasn't until I had the accident and died that I was reactivated, returned to duty."

The hairs on my neck prickled. "Is that…reincarnation?"

He shook his head. "This is my first time in a human form. I'm not strong enough to exist here without one anymore."

"Was it strange? Going from thinking you were human to…" I stopped myself. How *couldn't* it have been strange? It was like asking if water was wet.

"It's like not knowing you had another limb until it grows back. Then you know what it was and how to use it."

He turned the car along Alaskan Way and parked near the waterfront. City lights sparkled and danced off the water. Thick gray clouds covered the sky, except around the moon which had managed to peek through and light up the rippling waves.

"Why are you back now? After all this time?" I asked as we got out of the car. The sea air smelled of kelp and creosote from the docks, and its dampness made my skin tingle.

"I was in…recovery. Time doesn't exist the way it does here. I had no idea where or when I'd be assigned, but I knew eventually I'd have to come back."

"What for?"

He gazed out over the water and the wind caught his voice, making it almost inaudible. "To face you."

We crossed the street and headed to a Mexican restaurant nearby. When he opened the door, the warm smell of fresh salsa, chilies, and herbs washed over us, making my mouth water. The fluorescent lights were so bright I had to squint to read the menu on the wall. Even then, the words swirled as though I were drunk. I drew in a deep breath to steady myself. Michael touched my arm, standing so close to me I could smell the sweetness of his skin mixed with the scent of fresh lime that hung in the air. In that moment he seemed very real, very human, and *very sexy*.

A man working alone behind the counter took our order and offered to bring it to our table. We sat by the window. Michael held my chair for me, and even though it was casual we were definitely out *together*, like a date. I should have felt guilty about going out with someone else's boyfriend, but I didn't. Being with him seemed right.

My cell phone rang, startling me. I fished it out of my purse and saw Heather's number. Immediately thinking it was about Fiona, I answered. "Is everything okay?"

"You asked me to call you, remember?" said Heather. With everything that had happened, I'd forgotten. "I know I'm late, but I figured you were doing fine."

I checked the time. It was 8:45. So much for my plan to use a phone call to escape Damiel. If Michael hadn't arrived, I could have been dead by now. "Everything's okay."

"Have fun," she said and hung up.

I didn't realize how hungry I was until there was food in front of me. Before I knew it, I'd wolfed down a large bean burrito. As Michael chewed, the bright fluorescents revealed a tiny scar at the hinge of his jaw, a flaw that didn't detract from his looks but enhanced them.

"How'd you get the scar?" I asked, gesturing at it.

"Oh, *that*." The corners of his mouth pulled into a wide grin and the scar crinkled slightly. "I've had it since I was six. Thought I'd try shaving one day. Took my dad's straight razor, but forgot to use shaving cream."

I wasn't sure if it was the idea of him being six or the idea of an angel with a shaving nick, but it made me want to laugh. I stifled it—poorly.

He swallowed a bite of his food, noticing my expression. "What?"

"Sure. Demons can't hurt you, but shaving?"

"What makes you think demons can't hurt me?" He took another bite of his taco.

Of *course* they could. But if they could hurt him, I didn't want to think about they would do to me.

I scooped some guacamole with a tortilla chip. "You mentioned something before about other Watchers. What are they?"

"Grigori. It's the order of angels I belonged to."

"Not anymore?"

He chewed thoughtfully. "You could say I'm in rehab."

"Rehab? Like AA—only *Angels* Anonymous?"

He shook his head despairingly at my joke. "What else would you call it? Coming back to this world to live a human life." He lowered his voice. "While I try to be an angel again."

"Slumming?"

"There are worse places."

"Than high school?"

That made him laugh. "Okay, maybe not."

***

He picked up the tab for dinner despite my protests, and we made our way to the door as the restaurant filled with a later crowd. Not wanting our evening to be over yet, I lingered on the way out. His hand brushed my lower back to guide me and a tingle ran all the way down my legs.

Still warm from his touch, I didn't notice the cold sea air until we stepped outside and it cut through my clothes. I'd dressed for fashion, not warmth. Michael took off his jacket and draped it over my shoulders; it was warm and smelled of lightning and grass after it rains.

"Where to now?" I asked, hoping he wouldn't say *home*.

"It's too cold for a walk." His breath formed clouds of steam as he spoke.

"I'm okay if you are."

He guided me a few short blocks to the waterfront and piers. The tourist shops were closed now, but there was a well-lit path that led to the docks. Nearby, a group of young guys practiced tricks on their skateboards while a busker put away his guitar. Though it wasn't a dangerous area at night, it was close enough to some of the seedier areas downtown that I wouldn't have gone there alone.

We approached a long boardwalk lit by globe lights, our steps rhythmic on the wood below. "Damiel called you 'brother' earlier."

"That's what Grigori call each other."

"He's a Grigori, too?"

Michael slowed his pace. Sadness tightened the hollows of his eyes and reminded me that this *being* standing beside me—half-human, half-angel—was truly ancient. "He was. Before he fell."

"You said he was a demon. How can he be a Grigori like you and a demon now?"

"He's not like me," he said so quickly I was afraid I'd upset him. He took a deep breath. "When you're one of us, you don't just fall and that's it. Falling is a constant, endless thing. At first you feel the same, only you're alone—no longer connected. But then the other voices start."

He spoke about the voices as if he'd experienced them first-hand. The idea chilled me. "What kind of voices?"

"Dark voices," he said. "If you give in and side with them, you keep falling, which is what Damiel did."

"What about Hell?"

"Hell is just a place. Demons that are strong enough come and go at will so they can hurt people."

He spoke of Hell as though he knew it. Had he been there? Would Damiel be back? I wanted to ask him so much more, but the hurt and warning in his eyes had me deciding against it.

We stopped on the dock. Across the harbor, tiny lights from the streets and houses speckled the islands of Puget Sound. The ferry leaving Colman Pier sounded its horn.

Michael rested his hand on the railing, and I became very aware of his presence beside me: the deep slow sound of his breathing, the closeness of his body, and all the barriers between us. I reached for him, gently touching the backs of his fingers. As I did, I felt an electric current that made me want to pull him toward me. Afraid of the intensity of that impulse, I backed away.

Closing his eyes, he exhaled. Though he didn't move, everything around him seemed to come alive. Light radiated from his body, its outer edge shimmering with golden white sparkles. Trying to touch the light, I reached out. It moved around my hand like phosphorescence in the night sea and tingled like warm soda bubbles on my skin.

Michael turned to me at that moment, unfocused, as though returning from somewhere far away.

"There's something around you," I explained. "Gold and white flashes."

He smiled self-consciously and the light around him flared brighter. "You can see that?"

"What is it?"

"My halo."

"All the way around your body?" I asked, thinking of those old paintings of angels with their golden rings of light. They didn't even come close to what a real halo was.

"It used to go much further."

"I saw you that day I went to the hospital," I said, recalling the girl who'd been stabbed. "Then you were gone."

He leaned his elbows on the railing. "We're often invisible when we're working, but you've always seen me."

"And with Fiona?"

He shrugged. "Going to the dentist freaks her out, and she's not the best driver when she's distracted."

I smiled at that. Fiona was always getting caught up in the conversation, forgetting to look at the road, and she did have an appointment that day. He was trying to calm her down so she wouldn't have an accident along the way.

"Angels do that?"

"She's your friend," he said.

He closed his eyes again, and his halo flared and hummed around him. Stiffening, Michael said, "We should go."

"What is it?"

"I'm on duty tonight."

"On duty? What does that mean?"

He led us down the boardwalk. "The Grigori still watch over people, keep things safe."

"Safe from what?" I swallowed nervously.

"Things you shouldn't know about."

"I'm not a child, Michael," I snapped.

My reaction rolled off him. "I never said you were."

We turned down the street that his car was on, and I recalled that first day I'd seen him in the park. And the pieces started to come together. "That shadowy dog—you saw it, didn't you?"

He gave me a wary look.

"I asked and you... You let me think I was crazy!"

"I was trying to protect you. You're not supposed to see these things. They sense fear; they live on it. The more afraid you are, the more they can materialize. They'll drain your life force until you pass out."

"That old man! Is that what happened?"

He nodded. "After that, you're just meat."

"It was going to *eat* him?" Bile rose to my throat over the thought of being eaten alive, but I fought it back. "What the hell was it?"

"A hellhound," he muttered. "Scouts. Damiel sent several of them to find you."

"He did?" I shuddered at the idea of Damiel looking for me. "You were *watching* me even then?"

"I only knew there was danger. I didn't know I would see *you*."

Approaching his car, he clicked the remote and the doors unlocked. Within seconds, he was opening my door.

"What about that day I sprained my ankle?" I asked.

"Then too."

Partway through the ride home, my mind overloaded itself and shut off, and an easy silence grew between us. Though sometimes obscured by passing streetlamps, the light around Michael still glowed. His halo burned beside me, brushing and tingling my skin.

"You've been through a lot tonight," he said. "You ought to sleep. It'll help you process."

His sweatshirt draped open at the neck, exposing the edges of his collarbones and the dip in his throat where they met. Despite everything I'd been through, all I could think about was planting kisses there. Clearly, sleep was the last thing on my mind.

Catching my gaze, his face became shadowed. "Arielle said we should keep an eye on you."

"Arielle?" I asked. At the mention of her name, I had a twinge of envy.

"Sure. We work together."

So Arielle was a Grigori too. That explained a lot: her otherworldly beauty, the flickering lights that day in

the café, and even the way the shadows—hellhounds—
disappeared. "She's not your girlfriend?"

"No," he said, scrunching his nose. "It's not like
that."

A knot in my chest relaxed. It had formed the
moment I first saw them together at the movie theatre,
but I'd become so used to the feeling I'd forgotten it was
there.

Next thing I knew he was outside the car, opening
my door. As I got out, I accidentally brushed his arm, and
the draw to be near him was so strong I had to lean back
against the metal to steady myself. Then, as if in answer
to a silent prayer, he wrapped his arms around me and
closed the distance between us.

Pressing his lips to the crown of my head, he
breathed the words "I missed you" into my hair, softly, as
though it were a secret that only I was meant to hear.
Then, letting his arms drop, he stepped away.

All the lights were on when I got in the door and
the house smelled of pine cleaner. Mom scrubbed the
kitchen counter with the TV on, trying not to look like

she was waiting up for me. From the looks of it, she'd cleaned the whole house.

She greeted me cheerfully, focused on removing a spot from the counter. "Did you have fun?"

"Yeah," I said, trying to be understated. She seemed different to me now, still my mom, and yet not the same. Perhaps I was the one who had changed.

Realizing I was still wearing Michael's jacket, I hung it up in the hall closet before she could notice.

"He likes you," she commented.

"Mom," I said. "So *not* ready to talk about it." And I didn't just mean my date. The things Michael told me—that I *remembered*—shook me. *I'd lived another lifetime before.*

Mom didn't let up. "There's something really *good* about him."

I stifled a wry smile. "Angelic, even?" *If she only knew!*

"No, honey. Men are never angels," she said sagely. "Besides, it's the devil in them that we love."

Before she could ask any more questions, I kissed her goodnight and went to my room just so I could be alone. I doubted I'd be able to sleep. Every idea I had about my world was being challenged. Demons were real and came here to hurt people. The strange creature that chased me that morning in the park was a *hellhound*, and Damiel—who was a demon—had sent it to find me. Michael was a Grigori—an *angel*—albeit in rehab, and I'd shared a life with him *thousands* of years ago.

As soon as I closed my eyes, memories of the night flooded my mind with dizzying speed: Damiel at my door surrounded by black sooty shadows, Michael fighting him with the blue sword in his hand. I wanted to know more about the past, who I was back then, what had happened to me. To us. Had I lived other lifetimes since? But no matter how hard I tried, my present-day memories wouldn't give way.

An hour later I lay in bed still awake, shivering. It wasn't from the cold, because I'd already cranked the heat up and covered myself with every blanket in the house. The only thing that helped was thinking about Michael. I remembered the warmth of his arms around me as he hugged me goodbye, and a flush of restlessness flowed through me.

With Mom now in bed, the house was quiet and still. I crept out of my room to the hall closet and retrieved his jacket. I got back into bed and laid it beside me, enjoying the comfort of its smell. This time when I closed my eyes, I remembered the feel of his arms around me, the sound of his beating heart, and with these memories I relaxed easily into a deep sleep.

***

I awoke well-rested. Sunlight streamed through my bedroom curtains, filling my room with a peaceful, warm glow. My phone was crammed with text messages from both Heather and Fiona, asking how my date went. I replied with a quick *Good—I'll tell you later* which must have had them thinking Damiel was still around. But I couldn't explain his disappearance, or even the fact that he was a demon. When I got out of bed, Mom had already made a pancake breakfast, so we ate together in front of the TV. Mercifully, she was focused on getting ready for a mid-shift at the hospital and didn't ask about my date.

Shortly after she left for work, Bill called my cell.

"Hey," he said. "Everything okay?"

"Yeah. Why wouldn't it be?"

"I tried calling and all I got was static. Then I called back and some guy answered."

"Just now?" I asked, sitting on the couch. "I've been here the whole time."

"Yeah. Said he was expecting you."

I shivered in spite of myself. "Weird. What else did he say?"

"Nothing. The line cut out, so I called back and got you."

For a brief moment, I wondered what it could have been. Was it just a wrong number or something else? But Bill changed the subject. "You know that guy you asked me about…"

My throat constricted. With everything that had been going on, I'd completely forgotten. "Damiel?"

"Yeah. I checked him out. He's got no birth records, no school records. There aren't even any death records for him. This guy is totally off the grid. Technically, he doesn't exist."

Of course he didn't exist. He was a demon. A wave of panic pushed at me, but I fought to stay calm. "Wow," I said. "You checked all that?"

"Yeah, of course."

What if Damiel knew Bill was looking into him? I didn't know all he was capable of, but I knew he was dangerous. "Can anyone *tell* that you did all that? I mean, you won't get caught, will you?"

"Gee, paranoid much? Shouldn't I be the one worrying about you?" I could hear the tapping of his fingers on the keyboard. Always multitasking. "Who *is* this guy?"

"Nobody. Forget about him." The idea of Damiel getting anywhere near Bill terrified me. "Please?"

Bill stopped typing and when he spoke, he sounded worried. "Hey. He's not bothering you, is he?"

"No," I lied. "I'm fine."

"Stay away from this guy, Mia. I mean it. He sounds like a scumbag."

If he only knew. "I will," I said. "I promise."

A few minutes after Bill and I hung up, the doorbell rang, startling me. Still a little creeped out from my conversation about Damiel, I peeked out the kitchen window and saw Michael.

"Hi," I said. Rushing to open the door and hug him, I buried my face against his chest and felt the softness of his light gray sweater against my cheek.

"Hey." Caught off guard, he chuckled, but his body was stiff as he put an arm around me. Was he *nervous*? "I thought we could finish that walk we started last night. While the rain holds off."

LISA VOISIN

Chapter Fifteen

He took me to Alki Beach, partly because it was close and partly because it was one of the best places in the area to walk. I liked it there. I especially liked being there with him. By daylight, I could see out over Puget Sound, where the choppy gray water reflected the storm clouds above.

He was right about the rain. It looked as though it would come down any minute, and when I stepped from the car the cold air smelled of ocean, seaweed, and evergreens as it filled my nose. With the exception of a few joggers, the beach was deserted. The tide was low, and acres of rocks, teeming with marine life, stretched out along the shore.

Some of the nearby trees had already started to turn. Half-ochre, half-green, their leaves had dried around the edges, holding onto the memory of life. Others had fallen to the ground. As we walked, Michael seemed to notice them too.

"What was I like? You know...*before*?" I asked. "Was I different?"

When he turned to me, his eyes were the color of the Mediterranean Sea, and they had a way of looking at me that made me feel equally vast and deep. "What do you remember?"

I closed my eyes and recalled the house we lived in, the glow of sunrise along its walls. But mostly I remembered Michael. The way that being near him made me feel exactly the same as it did now. They were the same images and sensations over and over, no more than the night before, but no less.

I felt the heat of him and opened my eyes to find him standing only a foot away from me. *Could he see what I saw?*

As though catching himself, he stepped back. "Arielle suggested I spend time with you."

The mention of her name gave me a twinge in my chest. Obviously they were close. "You saw her last night?"

"Of course. We check in," he said. Turning, he headed toward the rugged shoreline.

I followed him, my sneakers crunching and slipping on the damp rocks. I had to watch my step. "Why did she suggest you do that?"

"She's trying to help me." A gust of wind blew his hair into his face and he lazily pushed it back. "When we first came here, many of us became sick and fell to one of the seven deadly sins—envy, pride, lust. It took me longer. I thought I was different, but I got caught up in it just like the others."

"Caught up in what?"

"Lust," he said and flashed me a sideways glance that was positively scorching. The effects rippled all the way down to my knees. As though sensing my reaction, he turned back to the white-capped waves crashing against the shore. "It wasn't just about sex..." He checked my reaction again, as though expecting me to shy away from him. I didn't. Hearing him use the words *sex* and *lust* made a shudder of want rise within me. "I forgot who and what I was."

Instead of saying more, he brushed his fingertips along my cheek, and his halo glimmered. I could hear the waves slapping the rocks behind us, the wind driving them in. That same wind whipped against my skin, but the touch of his hand on my face was all I could think about. It sent a current through both of us and filled me with longing for something I wasn't sure I understood.

"I'm sorry." He stepped back and shoved his hands into his pockets as the light around him faded. "You don't know what it's like. Being near you now, remembering those moments we had..." His hair blew into his eyes, but this time he didn't move. I wanted to brush it back, but I didn't know how he'd react. Would touching him be *bad*?

"You want to know who you were?" he asked. "You may look different, but you're the same. I look into your eyes and see *you*." He took in a deep breath, fixing his attention on the horizon. I'd seen and heard so much now that the logical part of my brain had long since given up arguing with me. I could feel what he was saying was true. All of it.

"What was my name?" I asked.

"Sajani." When he spoke, his voice was a chord, and the sound of my name echoed through me like I was an instrument being strummed. "It means 'beloved.'"

I drew in a deep, shaky breath, letting in a stream of emotion that practically drenched me. Very gently, he pulled me into a hug. The sound of his voice echoed through his chest as he spoke. "I'm supposed to let you go, but I can't."

"Then don't."

Placing a finger under my chin, he gazed into my eyes. His were filled with warning. "We can't...I can't be with you that way."

"What way?"

He pressed his lips into my hair and I flushed as I realized what he meant. I wanted to ask why, but didn't want to say anything that would interrupt this moment. His heartbeat pressed against my cheek as I breathed in the scent of his skin. Out of the corner of my eye, the sparkling glow of his halo surrounded us and a tingle of energy buzzed, stronger than anything I'd ever felt before. It awakened every cell in my body, and I thought if we could just do this, the feeling itself was incredible. *Surely this would be enough.*

"It's okay," I said, leaning to look up at him.

"It's not really fair to you, to be with you and not be able…" A lock of hair had blown into my face. He tucked it gently behind my ear. "I can never be with you like that, Mia."

"I don't care," I said. The heat of his touch lingered on my skin. "I don't think I could *never* have this again and be okay." My voice broke as I realized how much he meant to me, how much he had always meant.

"You'd be fine," he reassured me. "You're much stronger than you think. Stronger than me. You always were."

My eyes filled with tears. "What are you saying?"

"Shhh," he whispered. "Please. Don't cry."

His hands gliding to the sides of my waist, he leaned in close—so close I stopped breathing—and kissed a tear that had fallen down my cheek. Afraid he'd back away, I lifted my lips to his, brushing against them, softly, tentatively at first, awakening the current that trembled through me. Twining my arms around his neck, I drew myself into him. And with a sigh, he tightened his arms around me, parted his lips, and the culmination of thousands of years of waiting poured out of him like a dam had burst.

The energy around us built with the wind off the water, rushing past my skin, tangling my hair. I wanted to be swept away, carried above the clouds to the heavens. For a moment, everything was warm and bright like the sun.

In the distance, I could hear a gentle female voice in the wind, then a chorus of voices, speaking all at once, calling Michael by name.

His body tensed, but he pulled me closer, his kisses more urgent. The wind had died down, and a golden flare brushed my skin, searing me. I crushed myself against him, hips against his thighs, welcoming that heat. There was nothing I wanted more than this.

"Michael," the voice—or voices—said firmly, "you must stop now."

Why couldn't the voice just go away? I wanted to get closer to that heat, crawl into it, let it consume me. But with those words, he froze. Gently but firmly he untangled my arms from around him and backed away, not looking at me but at the ground.

Behind him, Arielle was furious.

"Is this your idea of being on duty? You were wide open. We could have easily had another breach," she said, her voice still sounding choral. "If I wasn't here, anything could have come through."

Michael shook his head gravely. "I didn't expect…"

"You were sent into the body of an eighteen-year-old male for a reason."

He glared at her, his expression all at once wild, dark, and haunted. "The ultimate test?"

"For your own recovery," she said. "You *know* you're not being punished."

They talked as though they were discussing some kind of science experiment and not the intimate experience we'd just had. Still reeling from the intensity of his kiss, I couldn't help but think that if she hadn't arrived, we might have enjoyed ourselves a little longer. What would have been so wrong with that? My heart sprinted in my chest, aching to be near him, and my body craved his touch. I was cold, so cold I started to tremble. I wanted—needed—him close to me. This was how an addict must feel. It was as though someone had just filled the needle and tapped it, about to plunge it into my veins, and then someone else came along and took it away.

Arielle gave Michael a stern look. "Your energy's way too much for her. You've enthralled her."

What did she mean, *enthralled*?

Michael clasped his hands behind his head and huffed out his breath. "Not on purpose."

"That doesn't matter. You know our laws are absolute. What if the others found out?"

As I listened to them speaking as though I wasn't there, I couldn't help but wonder how she'd found us and why she was telling him off. Did she want more than friendship from him? If she did, she had a funny way of showing it. My confusion must have shown on my face, because they both stopped talking and turned to me.

"It's not how you think," she said, her voice sounding more human. "I don't feel the way you do for him, and I don't disapprove of you, either." She then turned back to Michael and said in a more musical voice, "She doesn't know I'm your sponsor, does she? If you're going to keep her around, you might want to think about telling her."

"Hello, tell me what? I'm right here," I exclaimed. "Why are you talking about me when I'm right here? It's rude."

Arielle looked sharply at Michael. "She can hear us?"

"Of course I can hear you," I replied. "What do you mean you're his sponsor?"

Arielle spoke to me in the same voice I'd heard her use at the movie theater. "You can hear me now, right?"

"Of course!"

"What about now?" she asked. Her lips didn't move, but her voice was musical and clear. It was a different voice.

I nodded, my mind reeling. *How can I be hearing her speak when her lips aren't moving?* I wanted to cry again.

"She can hear us telepathically," she said out loud this time, and her serene, perfectly balanced face registered alarm. "I wonder how far along the network—"

"What's going on? What network?" I asked. Their serious expressions were beginning to annoy me.

"You can hear our thoughts, Mia," Michael said. "We've not known anyone who could do this before."

"*You've* not known," I said.

Looking concerned, Arielle took a step toward me. "Have you heard us before?"

"No," I said quickly, then recalled the morning in the park, the flash of light. I'd heard something that morning too. "Once, maybe. After I was chased. But it was really staticky. I thought it was just a radio or something."

"It's clear now?" she asked.

"Yeah."

"People hear things when their adrenaline is up, like when they're afraid, but having it come in so clearly…" She turned to Michael. "Another side effect of you kissing her. You have to be careful."

"I am…" he began, but stopped at Arielle's look. He ran his hands down his face and let out an exasperated sound. "Do you think its effect will wear off?"

"It better." I let out my breath, trying not to panic. "Because this is a little too weird for me."

"I'm sure it is," said Arielle, a wry grin on her face. It was difficult to dislike her, even though everything female in me felt threatened.

"We should watch her carefully. I'll keep an eye on her tonight, make sure she's all right."

Arielle frowned and a gust of wind blew tendrils of hair into her face. "No, Michael, I think *I* should watch her. You need to recover, too. You've both been impacted. You couldn't even feel me coming."

"I'll be fine," he said hastily.

"Will *she* be, if you're around all night?"

With a sigh, he acceded and turned to me. "Come on, I'll take you home."

We drove back in silence, not touching each other, not talking. The distance hung between us, palpable and heavy as a lead curtain. I tried to focus on the music instead, but it sounded harsh, so I turned it off.

"I'm sorry," he said, pulling the car in front of my house. He didn't look at me but at the dark clouds looming in the sky. Rain would come any minute.

"What?" I asked, biting my lip to keep my voice from wavering. "Sorry you kissed me?"

He reached a hand to touch me but let it drop. "Can't you see? You could get hurt. Really hurt. I'm not good for you."

I shook my head, not wanting to hear what he had to say next. "Please. Don't."

Turning to face me, he leaned against his car door and sighed, clearly upset. "The feeling that you couldn't get enough—I put it there. I don't even know how. I just wanted to be close."

So did I. "I don't see what's wrong with—"

"It's dangerous," he warned, cutting me off. "Had we gone any further..." He stopped talking, but the look in his eyes spoke of anguish and terror and shame. "I don't know how to control it."

I didn't understand all of what he was saying, but I knew *him*. I also knew how I felt, how I'd always felt for him. I'd wanted that kiss as much, if not more, than he had. "What if you could?"

"I can't—"

Before he could finish what he was going to say, I leaned across the console and put my finger to his lips. He didn't move but held my gaze, warily, as my finger traced the outline of his lips. When he raised a hand to my elbow, I thought he was going to stop me. But he didn't, so I leaned in and kissed him. His body tensed. I pulled back. I could see the struggle behind his eyes, the war raging within him. I should have been afraid—of him, of what I was doing—but I couldn't be. Instead, I kissed him again and felt him relax as his mouth responded to mine.

It was my own desire that made me kiss him, but his response tingled and rushed through me like a spell. I was playing with something strong and tempestuous and I wanted to be consumed by it. My life. Me. I didn't matter. *This* mattered. His hand gripped mine tightly as he leaned into me, and I thought my heart would explode in my chest. When his other hand moved gently up the side of my waist, it shook. It was time to stop. But, oh God, I didn't want to.

Just a simple kiss goodbye, that's all I wanted. I needed him to know it didn't have to be overwhelming or scary. But this, this was incredible. Squeezing his arm below the shoulder, it took all my self-control to slow down. My kisses shortened and, as though we were a single person, he responded in kind. I pulled myself away, basking in the warm haze that had formed between us. His eyes flickered blue around his dilated pupils. Intense as it was, this was normal desire, not enthrallment. I felt it, and I knew he felt it too.

But his expression darkened with shame and the warm haze turned to static. What he said next struck a blow.

"I'm sorry, Mia. I can't be with you. Not like this."

There was a whooshing in my ears and a sinking in my chest, as though my world was falling apart. I blinked back tears. "What?"

"It's too much." He swallowed hard, shaking his head, and he seemed so far away. "I can't...I just can't."

Chapter Sixteen

I cried until nightfall. Lying in bed with the lights on, I tried not to think about Michael, but I couldn't forget the taste of his lips. Or that look of shame in his eyes. I wanted to focus on reading my Gov/Econ homework, hoping to bore myself to sleep, to escape how repulsive and terrible I felt. I thought he wanted me. I thought it was safe to open up to him. We were meant to be together. But he'd pushed me away, and I couldn't help but wonder *Now what*? Was he going to avoid me again, just when he'd finally let me in?

There was a faint tap on the window. Arielle was outside.

"I saw you were awake."

"I'm not sure I want to talk." I opened the window anyway and she leapt through it with the grace of a lioness. A light rain had been falling and the drops sat in her hair like jewels, as though she'd been sprinkled with it, not drenched. Her long blazer and T-shirt were mostly dry. When she turned, I noticed vents in the back of her jacket, but I was too nervous to ask where her wings were. She was that intimidating.

She paced my room, taking in the full bookshelf in the corner, the old Ikea armchair, my white dresser and desk. Having her there, I was suddenly glad I kept my room tidy. If she noticed Michael's jacket next to me on the bed, she didn't say anything. It smelled like him, and I didn't want to talk about how that comforted me. I didn't even want to think about it, in case she could read my mind. After all, if I could hear the angels' thoughts, it only made sense they could listen to mine. *Does that mean Michael can hear me as well?*

Suddenly the light around her, which I assumed was her halo, shone, a ring of golden flame. Behind her was the same blue outline I'd seen on Michael the night he fought Damiel. But on Arielle, the outline was even more pronounced, a gossamer grid of blue light extending from above her shoulders to below her knees.

"Wings!" I said a little too loudly then covered my mouth, hoping my mother didn't hear.

"You can see them?" she asked as she paced the confines of my room.

"I thought they'd have feathers," I said, trying to not look too amazed as her wings shimmered and glistened like jeweled light behind her.

"They're cloaked right now. I bring them out when I'm flying or if I need to deliver a message. When people see the white feathered wings, they know you mean business." She peered back over her shoulder at me. "But I don't need to do that with you, do I? You know what I am."

"No, I mean, yes. I know what you are," I said, still intimidated by her.

"Most people can't see them when they're cloaked," she added. I could tell she was making an effort to put me at ease. "Have you always seen things?"

I remembered Bill telling me how I saw angels as a kid, and then the hellhound a few weeks ago, the flickering lights around Michael. Yet there had been nothing for all the years in between. "Once when I was a kid, maybe, but I think it's more of a recent thing."

She stopped pacing and turned to face me. "Around the time you first saw Michael?"

"I saw the hellhound first."

"Michael was near. Given your connection, I'm not surprised." Tilting her head, she closed her eyes and smiled. The gesture made her look pensive, connected to another world. "Sight is a gift that God gives people when He wants them to see the truth."

I wondered exactly what kind of truth I was supposed to be seeing, when her manner changed. She stood up a little straighter, became more formal, courteous.

"I came to see how you're doing," she said.

"Fine," I said, though I was anything but.

"I'm sorry you feel hurt by what happened."

Something about her apologizing brought up all my sadness again. Did she know Michael had dumped me? Did he tell her? I tucked the duvet around my legs, though I wasn't cold, and fought back the urge to start crying all over again.

Not wanting to get into it with her, I changed the subject, remembering something she'd said earlier. "What's a sponsor?"

She sat beside me on the bed, and the shimmering gold light from her halo washed over me like a spring breeze. "When Michael came back, he needed help to rejoin the ranks of the Grigori again, so I was assigned to help him."

"How do you help him?"

"However he needs me to, which is a pretty big job description." She smiled. "Michael has a very difficult journey ahead of him. Lust was his weakness and he just came back from…a type of limbo, essentially. He's lucky he didn't fall further. We've never had a Grigori come back before, so Michael's an experiment, a prototype. He's the first angel in a real human form."

"Don't you have one?" I wanted to ask her how far Michael fell, how bad things really were, because I didn't know anything about that part, but something stopped me. *What if he'd done something so terrible I could never forgive him?*

"My form," she said, motioning to herself, "is made of light. I can make it solid at will. Michael doesn't have the strength for that. Having a human body is new to him, to all of us. It may give him a type of strength, but it may also backfire and become a weakness."

"I don't understand what you're getting at."

"You will. In time."

As though remembering something, she looked at me intently, her golden eyes fierce and beautiful as a big cat's. As her halo flared slightly, I heard the sound of white noise in my ear.

"Did you hear anything?" she asked.

"Just static," I replied.

"You can't hear my thoughts anymore, which is good." She relaxed and her face softened. "You are better."

"I knew I would be," I said.

"Do you mind if I show you something?" she said. "I don't know if it will work, but I'm curious and I thought it might be worth a try."

"What are you going to do?" I asked nervously.

"Take you down our communications network and show you what Michael does."

"Your what?"

"As you discovered earlier today, we communicate telepathically. But it's more than that. We're linked into each other like a network, so we can see what's going on with each other when we need to."

So that was how she had found us earlier. "You mean you can see…" *Michael and me kissing?*

"Only when he's working," she replied quickly, as if she'd read my mind.

Can she hear my thoughts? I stared at her intently. *Is she listening now?*

If she was, she didn't let on. "The network's in place so we can back each other up. It's how we communicate. If an angel on duty disconnects from that network, the way Michael did today, we have to check on each other, in case of injury. It's for our safety. Any number of things could attack us when we drop our connection." She turned to face me. "I didn't know what I'd see."

"Oh." Her explanation didn't make the idea of her being able to see us any easier, but at least she couldn't read my mind. "How do we do this?"

Still sitting beside me on the bed, she took both my hands in hers. "You relax and look into my eyes. I don't know exactly how it will appear to you. It could appear as a vision, but it may seem like you're there."

I looked into her beautiful golden eyes, and a light flashed behind them, like sunlight through amber. I had the sensation of being pulled in, as though I was falling into her. I gasped.

"Don't be afraid," she said. "Just breathe and let me do all the rest."

I kept staring into her eyes as my bedroom disappeared around me and I was speeding down a wide tunnel of misty, silvery light. I flew through it as it bent and twisted several times and then opened into a room—a dirty, rundown apartment with cracked paint and water stains on the walls. It was so realistic, as if I was actually there, and yet I knew I wasn't. Arielle's presence blazed behind me as I took everything in.

There was no furniture—even the sink had been torn from the wall—and the carpet was stained with blood, vomit, and God knows what other bodily fluids. On the floor, amidst tattered clothes and broken glass, lay a sandy-haired guy in his early twenties, not much older than Bill. His eyes were glazed, haunted, and slightly open, and it seemed as though he hadn't showered or eaten in days. Beside him, pieces of tinfoil were scattered among a filthy-looking needle, a dirty ashtray, and a threadbare red bandana.

Most notably, on—or rather through—his chest sat something fuzzy and black, half the size of a man. It looked like lint, if lint could be animated, and it had hollows for eyes. Something about seeing it made my stomach churn, my chest tighten like the skin of a drum.

"You see it, don't you? I wasn't sure if you would."

"Oh my God," I said. Realizing I was cursing in front of an angel, I covered my mouth. "What is that thing?"

"A lesser demon. I guess you'd call it a minion of sorts. It's feeding on his addiction and despair." Her hand touched my shoulder. "They're parasites. They stir up negative emotions so they can feed off of them."

The thing writhed silently on the guy's chest and, suddenly agitated, the guy staggered to get up and reach for the tinfoil beside him, what I assumed were his drugs.

"How did it get on him?" I asked Arielle.

"They attack people and make them do horrible things, but nobody knows they're there. People think they're doing these things to themselves, but really they're feeding a parasite."

"So when people say 'a monkey on your back,' it's almost true." I shuddered at how it was more *through* than on him. I thought of Fiona, how she'd said she wasn't the one who hurt herself. "Do they attack everyone?"

"All the time, but it's about the choices people make. If someone chooses to hurt themselves or someone else, these things get in. If someone is happy and loving, it sours the milk and they leave."

"What about my friend Fiona?" I asked. "She wouldn't hurt herself, and yet…"

Arielle put a hand on my shoulder. "Fiona is insecure about her attractiveness. Damiel used that vulnerability to get in."

"She didn't do anything to deserve that."

A note of sadness crossed Arielle's face. "People seldom do."

I was trying to get my mind around this strange reality she was showing me when Michael appeared in the room. My chest tightened until it ached.

Despite the filth around him, his expression was serene, as though he were untouched by the grime. He was bathed in a golden light that made him awesome to behold, but the guy didn't even see him. Instead, with clumsy shaking hands, he fumbled to open the folded tinfoil.

Michael crouched behind the young man and whispered in his ear. Though I thought I'd seen Michael work before with Fiona at school, I couldn't ever hear what he'd said. This time I could. Arielle must have made it possible.

"Dear One, I bring you a message. Will you hear it?" He spoke in tones so beautiful my own heart leapt in response.

Tears filled my eyes as the man emptied the contents of the tinfoil into a spoon, preparing his next fix. The beast on the man's chest writhed and snarled. Michael spoke to him again, touching his shoulder and addressing him by name.

"Steven. You must stop this. This dose will kill you."

If he heard him at all, the man named Steven did not acknowledge it. The beast grew larger, its writhing more animated, as it snarled at Michael.

"Why doesn't he kill that thing?" I asked Arielle.

"He can't. Not unless the man releases it. We must respect his free will," she said. "Otherwise, another will just take its place."

"What about Damiel? Michael fought him."

"Demonic possession is different. If the host isn't willing, we can dispel them. This man, Steven, has given his will to the parasite."

Michael continued, "This is not the only way. You are loved. You are forgiven. Everything you have done is forgiven."

The man filled and tapped his syringe, ignoring him. The scene shifted and blurred as Arielle pulled me out back through the tunnel. I felt dizzy and strange as my eyes grew accustomed to the soft incandescent lighting of my room. The bed beneath me was soft and warm. A stubborn lump formed in my throat and I swallowed it back before I could speak.

"That's what he *does*?"

"Some of it."

"He's amazing!"

"He'd be even more amazing if he realized that the same forgiveness applied to him." There was sadness in her voice that made me feel foolish for gushing. "How do you feel?" she asked, changing the subject.

"Fine," I said. Actually, I was bright and awake and, for some reason, my mouth tasted of orange peels.

She did that thing with her halo again to see if I could hear her telepathically. "Well?"

"Just static," I replied.

This seemed to satisfy her. "I wanted you to see that...I know you look at him and see an angel, and I know that's astounding to you." She stood and turned toward the window, as though checking the night, and when she turned back to me, her expression was filled with sadness and a quiet determination. "He has his choices to make, and I will respect them. But I really don't want to see him go down again. Not when there's so much at stake."

She saw me as a threat to Michael's well-being, even now that he'd chosen to push me away. *Surely I wasn't still a threat?*

"He doesn't want to be with me," I said, hoping she couldn't sense my shame. I'd been so caught up in my feelings about him that the fact he was a messenger of God hadn't really sunk in. I never considered how wrong it might be for him, how wrong it always was.

She placed a hand on my shoulder. "You have nothing to be ashamed of. It's natural for humans to be in awe of angels. That awe is part of who we are, what we do. For an angel to act on that is wrong in so many ways. It's strictly forbidden."

"Why is it forbidden?"

"Because of the impact we can have—that awe—it's so easy for us to affect you. Being close to one of us can lead to a type of enthrallment, which you experienced earlier today. It becomes intoxicating for you, addictive, for both the human and the angel. We were never designed to be with you physically. That is considered perverse among our kind. It's an abuse of our power, a line we're not meant to cross. Those who do suffer immensely for it." She got up and paced my room again, ruffling her wings, and specks of blue light danced around her.

"What happened to them?" I asked.

"Many became addicted to the enthrallment, as did the people they enthralled. Eventually, the fallen learned how to use it to manipulate and control. The further the angel fell, the more dark and self-serving the enthrallment became, where they drained the life force of their victims until there was nothing left." Arielle turned to me. "You've seen Damiel do it. It's what makes him so dangerous."

I recalled the way I'd had a hard time breaking my date with Damiel, how tired he'd made me, and shivered. I was lucky Michael had come along when he did. Damiel had used that same charm on Fiona and look what happened to her.

I wanted to ask Arielle if Michael had done that with me but didn't know how to ask. I searched my memories from both lives, old and new, but found nothing, nothing that seemed like I was being controlled. Instead, Michael shut himself down, trying to keep us apart, as if he had the right to choose for both of us.

"You said before it was a line you're not meant to cross. Where—exactly—is it?" I asked. Michael had said he couldn't be with me *that way*, but he'd kissed me. Had we already crossed it?

"It's not easy to define, since it's a matter of enthrallment and addiction. There are some alcoholics who can have a glass of wine and not go on a binge, while others can't take even one sip," she explained. "Our way has been to avoid human contact altogether, and Michael's track record hasn't been very good."

It still didn't answer my question. Was there something else she wasn't telling me?

"I don't know everything that happened between you and Michael," she said. "But I do know it impacted you. Why else would you have been intrigued by ancient history for so long, and not only in this life?"

I'd been into ancient history before? In other lifetimes?

"Being near Michael brought forward some of your memories, but when Damiel tried to force them all to come in at once, it opened you right up," she continued, "so even though your mind might not remember all the details—your soul does."

The whole idea of my soul remembering things made my head hurt. I could sense more memories lurking in the back of my mind, threatening to reveal themselves, and I was suddenly tired. "Why did Michael come back? He said he'd been given another chance."

Arielle put an arm around my shoulder, her presence as soothing as I imagined a sister's would be. "I don't know all of God's plan. But I know one thing. You and Michael were brought together again for a reason."

Chapter Seventeen

The next morning, the sound of growling startled me awake. The air in my room felt cool and damp against my skin, and through my open curtains, clouds hung in the sky like huge black sponges, blocking the sun. I sat up, kicking the blankets off, and listened. Over the sound of heavy rain beating on the roof, I heard another snarl. Close. I'd know that sound anywhere.

Hellhounds.

Could they see me inside my house? Tell if I was awake? They were ghostly at times, neither in this world nor out of it. Could walls keep them out, or would they just come rushing in? *The more afraid you are, the more they materialize*, Michael had said.

Great, I thought, realizing that my skin was already starting to prickle with cold sweat; my mouth tasted of iron. *Now what?*

I didn't know how well they could see, but I didn't want to take any chances. Avoiding the windows and leaving all the lights out, I grabbed my housecoat and sneaked into the hallway.

I checked Mom's room and heard her slow, rhythmic breathing through the door. She was still asleep.

Should I wake her and try to explain what these things were? If I did, *if* she believed me, it would only frighten her. I'd be willing to bet that two scared people were better than one when it came to materializing hellhounds. I couldn't take that chance, not when I didn't know how to fight them. Last time I'd encountered these things, Michael had been there to scare them away.

Something twitched at my throat, the necklace from Fatima thrumming as it had around Damiel. Was he nearby too?

Standing in the hallway, I took deep breaths, fighting the urge to panic. The clicking of the old furnace, the humming of the fridge, and the incessant pelting of rain against the roof were almost deafening. Drowning it all out was the sound of my own breathing, the hammering of my own heart. I wished Michael had told me more about hellhounds. I had no idea how to fight these things and I couldn't outrun them. But the growling had stopped. Perhaps they were gone.

I went to the kitchen and grabbed a big knife. In the dark, I showered and quickly dressed, all the while listening for any more growls and not hearing any. I was so tense that when my doorbell rang, it was all I could do not to scream.

I checked the door. Michael stood there, shaking some of the rain from his hair.

I forgot all about hellhounds. "What are you doing here?"

"Making sure you get to school alive." He motioned to the cedars in the far corner of my front yard. Behind them, a lone hellhound paced. It was solid, its wet fur matted. Seeing me, its red eyes flared and held mine, sending a terrible chill up my spine. If I'd gone out alone, it would have attacked.

I stepped back from the door. "I heard it this morning."

"There was another breach last night," he said. "Damiel, probably, sending spies. That's just one of them. There are several."

"Oh," I said, swallowing a hard lump that had formed in my throat. Seeing him all serious and protective made my heart hurt. "What about my mom? She's still asleep."

"We put sigils around your home. They can't get in."

"Sigils?" I said. "What are they?"

"They're a warding system. Symbols we use to keep lesser demons away."

My limbs transformed into jelly. "It would have been nice to know about that."

"We just did them." He looked a bit sheepish, but it didn't change his demeanor, which made it clear that he was only here on business. He wore a different jacket—waterproof. Good. I wasn't ready to give up his other one yet.

My attention wandered back to the hellhound. Its teeth were wet and slimy and its eyes blazed with hellfire. The hairs on my neck bristled from the sheer brutishness of it. Like prey, I couldn't help but stare. It was a creature of destruction, and without a doubt the most horrifying thing I'd ever seen.

"Stop that," Michael said.

I flinched. "What?"

"Staring at it."

"Sorry," I said. His eyes, crystal clear, flickered with light. Just wanting to stare into them as well—but for different reasons—I looked away. "What about school? Should I stay home?"

"We put sigils around the school a while back. So it's safe."

"It didn't keep Damiel away."

"Damiel's no hellhound." There was an edge to his voice—irritation? Fatigue? "I've yet to find a symbol that will keep him out. Believe me, I've tried."

He turned to me and his expression softened. I hoped he was going to say something romantic, like he wanted to be with me, or even that he was wrong to push me away. But he didn't.

"Well, your home is safe, and your school is safe," he said briskly. "The trick is getting you from here to there." A wet tendril of hair fell into his eyes and he raked it back with his hand. "Want to take your chances on the bus?"

No. Not likely. I was horrified until I realized he was smiling. "A ride sounds good," I said.

Grabbing my school bag and umbrella, I took a step outside. As soon as my foot hit the pavement, the hellhound launched, charging right for me. My breath hitched, and in that moment time stood still. The warding necklace pulsed at my throat, and Michael's halo pulsed a bubble of white flame around both of us, stopping the beast in its tracks. Then Michael drew his sword and sliced through the hellhound's neck. It vanished into a puff of slimy black smoke before its head could even hit the ground.

From out of nowhere, a second hellhound materialized to our left. *Where had it come from?* It lunged for my throat. Jolting, I staggered backward and almost fell, but Michael caught me.

He flared his halo around us again and the hellhound backed up, snarling. Testing the fiery barrier, it inched closer, snapping its jaws at me. Michael raised his sword to strike, as another hellhound appeared to the right.

"Get inside," he said to me.

I turned to make a run for it, when another hellhound formed between me and the door. Roiling smoke blocked my way.

"I can't."

"Hold still," he said.

In a single arcing motion, Michael's sword sliced both left and right, taking out two of the hellhounds. Smoke, black as coal dust, exploded everywhere. I held my breath. Reaching over me, he slid his body around mine and lunged at the third, piercing its heart. Black fluid oozed an oil stain from its chest. It took a step closer, and with a shudder it collapsed on the walkway before it flickered and disappeared.

Thinking it would come back any second, I stared at the empty space the last hellhound left behind. When Michael stepped into view, his sword was already gone. I wanted to know where the weapon came from, if he carried it all the time, but I couldn't think of that. Not yet. I was too busy swallowing the bile at the base of my throat and trying to deal with what had just happened. Not knowing what to say, I looked at up him. He always seemed so strong, like nothing could hurt him. After he fought Damiel, I had a sense that fighting was a part of who he was—perhaps what he was here to do. I also knew that a part of him was thousands of years old, but with his hair damp from the shower and curling at his temples, he looked *my* age and very human. It made him seem vulnerable.

"Thanks," I said.

He shrugged. "They usually won't try to cross the halo, but with you here…"

"You used me as *bait*?"

When he looked at me, his eyes still held all that vulnerability, as though my accusation hurt. "I'd never do that."

All business again, he surveyed the area before leading me to the car, and it was like he'd put a wall up between us. A cool and formal wall that said he was just doing his job. I wasn't sure if it was the shock of seeing the hellhounds again or what had passed between us the day before, but something unsettled me.

I wanted to speak but didn't know what to say. The silence between us grew, and I wished he would say something, anything, to lighten the mood. The cold gray light from the sky made him look paler than normal, and I noticed the stubble on his jaw line, rings under his eyes. He hadn't been home.

"Did you get any sleep?" I asked.

He shook his head. "It was a busy night."

"None at all?"

"We used to be called the Ones Who Never Sleep. But sometimes I need to rest."

"Is that one of the side effects of being part human?"

He gave me a puzzled look. "Why do you ask?"

"Arielle said something about it."

"She did, did she?" He smiled at that. "When?"

"Last night. She wanted to see if I was okay." Everything she'd told me was too wondrous, too strange. I was still processing. I had huge pangs of guilt for wanting him so much, but I needed him to know that kissing me hadn't hurt me. "I am. Fine. By the way."

"Good," he said, but his expression was unreadable.

When we arrived at school, the parking lot was already full so Michael pulled the car into a no-parking zone around back to drop me off. As soon as the wipers stopped, rain pelted the windshield, making it nearly impossible to see outside. Sitting beside him in a parked car, I was close enough to smell his skin. It reminded me of our kiss the day before, and I wanted to be close to him so badly it made my head spin. I had to get out of the car.

Gathering my things, I opened the door and stepped outside. The rush of cold wet air forced a gasp from my lungs. I ran for shelter.

Michael followed. "Wait."

I stopped, and he slowed his pace as he approached, taking shelter under the wooden awning.

"About what happened yesterday," he said. "It's for the best."

I wasn't sure how to take that. On one hand, I knew the stakes were high, but on the other, I couldn't bear not seeing him. "You're not going to *ignore* me again, are you?" *Like my dad does.*

I'd lost my dad the day he chose another woman over our family. Bill had a life of his own at school, and Mom was always working. Maybe I was destined to lose people no matter what I did.

"Of course not," he said, folding his arms protectively across his chest. "But I can't change what I am."

I let out my breath, not realizing that I'd been holding it. "I don't want you to," I said, and opening the door I ducked into the school.

When I arrived at my locker, Elaine was shaking water droplets off her umbrella. I said a polite, if cool, hello. Her mousy-haired friend Lor joined her almost immediately.

"Did you hear about Fiona?" Lor asked, her face shining with the excitement of new gossip. I flinched.

I thought about turning back to my locker and pretending not to listen, but I didn't. Instead, I made my eavesdropping obvious, as they tried to ignore me.

"God, the way she left—on a stretcher. I mean, everyone saw her." Elaine gave a big dramatic shudder. "I'd be mortified."

"How can you talk about her like that?" I snapped at them. Elaine wouldn't hesitate to retaliate any way she could, but I didn't care. "She was nice to everyone, even you."

"Get a grip," Elaine said all high-and-mightily, then turned to Lor. "We were just sayin' it won't be easy for her to come back. Now that everyone knows."

"Whose fault would that be?" I said, straining to keep my voice down. "You're the one who's been saying shit, spreading lies about her."

"We don't spread *lies*," Lor protested.

"We find out the facts that people want to know," Elaine said. "But if someone's life is a total screw-up and people want to know about it, we can't help that."

"Fiona's life's a *what*? You don't even know her!" I wanted to choke both of them so badly my hands were shaking. I balled them into fists.

Elaine grabbed Lor's arm and, even though I was at least two inches taller, she somehow managed to look down on me. "Come on, Lor. We don't have time for her issues," she said, and they headed down the hall, arm in arm, snickering.

As I grabbed my books from my locker, I remembered those horrible black things—minions—that Arielle had shown me the night before. Perhaps Elaine had one of them on her. If they attacked Fiona, surely they attacked other people as well. With those bitches Elaine and Lor around, coming back to school wouldn't be easy. Fiona was going through enough. There had to be something I could do to help.

Maybe there was. I had an idea. I only hoped Michael would go for it.

***

In math class, I realized I'd forgotten to text Heather back about my "date." She was so curious she texted me as soon as our teacher's back was turned.

I replied with a quick message that said *didn't happen.*

When she read it, she mouthed the words *What happened?* at me. I shrugged, not wanting to get into it in class.

After class, Heather caught up with me and walked with me to my locker. "So, I thought you and Damiel had a date?"

I tensed at the mention of his name. "We did." I was afraid to let on too much. Damiel might not have any records because he didn't technically exist, but he was still real to everyone here. If people knew he came over, they might get suspicious. Not sure who could be listening, I kept my voice low. "But Michael came by first, and we hung out instead."

"You blew him off? For Michael?" When I nodded, she continued, "How did Damiel take it?"

I didn't know how to respond to that. She wouldn't come up with the truth on her own. After all, it's not every day that you narrowly escape dating a demon. "Okay, I guess," I replied, bluffing. "It wasn't serious or anything."

"You got any idea where he is today? He hasn't been around."

Hell? I thought as I shook my head.

"I guess you wouldn't. I've already heard a few girls whispering about him."

I resisted the temptation to tell her my thoughts. She wouldn't believe me if I told her the truth about him. The word *demon* was hardly in Heather's vocabulary, but I did wish I could talk to someone about what was happening to me. Someone other than Michael.

"So, Michael, huh? I'm glad. He's way more your type than Damiel. The bad-boy thing is really only good for exploring the Jungian shadow side of your unconscious."

I didn't have a clue what she was talking about. "Jungian what?"

"Carl Jung believed that everyone has a shadow, or dark side to their personality."

"Oh." I didn't think Carl Jung, whoever he was, could explain *Damiel's* dark side.

She waved her hand dismissively. "Anyway, I knew you really liked Michael ever since that day we went on the hike."

I remembered that day, how his carrying me seemed so close, so intimate that it scared me. Now, I couldn't get close enough.

"Has he kissed you yet?"

I didn't want to answer her question, but my face gave it all away.

"I'll take that as a yes." She grinned.

"No," I said, blushing. "It's not what you think." How could I explain how complicated things were? That he and I had been in love before, and I was so in love with him now that it hurt to think about it? If Heather thought there was a chance between us, she'd only look for ways to set us up, and that would only drive him further away.

**

When I didn't see Michael all morning, I began to worry. If he was still battling hellhounds, there had to be a lot of them. Were other people getting hurt? Was Michael? What if they got to my mom? I thought of her lying on the ground outside our house, unconscious, while those creatures feasted on her flesh. The image haunted me so strongly that when I finally saw Michael in the hallway before last class I rushed up beside him.

"Is everything okay?" I asked.

"It's fine." He leaned toward me and our sides touched. It was electric, and he backed away slightly, as though he felt it too. "We got all the hellhounds, if that's what you mean."

I let out the last of my breath, and the knot that had formed in my stomach relaxed.

"Hey," he said, leaning in again. "Are you okay?"

"I was worried about my mom. You know, in case…"

"She's fine," he reassured me. "Arielle and I double-checked your place."

"Thanks." Hearing Arielle's name reminded me of what I wanted to ask him. "Arielle told me what happened to Fiona."

"What do you mean?" he asked.

We reached the door of my Latin class. I lowered my voice, looking around to make sure no one could hear us. "She showed me those minions—parasites, whatever—that get on people, the ones Damiel sent."

"She showed you that?" he asked.

"Yeah, and I thought maybe we could tell Fiona…"

One of my classmates, a tall, freckled blond guy whose name escaped me, wanted to get in the room. Michael backed me out of the doorway into the hall. "Tell her what, exactly?"

"That it's not her fault. That she was attacked by something terrible," I said. "That she didn't do it to herself."

"No, Mia. You can't tell her that. Nobody can know what you know."

"Why not? *I* know these things."

He took a moment to consider his answer. Out of the corner of my eye, his halo flashed like paparazzi cameras on Oscar night. "Telling you was a tough decision to make. I did it because you're different. You already see these things, and if you'd listened to me about Damiel in the first place…"

I stiffened. "That's the only reason you told me? Because you *had* to? The cat was already out of the bag?"

"It was a sign that I *could* tell you. You were in danger."

"My friends are in danger, too! I can't *not* let them know what's coming at them. How can they fight it?"

A few more students made their way into the room. Class was about to start. I had to get inside. Michael held my arm, quiet and serious. "Believe me. Knowing about these things only makes it worse. I told you—"

"She's my friend."

"What do you think would happen if you told her? After everything she's been through? With all those doctors questioning her?"

Ms. Nelson, my Latin teacher, approached. "Class is starting." She turned to Michael. "Are you joining us today?"

"Nos iustus postulo paululum," Michael said. *We just need a moment.* His accent was perfect, his voice a chord.

Nodding, Ms. Nelson backed off and shuffled into class.

"Did you—?"

"I bought us a few minutes," he said quickly. "What if Fiona says something?"

"She won't." I remembered how Elaine found out about Michael rescuing me in the woods. Fiona wasn't the best at keeping secrets. "They'd think she's crazy."

"Yeah, and that's the last thing she needs right now."

He was right. There was nothing I could say to Fiona to make it all better. The only thing I could do was be her friend, even if that meant hiding something from her. At least it was for her own good.

My cell phone rang, making me jump. I'd thought I'd turned it off. The number was blocked on my call display, but I answered it anyway. From the other end came an inhuman screeching that sent tendrils of ice down my spine. Around my neck, the warding necklace from Fatima twitched.

I was about to hang up when I heard a voice. Tinny and metallic, it sounded dreadfully familiar. "I like it when you wear your hair down. It's so sexy."

My breath froze in my chest. "Who is this?"

Beside me, Michael tensed. My phone was loud enough that he could hear everything.

"Don't tell me you've forgotten me already," Damiel's voice purred on the other end of the phone. "I haven't forgotten you." I pictured his eyes the last time I'd seen him, the way they shone that terrible red. But then he was in a body—Giulio's body.

Could he *see* me? Right now? "I thought you were gone."

"Oh, you mean what Michael did?" He laughed— a cold, evil sound. Behind his voice, I could still hear the screeching. "It takes more than that to get rid of me."

Michael clasped his hands behind his head and turned away. "Just hang up," he said.

"Tell Michael to remember who he's dealing with."

"Leave us alone!" I said and hung up.

Michael muttered something under his breath. If I didn't know better, I'd think he was cursing.

My hands shook, so I clasped them together. "Is he back?"

"If he was back, he wouldn't bother to call," Michael said. "He'd just show up."

"He said something about my hair." I shuddered, remembering the sound of his voice. "Can he *see* us?"

"No, but the hellhounds saw you this morning and he works closely with them. They're his eyes and ears. He's messing with your head."

"I thought he was in Hell. How did he call—?"

"I'm not sure," he said. "He could have intercepted an incoming call."

"Can he *do* that?" I asked. A terrified, crazed animal paced in my chest. I wanted to run as far and as fast as my legs would take me, but they'd turned to liquid beneath me.

Noticing my reaction, he backed me into a locker so I could lean against it. I pressed my fingers into the metal behind me until they hurt.

"You mustn't be afraid," he said. "He won't get anywhere near you. I won't let him." The halls now empty, we were alone. In the background, I could hear Ms. Nelson starting the class, but Michael stood so close I didn't care about being late. He let out his breath slowly. "I'm sorry I brought you into this."

"You didn't," I said.

"Oh, but I did." He slid his hands to the sides of my head, stroking my hair. It was meant to be comforting, but my spine melted from his touch. Leaning his forehead into mine, he whispered, "I won't let anything happen to you. I promise."

Chapter Eighteen

The next few days were almost normal.

At school, I marveled at how Michael passed for perfectly human. Nobody else could see the intermittent flashing of his halo or the vague outline of his wings. The fact that I knew what he really looked like was an intimate secret between us, almost like seeing him naked would be. Okay, nowhere near as good as *that*. But I was beginning to enjoy it.

Elaine published an article on her blog saying I broke Damiel's heart and rejected him for Michael and that's what made him go away. The article upset me a lot more than it did Michael, who just ignored it, but he wasn't the one being called the next whore of Babylon—

something I had to look up the meaning of online. The girls who liked Damiel gave me dirty looks in the hallway. It made me almost wish Damiel would come back, as long as he left me alone.

At night, Michael watched out for me, but kept his distance like I was some kind of VIP and he was my angelic security service. Though they'd cleaned up the hellhound problem, something was worrying him. Something he didn't want me to know.

Fiona came back to school on Wednesday, and Heather and I stayed close. We wanted things to be as normal as possible and she didn't need people gossiping or staring at her. At least Elaine didn't print anything in the school paper, which, for Elaine, was actually decent.

I was on my way to lunch with Michael when I noticed Fiona alone at her locker fumbling with her books. She dropped one, and as soon as she went to pick it up another one fell. She didn't seem depressed this time, but a few people were chuckling at her while they gossiped amongst themselves. I could tell it made her uncomfortable.

"We should go talk to her," I said to him. "Take her to lunch."

"Wait a sec," he said. When I gave him a questioning look, he added, "You'll see."

"Are you going to wave a magic wand or something and make it all better?"

He whispered in my ear, "I'm an angel, not a fairy godmother." The heat of his breath traveled all the way down my neck, and I had to fight the urge to press myself against him.

Arielle appeared in the hallway. At first I thought she might say something to us, but other than giving Michael a nod, she walked right past. "Hey," I said, lifting my hand to wave at her.

Michael caught my hand. "Shhh," he said, his voice barely a whisper in the noisy hallway. "Don't draw attention to her; she's working. It's going to help."

"We're the only ones who can see her right now?" I felt utterly foolish. *Of course she was working. She doesn't go to school.*

If anybody else had seen me, they'd already moved on. Arielle approached Fiona and touched her arm. Fiona didn't seem to notice, but this was how it worked. Arielle would whisper words of kindness, unseen, and Fiona would start feeling better. She'd already brightened. A smile crossed her lips.

Michael squeezed my hand and led me down the hall to the cafeteria. It was amazing how much it meant to me, this simple touch, showing that he cared.

We arrived at Heather and Jesse's table and he let my hand go. If they saw us holding hands, they didn't say anything. Michael and I acted like friends but they must have noticed the way I behaved around him, the way my breath would catch whenever our eyes met, or the way my skin would burn if he stood or sat too close.

"May I join you?" It was Farouk. He had a girl with him. Her dark brown eyes were so intense they seemed to look right through me.

"Is this Fatima?" I asked.

"Hello, Mia," she said. Although Farouk hadn't mentioned it, she was a junior, the same year as him— which meant they must be twins. Her accent was less pronounced than her brother's, but she had the same curly black hair—only hers was long and wild, giving her an exotic beauty.

"Your hair is gorgeous," I said.

"Thanks." She tugged at one of her curls, examining it. "It needs a trim."

"I'm glad to have a chance to finally thank you for the necklace," I said.

"You're most welcome." She grinned at me, then leaned forward to ask, "Did it help?"

I recalled having Damiel at my door, the hellhounds around my house, and the way the necklace had vibrated each time, some kind of warning. It must have been letting me know when I was in danger. "Yes, it did."

"You might not need it so much now." She glanced knowingly at Michael, who was chatting with Jesse. "But you never know."

Could she see Michael, too? The way I did? I didn't know how to ask without giving away his secret, so I kept quiet, almost awkwardly so, and looked out the window at the rain that wasn't letting up.

Fatima and Farouk finished lunch early because they had to study for a biology exam. They left as the topic changed to our weekend plans.

"Hey, this weekend Kevin Foster's parents are out of town and he's throwing a big party," Jesse said.

"How big?" Heather asked.

"Everyone's invited. He's got a huge place," he said, looking at all of us. "You guys should come."

I was eating a chicken salad that seemed oilier than usual. It slid down my throat and sat in my stomach like a lump.

"Who's Kevin Foster?" I asked, not sure I wanted to go to a stranger's party.

"He's in his junior year at Sealth," Jesse answered, then turned to Michael. "You remember his brother Dave? His parties?"

"Yes," Michael said, gazing out over the cafeteria, absently keeping watch.

"Dude, you should come. It'll be awesome."

"Don't think so."

"Chloe will be disappointed." Jesse gave him a suggestive smile.

Michael shot Jesse a look that silenced him. Jesse's gaze darted quickly in my direction and then fixed on the table in front of him.

Who was Chloe?

Michael shifted in his seat and squeezed a packet of ketchup onto his plate. He had hardly touched his burger. I was going to ask right then and there who Chloe was, since everyone at the table seemed to know something about her. But Fiona and Dean joined us, holding hands, and Heather took the opportunity to break the awkward silence by chatting with them. Michael excused himself quietly and left.

For the rest of lunch, I listened to Heather and Jesse chat about the upcoming party with Fiona and Dean. I felt more out of place than ever. While Heather managed to look mystified—she didn't know anything about Chloe—Jesse ignored me. It was as though the space I occupied no longer existed. As soon as lunch was over, he took off.

I asked Heather, "Who's Chloe?"

"I've never heard of her, but I can ask Jesse if you want," she offered.

LISA VOISIN

"No. Let me try Michael first. I think I need to hear it from him."

In English class, Michael sneaked in a few minutes late. We were still reading *Hamlet*, and Mr. Bidwell called on me to read Ophelia's lines in Act III Scene II. In the scene, Ophelia was upset over the way Hamlet had been treating her. I could relate. After all, who was this Chloe, and why did Michael walk away after her name was mentioned? Jesse was reading Hamlet. Ophelia's lines were short, but I read them right at Michael, hoping for a reaction of some sort. I got none.

After class, Michael caught up with me. "I'm on duty after school today," he said, "but I can drive you home."

"Who's Chloe?"

He scanned the crowded halls to see if anyone was listening and sighed, running his fingers through his hair. "Dave and Kevin's older sister."

"You know what I mean! Why did the conversation— *How much older*?"

"She's in her third year of college now, I think."

Third year of college—that meant she was Bill's age. Michael had dated older women. I could never compete with that. "Were you seeing her?"

Grabbing my arm, he guided me into the nearest empty room, the chemistry lab. All the tables were clear, and someone had lined beakers and bottles in neat rows along the shelves. He closed the door before he spoke. "I haven't seen her since before the accident."

"Were you…?"

"I was drunk. We both were."

"And?"

He leaned against the desk at the front of the room, his hands gripping the wooden desktop so tightly that the veins popped at his wrists. Tilting his chin, Michael looked up at me, and I knew without a doubt that something had happened between them.

My stomach lurched, and the chemical smell in the air hit the back of my throat like I was going to be sick. I leaned against one of the tables to steady myself.

"I was much different then," he said. "She was a friend… It was before everything."

"How could it be before *everything*?"

"You know what I mean. Mia, please…" He reached for my hand, but stopped. I wished he hadn't.

"Look. I know we have this ancient history and all, but—"

"Nine thousand years," he said plainly.

If he planned to distract me, it worked. My mind reeled with the thought. "Is that how long—?"

"Do you really think that *one night* at a party could compare to that? I was very drunk… We both were. I hardly remember it." He looked maddeningly far away. Was he *thinking* about her?

Hot, furious tears filled my eyes. I wiped them away with my sleeve, aching to be close to him and knowing my words and actions were pushing him away. I hated myself for it, but I couldn't help but think about *her* and how she would know him, be close to him, in a way I never could.

"I wasn't the same person then." He leaned closer to me and the presence of his halo, warm and tingly, soothed my skin—even through my clothes.

"No," I said, shaking the feeling off. "From what you tell me, you were exactly the same *person*; it was just your spirit that was different."

"A person is *both*," he said firmly. His halo still hovered around me, even though I refused the sensation. I wanted to feel cold. Alone. He sighed. "I told you, Mia. My sin was lust. If you think this is bad—"

"You just said you were a different person then."

Slouching, he shoved his hands in his pockets and crossed to the side of the room, moving even farther away. "Please, you're making too much out of it. This, this was nothing compared to—"

"How can you even *say* that to me?" I cut him off, more loudly than I expected. I was going too far but couldn't stop myself. "Are you really *that* unfeeling?"

His halo flickered and dimmed. The effect made the glass bottles on the shelves behind him appear to shake. What I'd said had hurt. He ran his hands down his face and drew in a deep breath.

"I can't argue with you about this," he said and walked out of the room.

My insides jumped and stung like I'd swallowed a hornet's nest. I stood in the classroom and cried. Outside, the rain had stopped but the sky was covered in a blanket of clouds, and though I was indoors, wind rushing through the trees chilled right through my bones. It seemed to take forever for the halls to empty so nobody would see me leave.

Since Labor Day, I'd been avoiding the park. But now the hellhounds had been caught. The muddy trails were slick and covered in wet leaves, so I had to watch my step. Above me hung a thick canopy of evergreens that made it seem more evening than afternoon.

Our argument played over and over in my head. No matter how I looked at it, I'd overreacted. It happened before he even met me, and yet I was insanely jealous of this girl I'd never met, all because she knew him in a way that I never could. It had nothing to do with us. It was his past. But so much of us was the past, too. I'd clung to what little I knew of it, hoping that if he felt something for me back then, he might feel something for me now.

But it was too late. I'd hurt him. I may have even lost him—as a friend, or whatever we were to each other.

In the middle of the park, one of the trails veered off toward an empty playground. Swings blew sideways in the wind, their chains rasping like metallic ghosts. I sat on one and ran my heels along the wet grooves made by other people's feet in the dirt. I didn't feel like swinging, but it was better than going home. Mom would know something was wrong and I didn't want to talk about it, not yet.

Over the sound of creaking chains and whispering leaves, I didn't notice anyone approach until I saw movement and light out of the corner of my eye. A mixture of emotions flooded me as Michael sat himself on the swing beside me: relief, shame, and even jealousy. His mouth was set in a straight line and a river of anger and sadness flowed off of him, both of which I was pretty sure I'd put there. He'd held my hand today. Had he decided I wasn't worth the trouble and come to tell me to get lost? *Was this it? Was I going to lose him?*

His voice was surprisingly gentle when he spoke. "If you can't accept this, I don't know how you can ever accept the past."

"It's different," I said.

LISA VOISIN

"It is. We'd both been drinking, but it was her choice." He turned his swing toward mine and the metal hinges creaked. The wind caught his hair. "That night. You *deserve* so much better."

Hearing him talk about it only made me feel worse. I started to cry. "It's not that."

"What is it, then?"

"It's that I'll never…" The tears choked out of me in embarrassing sobs. How could I tell him that I'd always want more? And the fact that he'd been with someone when I couldn't be with him *at all* was almost unbearable for me?

And then he got it. Somehow, intuitively, he understood. Standing, he lifted me to my feet and took me in his arms. He kissed my hair, my forehead, making me shiver inside. When he whispered my ancient name, "Sajani," his voice came out in deep, low tones like a cello, and the force of it echoed through me. "You *were* with me that way."

I sobbed, heated by his arms, as a blissful thrum of energy flowed between us. His hands shook as he stroked my hair, gently rocked me until I cried myself out. When I was done, he took me by the hand and walked me home as the shock of a blood-orange sunset broke through the clouds.

Chapter Nineteen

The next morning at school was soured by Heather arguing with Jesse over bringing up the subject of Chloe in the first place. Fortunately, they made up at lunch. At least things with Fiona seemed to be good. People were acting normal around her again, and she and Dean were closer than ever. She'd stopped flirting with other guys. Though I was happy for her, I was still a bit sad.

Michael wasn't at school, and his absence made me irrationally suspicious. My night had been filled with crazy jealous dreams of him sleeping with every girl in school but me—even Elaine—as if I meant nothing to him. Though they were only dreams, they reminded me that I would never be able to be close to him *that* way. The way all my friends could be with their boyfriends. The fact that Michael and I were destined to be only friends ate at me like acid in my veins.

When I got home after school, Mom was just getting up, having spent a few days changing her sleep patterns to prepare for the overnight shift. I made us chicken curry for dinner—which I'd been craving lately—and we ate together in the dining room instead of our usual spot in front of the TV.

"Mia, I think we need to talk," she said after we'd finished eating.

I shifted uncomfortably in my seat. Conversations with Mom that started with *We need to talk* usually sucked. The next line was usually something like *Your father and I are going to live apart for a while* or *We're moving to Seattle.*

"You know you have the house to yourself tonight," she said. When I nodded, waiting for the bomb to drop, she continued, "I've noticed that you and

Michael have been spending a lot of time together. I remember being your age—"

"Mom!"

"Mia," she said back. "I can see that you really like this boy. But I don't want you to rush into anything just because the opportunity may present itself."

"Mom, it's not like that." I squirmed, unable to believe I was having this conversation, that she was using the *we need to talk* code for my non-existent sex life. After everything I'd been through with Michael over Chloe, this had to be some kind of cruel joke. I didn't even know when I'd see him again outside of school.

"Okay. I don't want to have to make rules about when he can come over. Can I rely on you to be sensible about it? Make sure he goes home at a decent hour if he visits?"

"Yes, Mom, I'll be sensible." And if I wasn't, he'd only run away again.

"I've seen too many teenage pregnancies in my line of work."

"We're just friends. Really."

"Oh," she said, and for a moment I thought she'd have the good sense to stop but I was wrong. "Well, if that changes, you remember our talks about this? You'll make sure to stay protected?"

God, would this conversation *never* end? "Yes. *If* it does—which it won't—I will." She had only told me about a hundred times since I turned twelve, for all the good it would do now.

And then, finally, she decided it was time to leave. Having not heard from Michael all day, I prepared myself for a long, boring night with my textbooks. Unable to decide whether to do my Latin or Gov/Econ reading first, I curled up on the sofa with both of them. I had just finished reading a chapter when the doorbell rang.

Jumpier than I expected, I checked who it was through the kitchen window, and when I realized it was Michael I rushed to the door. Still embarrassed about my outburst the day before, I greeted him nervously and invited him in.

"Are you busy?" he asked.

I shook my head. "Just homework. Why? Do you have the night off or something?"

"I never technically have a night off, but I'm only on call tonight."

Never had a night off? God must be one hell of an employer!

He made his way toward the kitchen area and leaned against the counter. "Are you alone?"

"Yeah. My mom's working the night shift."

"She works them a lot?" he asked.

I leaned on the counter beside him. "She has to support us."

"Do you ever get lonely?" Folding his arms across his chest, he looked down at me, his eyes hooded and soft. In that moment, I couldn't tell if he was asking because he was curious or if it was part of his job as an angel.

Either way, I didn't want to answer. The truth would make me sound needy, and Heather said guys hated that. I was pretty sure my dad did.

I shrugged. "I'm used to it."

He didn't press the subject. "Well, there's something I want to show you tonight." He scanned my outfit thoughtfully. "Though you'll need to dress more warmly than that."

My cheeks pinked from his appraisal. "What exactly am I dressing for?"

"We'll be outside—near the water."

I went back to my room to change. Out my window, the sky had cleared and a ring of blue light circled the almost-full moon. Thinking a moonlit walk on the beach would be nice, I put on a few extra layers, trying to make sure everything matched and didn't look bulky.

Michael was sitting on the kitchen counter reading the paper. When I came out, he looked up. "Much better. I don't want you getting cold."

"What about you?" I asked, noting he wore only jeans and a sweatshirt, whereas I was in layers of polar fleece.

He slid off the counter in such as way as to make even that look graceful. "I'll be warm enough, trust me."

He removed his sweatshirt and tied it around his waist. Underneath, he wore a white tank with a t-shaped back that showed off the muscles in his arms and shoulders. Golden light sparkled and flickered between his shoulder blades.

He opened the door and held it for me, waiting. "Ready?"

"For?"

"I'm taking you flying."

"Flying? Wait. *Flying* flying? You don't mean in a plane, do you?"

"No." His smile grew brighter and fuller as he watched my realization that *he* would be flying *me* sink in. "Do you want to?" When I hesitated before nodding, he asked, "Are you scared?"

"Yeah. A bit." Actually I was scared a *lot*, but the idea of seeing his wings more than made up for it.

"You'll be safe. I promise," he said, closing the door behind me.

When I stepped out onto the front yard, he scooped me up into his arms as though I were weightless, like that day I'd injured my ankle in the woods.

Marveling at the strength it must take to do that, I swallowed a girlish squeak.

"Ready?" he asked.

As soon as I nodded my answer, he bent his legs and leapt into the air, taking me with him. Uneasiness stirred in the pit of my stomach. I fought the urge to scream as the ground disappeared beneath us, the houses and lights shrinking at a dizzying rate.

"Relax. You're safe," Michael said. "Breathe."

I was so fixated on the ground speeding away from us that every muscle in my body tensed. I forgot I'd been holding my breath and gasped for air. Although Michael's arms were strong and solid beneath me, I needed something to hold on to, so I linked my arms around his shoulders. Even in the cold air, his skin was warm to the touch.

And that was when I saw his wings. In the past, I'd only seen a faint blue outline around him or blue gossamer around Arielle. Nothing, not even my dreams or memories, prepared me for how his wings really looked. They were huge, not white exactly, more iridescent, with a featherlike covering that reflected all the rainbow colors, even in the dark. They weren't actual feathers, not the kind you'd see on a bird; they were filaments of solid light. Joining at his back, they stretched out at least ten feet on either side from base to tip. Beating powerfully behind us, they made a sound in the air like wind hitting silk sails.

"Can people see us?" I asked. The wind rushed my ears and I had to speak loudly even to hear myself.

Grinning, he shook his head. "Don't want to set off Homeland Security." For the first time, I noticed that his halo had enveloped both of us. It shimmered and rippled, a mirror reflecting the night sky. We were invisible.

While everything in me said that flying was impossible and that I should be terrified, I wasn't afraid. The wind carried us so high that cars buzzed like fireflies on the streets below, and across Elliot Bay, the freighters and boats could have easily been toys. Michael swooped low over water reflecting distorted city lights and we glided under the West Seattle Bridge. His wings beating against the wind currents, we looped around and ascended again over the tall buildings of the downtown core.

The wind kicked up colder and whipped my hair against my face, and yet in his arms I was surprisingly warm. My blood thrummed through my veins. I looked at Michael's face again and realized he was completely in his element, completely at ease. Flying was as much a part of him as breathing was for me. I was safe, and with his heart beating against the side of my ribs, the strength and warmth of his arms around me, I felt closer to him than ever.

After making another wide sweep of the harbor, we glided effortlessly back across the water to the beach at Lincoln Park. Although his landing was smooth and graceful, as soon as my feet touched the ground my knees buckled. Michael quickly grabbed my elbows to steady me.

"You okay?" He furled his wings securely behind him. "Did you have fun?"

I opened my mouth to speak but no words came out, so I nodded my response. My heart pounded wildly in my chest and I realized I was shaking. My whole body hummed with adrenaline; I had to remember to breathe.

"You're sure?" He released my elbows and backed away from me. "You can stand on your own?"

I had foal legs, but I could stand. The edges of his halo shimmered as he tucked it around himself, and his wings shifted to their blue outline as though he had sheathed them with the air.

"It was amazing!" I said once I found my voice. My heart hammered against my ribs.

"Walk a bit. It'll help you adjust to being on the ground again."

He took my hand, dispelling any cold from the night air, and we strolled along a dimly-lit path that followed the rocky shore. His wings stretched out behind us as iridescent as starlight, visible only to me. Since it was the first clear night in days, there were a few other people on the path and Michael adjusted his wings to avoid touching them.

"How do your wings work?" I asked after I'd fully recovered from flight. "I usually see them as a blue outline, but when we were flying they were more real."

"They're inter-dimensional."

"They're what?" I asked in disbelief.

"They exist in another place, a different dimension so to speak, and I bring them into this one when I fly."

I was completely baffled.

"It might be better if I show you," he said, walking us out onto the beach, away from the street lights, out of the view of the ferries and houses in the distance. "We're going to be invisible for a bit. Best to not attract attention."

His halo tingled as he extended it around both of us, its phosphorescence rippling against the dark sky. A golden light glimmered behind him, extending from his back, and the blue outline of his wings flickered. Then, soundlessly as morning snow, his wings appeared, as though pulled from an invisible sheath.

He unfurled them, and such a sense of peace and stillness came over me. Full and white, they were glorious. Observing them filled me with a sense of wonder, as though I were witnessing something profound and exquisite, so much greater than myself. Their presence humbled me, made me realize that everything I'd ever known or believed was a tiny piece of a greater, more magnificent whole, and I was honored to even be a part of it.

Studying my face, Michael closed his wings and took a few steps toward me. "This isn't too much, is it?"

I smiled at him and fought the strange urge to cry. It wasn't from sadness but more the way a beautiful sunset might affect you if you'd been blind your whole life and were suddenly able to see it. Silently, Michael retracted his halo and slid his wings back to their usual placement, all the while observing me as though expecting me to freak out.

The wind picked up, blowing through my hair. Not wanting it to tangle further, I finger-combed it and tied it into a braid, wishing I'd done that *before* we went flying. I had a few tangles but was lucky it wasn't a mass of knots. Not having an elastic band, I used a piece of my own hair to secure the end and then tucked the mass into my collar. It wouldn't last long, but it would have to do.

Michael leaned against a nearby rock, still watching me. With the orange-cast light from the street lamp playing off his skin, shadowing the muscles of his shoulders and arms, and the flickering of golden light his halo cast around him, he looked positively heroic, like a statue of an ancient god.

"Where to now?" I asked, approaching him.

The wind had swept his hair into a tangle of curls splayed in every direction, forming a dark, shadowy crown of their own. I reached over to smooth it, like doing so was the most natural thing in the world, and he brushed his hand up my spine. Even through my jacket, a burning heat coursed through me. Touching the back of my head, he found my braid and pulled it out from my jacket. He twisted it between his fingers, examining it, then looked up at me, his gaze open, unguarded, his pupils as wide and black as the night sky. A flush warmed the back of my neck and I stood there mesmerized by him, unable to look away.

Arcing his other arm around me, he pulled me toward him and whispered, "I shouldn't," against the side of my face, as though it were a confession. Then, his lips cool and salty from the sea air, he kissed me with such tenderness it made my chest ache.

But I didn't need tenderness. I needed *him*. Since the last time we'd kissed, I'd been so careful around him, trying not to cross the invisible line that would either damn him or scare him away. I couldn't be careful anymore. Gripping the front of his shirt, I pulled him closer, and he locked his arms around me like I'd always wanted him to, like maybe he'd never let me go. Sitting on the rock, he gathered me into him, sliding me onto his lap. My thighs straddled his hips and he let out the softest of moans, his lips grazing my throat, the side of my neck, the line of my jaw, before returning to mine.

With a sharp inhale, he tensed and stopped kissing me. His eyes flashed a warning look—full of fear, as though he'd gone somewhere fathomless inside himself that he'd sworn he'd never go. Standing, he guided me off his lap. When he spoke, his voice took on a deep timbre.

"We're not alone."

Chapter Twenty

An oily film of darkness rolled in like a black fog above us, extinguishing the street lights and stilling the air. The breeze from the water stopped, and even the waves themselves seemed to slow their undulations against the rocky shore.

Michael clenched the fleece of my jacket, in obvious pain. Behind him, something black and formless landed on his wings. Only it wasn't formless at all: it was something whose shape was so terrifying my mind couldn't process it. It was shiny, fanged, and blacker than the night itself. I'd seen hellhounds before, and minions that fed on negative thoughts and made people do terrible things, but this was different. Somehow it was even more frightening.

"Are you okay?" I asked, unable to keep the alarm out of my voice.

He nodded, but winced as another shapeless creature landed on him.

"I thought these types of things couldn't get across the halo."

"My defenses were down."

The kiss! So it was *my* fault.

"Can you fight it?" I asked. My throat was so tight I barely made a sound.

"If I move right now, it might come for you."

I started to back away, but he gripped my arms so I was planted to the spot.

"It hasn't seen you yet," he said. "I'll let you know when to move."

It? As far as I could see, there were two of them. I stood perfectly still as another creature landed on his wings. My only movement was that of my stomach plummeting to my knees. "Why does it want me?"

"I think it wants *me*." Still clasping my arms, he touched his forehead to mine, his body shaking as more of the creatures landed on him—making six by my count. "If anything were to happen to you…" His voice trailed off and I was left to wonder, horrified at what kind of danger he was expecting.

On the path between the water and where we stood, a young couple walked a Dalmatian. Did they notice anything unusual? A chill down their spines perhaps? A pang of fear as they walked through the thick, artificially darkened air? What true horrors had the Grigori held back from us unnoticed, had Michael held back, engaged in a constant battle against darkness?

Michael gasped, steadying himself as another two creatures landed on his wings. That was eight. Just as I was beginning to wonder exactly how much pain he could tolerate, he gave me a slight nod. Instantly, he flared his halo around us and I heard faint shrieking, followed by a sizzling sound. Black smoke emanated from the creatures on his wings. A few of them fell to the ground, writhing and melting like boiled tar.

"This way," Michael said, ushering me into the bushes.

We stopped near a twisted old tree. Its branches nearly bare for winter, it offered little shelter, but its trunk was thick enough to protect my back. Black forms gathered and surrounded us and an unnatural hissing filled the air.

I knew Michael would do everything in his power to keep me safe. But what about him? The creatures growled and shrieked behind us in a clamoring approach, and Michael was quiet and still, letting them near. Why was he doing this? I began to think he was sacrificing himself to protect me. I wasn't worth it, no matter how glad I was that he was there.

In the darkness, Michael's eyes flamed with golden light as they searched mine. "Is there something you love?" he asked, his body vibrating from the creatures attacking his wings.

"You," I blurted, surprising myself. Heat rushed to my face.

He grinned, despite the obvious pain he was in. "You love me?"

"More than myself sometimes."

That startled him. "Never more than yourself. I'd never want that."

"I can't help it."

He leaned in and kissed my forehead, his lips cool and smooth against my flushed skin. There was a gentle shift in the air as he shook out his wings. "I need you to feel that love, focus on it right now. Not fear, not worry…no matter what you see. Close your eyes if you have to. This thing will try to horrify and fascinate you, so remember that love, okay? It sours the milk. Can you do that for me?"

With the heat of his arms around me, I could do anything. I nodded and he turned, flaring his halo again and stretching out his wings to their full size as though he were in flight. Only this time, instead of luminescent white they were gold, the color of the fire in his eyes.

The creatures that had clung to him fell off in clumps and skittered away. Reaching over his shoulder, he turned, and from his hand blazed his blue sword. At this close range, it appeared to be made not only of steel but of fire and light as well. He held it up menacingly, with a dangerous smile on his face, challenging them.

The sky blackened and thickened, heavy with dread, as more of the creatures arrived. There must have been a hundred of them. The air smelled foul and close, like the inside of a garbage can only a thousand times worse. There was no breeze to dissipate the stench.

Michael stood his ground as the black shapes roiled and writhed, forming a massive single unit. My chest tightened in horror as it teemed and grew taller, forming into a long-necked multi-headed creature the size of a Mack truck. It must have had over twenty heads, each of them with glowing red eyes fixed on Michael, who stared unflinchingly at the center of this black massive creature, presumably where its heart would be—if it had one.

"Be gone!" Michael commanded, his voice strong, musical. I realized this was how it was with the angelic force upon him—a chord rather than a single note. Angel versus human.

The beast recoiled slightly, then let out a ghastly laugh. "Damiel sends his greetings," it hissed in a wet, glutinous voice.

"You'll never win, Azazel," Michael said. "Neither will he."

One of the demon's heads nipped at him in defiance. I flinched reflexively, horrified by the damage those teeth could do! Unyielding, he parried with his sword, and the beast rose on its legs, directing its many heads right at him.

Michael dodged and blocked the onslaught of claws and teeth with incredible speed. Caught up in the action, I gasped at the sight of him. He heard it and glanced my way long enough for the creature to land a blow to his back. He flinched, letting out a low, angry sound, almost a growl, and part of me wanted to run to him, to distract the creature, to make it leave him alone. But I stood motionless, frozen in place. I couldn't look. I couldn't bear to see him miss, to see the beast hurt him again.

I closed my eyes. *Love.* Michael had told me to love. I loved him with every cell of my body and every beat of my heart. I knew it as I knew my own name or the color of my own skin. My feelings for him were absolutely true, but I couldn't feel them. That's all he'd asked me to do. *Feel that love.* Just moments ago I had burned with longing, but now I was cold and spent, like steel and ashes. I had failed. What if it were the idea of him that I loved, and not really him? Conjuring images of him would usually make my head spin, but not tonight. Tonight I felt nothing.

Lost in thought, I hadn't noticed the air getting thicker and heavier around me, or the smell of decay growing in the air until I practically choked on it. The warding necklace Fatima had given me pulsed at my throat. I heard the demon's menacing laughter but couldn't see how the fight was going. If Michael was winning or in grave danger, I had no idea, but instinct told me to open my eyes.

Just inches from my face, one of the demon's heads sniffed me, as if I were food. It smiled a sickening grimace; wet, black flesh hung loosely from its teeth, and its breath was nauseating.

My lungs tightened, making it hard to breathe, and I clenched my hands to keep them from shaking. After distracting Michael the last time, I refused to react audibly and put him at risk. It was going to attack me and there wasn't anything I could do about it. In a way, it already was. Its presence devoured the love from my heart the way an inferno sucks the air from a building. I'd accept this willingly if it meant Michael would get free. The head of the demon closest to me stuck out a forked tongue, tasting the air around me as a stream of light and energy escaped my chest. Slowly, I backed away, refusing to look directly at the demon. Looking at it only made me feel worse.

Instead, I focused on Michael. Engaged in battle, he was ferocious as a tiger and equally as deadly to this creature. His blue sword slashed and chopped at the demon's other heads in a whirlwind of light and fire. His shirt, damp with slime, clung to his muscled torso, and I remembered those strong arms encircling me. How safe he had made me feel. How loved. My body burned with the memory of it. A memory that gave me hope...I absolutely did love him! I was wrong to doubt it, to doubt myself. And with this knowledge, I faced the demon, its mouth open, teeth dripping with slime. It was about to sink its jaws into me and it didn't matter. Everything would be okay.

The creature hesitated, watching me with black steam rising from its mouth. The necklace thrummed at my throat, moving like I'd never felt before. With a high-pitched hum, it shattered and fell from my neck as though it had overloaded.

Michael thrust the blade through the demon's neck. Black ooze gushed from its head. I recoiled, refusing to shriek, as the demon's head fell to the ground. Somersaulting, Michael leapt over the severed neck to tackle another head, which he sliced off in a single blow.

The creature bucked and writhed and its remaining heads turned toward Michael, snapping all at once.

He held his ground and raised his sword above him. "Azazel, firstborn of the demons," he commanded, his voice echoing a baritone chorus, "as Watcher and protector of this realm, I call upon the law to banish you. Back to Hell!"

With his words, a massive purple and gold light erupted around us, surrounding the demon. In the presence of the light, its body swirled and dissolved into a black, oily liquid. Then a huge rip opened in the grass behind Michael and the beast slithered right into it. When the tear sealed itself, I heard a sound echoing through the trees, like the slamming of an enormous steel gate.

The street light flickered back on. I let myself breathe again and the air around us became light, ebullient, freshened by a crisp sea breeze. Michael retracted his sword. It pulled back into its handle and extinguished before he tucked it somewhere between his shoulder blades.

"Are you okay?"

Shocked by everything I'd seen, I blinked at him a few times before I answered. "Yeah."

He scanned the horizon once more: the empty trail, the line of trees, the waves crashing from the harbor against the rocky shore. Then he turned to me and asked, "Wanna get a pizza?"

My stomach hardened as though I'd swallowed a lump of concrete that was beginning to set. I stared at him in disbelief. "You're *hungry*?" My voice was almost a squeak.

His face broke into a wide, boyish grin. "Starving. Like I haven't eaten in *days*."

He shook out his wings, scrutinizing them for damage. After a fine mist of black liquid sprayed off them, they looked flawless and clean again, undamaged. But there were wounds on his shoulders where the demon had struck, big open gashes from teeth and claws. His shirt was torn and soaked with blood and black slime. His face and hair were also covered, his jeans ripped and spattered, yet he glowed as though his skin were lit from within. His hands radiated light as he waved them over his wounds, and the bleeding stopped. Torn flesh inched its way closed, leaving no sign but the stain of damp blood on his skin.

He looked down at the state of his clothes and let out a grunt of distaste. His expression was almost sheepish. "I guess I should clean up a bit."

Sheathing his wings, he walked to the beach and took off his shirt, exposing a lean, muscled back, taut golden skin that looked almost bronze in the streetlight.

Crouching at the shore, he splashed himself with sea water, then completely immersed his shirt and wrung it out—once white, now it was gray and pink from rinsed slime and blood. He soaked his hair, his skin, and steam rose off of him in the cold night air.

As he approached, I noticed the water trickling down the few hairs of his chest and the tiny goose bumps that formed on his skin. "This is the best I can do for now," he said lightly. "I'll need to go home and change. We can pick up something to eat on the way."

I tried not to stare at his naked chest, the six-pack below it, or the damp line of hair between his navel and the top of his jeans. Flushing, I looked up at his face and caught a smile. With his wet hair pushed back, he was painfully beautiful, and I felt ashamed, somehow, for admiring him.

If he noticed me staring, he didn't say anything. Instead, he put on his tank top wet and tied his sweatshirt around his waist.

"Are you okay to go back now?" he asked. His voice was smooth, low, and surprisingly human.

"Your shirt is wet and it's freezing out" was the only thing I could think to say.

He let out a short, surprised laugh. "We were attacked by a demon and you're worried about a wet shirt?"

"You're worried about pizza," I replied defensively.

"Hey, a guy's gotta eat," he said, still smiling. Then, serious again, he unsheathed his wings and stepped closer. "Ready?"

Taking a deep breath, I nodded, and he lifted me into the air. I draped an arm around his damp shoulder, and the beach disappeared beneath us. The concrete ball in my stomach rolled a few times but settled quickly as I relaxed in his arms.

Chapter Twenty-One

After stopping to pick up an assortment of pizza slices which I ended up carrying, we landed in the backyard of a large, modern-looking house. It was completely surrounded by evergreens except for the view of Seattle's harbor peeking through the trees. Michael took me by the hand and led me along a dimly lit path toward the house, then through a glass door to a ground-level studio. As the lights flickered on, I noticed a large, open-concept living room with a tiled kitchenette. A plush off-white sofa faced a huge flat-screen TV over a gas fireplace framed on both sides by built-in bookshelves. On the other side of the sofa, a king-sized

Murphy bed lay open, covered by a soft-looking gray duvet.

"Wow, is this your room?" I asked. "Complete with its own entrance?"

"Yeah. My parents had this place built with the idea of housing me through college."

"It's fabulous."

He shrugged. "I like it."

My legs were a little wobbly, so I placed the pizza on a side table and perched on the couch. "Do your parents know what you are?"

"No. It's safer that way, for all of us," he answered and walked to his bedroom. "I'm going to shower." He pulled open a dresser drawer and grabbed some clothes and a towel. "Help yourself to a slice. I won't be long."

I couldn't eat. My stomach was queasy from flying and other things, like being attacked by a demon. "What do your parents think?"

"Nothing's changed. They think I'm the son they've always had." Holding his clean clothes in one hand, he grabbed a slice of pizza with the other, raising it in a toast. "Cheers." He put it in his mouth, swallowed a large bite, and left the room.

While I waited, I wandered over to a bookshelf. Unlike his music collection, his books were more what I'd expect from an angel. There were copies of Dante's *Divine Comedy*, Milton's *Paradise Lost*—which we'd be covering in English later this year—several versions of the *Bible*, the *Talmud*, and the *Qu'ran*. I also saw an old leather-bound book on demonology, and one called *Demon Lore*.

On the table was a smaller book called *The Book of Enoch*. Curious, I opened it and noticed that one of the pages had been folded down. I read:

1. And it came to pass when the children of men had multiplied that in those days were born unto them beautiful and comely daughters.

2. And the angels, the children of the heaven, saw and lusted after them, and said to one another: 'Come, let us choose us wives from among the children of men and beget us children.'

It was the story of the Watchers and how they fell, which was what happened to Michael. The book went on about the children of the Grigori and human women. It explained that they were giants, called Nephilim, and they were led by a demon called Azazel.

Azazel! My mind darted back to the horrific creature we had seen earlier that night. This demon was a leader of giants? What about the half-human, half-angelic beings? What did they look like?

Images flickered in my mind, dark images where I was screaming, sweat pouring down my face, my hand gripping Michael's with waning strength. The shards of memory were hazy and weak, but I could tell I was giving birth. I was in a dark, cavernous room with stone walls lit only by firelight. I had an old woman helping me. Her eyes were blue and cloudy with cataracts but her hands were deft, experienced. She touched my forehead with a cool cloth, encouraged me to breathe.

I was halfway out of the memory when Michael came into the room. His feet were bare, his hair wet, and his gray T-shirt was slightly damp at the hollow of his chest. The smell of steam and soap wafted behind him.

"We had a *child*?" I asked. I had no breath. The recollection came upon me fast, too, like vertigo. My

THE WATCHER

stomach lurched, and I was suddenly glad I hadn't eaten. "A giant. Like Azazel."

Michael removed the book from my shaking hand and placed it on the table. "We did."

"I gave birth to a demon!" I all but shrieked.

"We didn't know *what* it would be," he said.

My legs wouldn't support me anymore, so I collapsed on the couch. "W–what was Azazel doing here? Was he—it—my…" I couldn't bring myself to say the word "son."

Michael shook his head, his face blanching. "That creature was destroyed a long time ago."

"What happened?"

"It developed a taste for human flesh," he said. "I couldn't let it loose on the world. Not after what it did to you." Then, as though the horror of what had happened had resurfaced, he raked both his hands through his wet hair. "I killed it. I had to."

I couldn't remember the pain, but the memory of it showed on his face. I didn't have to ask what it had done to me. He had been there the whole time, watching, and in spite of all the power he'd once had, he could do

331

nothing to stop it. I saw him holding my hand, his tortured expression, his helplessness. I remembered a heat ripping through me, as though the baby would tear itself out with its claws if it had to. Apparently it did, and Michael had killed his own son because it was a monster.

As if we were both seeing the same memory, he added, "What we did. What *I* did. It *killed* you."

The memory was painful, but it wasn't his fault. Women had died in childbirth throughout history. Granted, these were different circumstances and it was *me* he was talking about, but it was a long, long time ago.

"It doesn't have to be that way," I said. "We don't have to have...offspring."

"It's not that simple," he snapped. "I broke laws of a very high order, and that was an abomination in itself. My offspring, as you put it, was simply its manifestation."

"Why would you be punished for love? You told me to feel love earlier and it kept the demon away."

"It does. *Love* does. But not lust, not enthrallment. There's something wrong with me. Angels are supposed to be impartial. You were in our care. We weren't supposed to desire you—let alone be blinded by it. We were supposed to watch over you, guide you, *protect* you from temptation—not *lead* you into it. God, Mia, I was so easily tempted to want more, to cross that line… Now, it's how I'm tested. How the demons get in."

So he was being tested. That was why he pushed me away. Even though we came from different worlds, we were drawn to each other so intensely it could hurt both of us. Just kissing me appeared to weaken his defenses, leaving him open to being attacked like we were tonight. Could things be any more impossible between us?

"Was Azazel a test?" I asked, still confused by it.

"Yes. No. He took advantage of the moment. It's what demons do. They'll exploit any weakness."

"He mentioned Damiel."

"Azazel wasn't acting alone, that's for sure. He was delivering a message. Damiel will be back soon." He leaned against the fireplace and folded his arms across his chest. "From the looks of it, he's bringing backup."

LISA VOISIN

What he said had to be true, but that didn't stop me from wishing it weren't. For the last day or so, I'd put the idea of Damiel's return aside, hoping it wouldn't happen, but now it was something I couldn't run away from. When I'd last seen him, Damiel had been in human form. Michael's battle with him may have been quicker, less gory, but I knew from the way he had been protecting me that Damiel was a much bigger threat than Azazel ever was.

"What do you mean by *backup*?" I asked, but on some level I already knew the answer. The demon had given us Damiel's regards.

I pulled my knees into my chest and hugged them for support. Michael didn't move closer to comfort me. Instead he flipped a switch on the wall and with a hiss of gas a fire ignited in the fireplace. "When I fought him that night, I knew he went too easily. All I did was dispatch him, temporarily freeing the body he'd been possessing, but I did him no real damage." I noticed how talking about Damiel agitated him, tightening his shoulders and hands, making the tendons pop. "What

334

Azazel said tipped me off. Damiel's up to more than I suspected."

"What is he up to?" I asked.

He reached between his shoulder blades and pulled out a long silver handle that curved to fit perfectly in his grip. "He's building an army."

"Why? What is he going to do?"

"I don't know his plans, but it's a very old grudge between him and me." He examined the handle. Carved with ornate scrollwork and ancient lettering, it was beautiful. "I don't think it's just me he's after. I think he wants you, too."

"Me?" The blood chilled in my veins despite the fire. "Why?"

"That was my fault. I trusted him."

His mouth forming a hard line, Michael focused on the object in his hands. His sword expanded from it, faster than a switchblade and at least as long as his arm. It made me jump.

"Where did that come from?" I said.

"A sheath between my wings."

Between his wings? Had it been there all the time?

The sword's blue light glinted in his eyes. Something about it turned his expression from grief to something quiet and determined, deadly even.

"Let me guess, it's inter-dimensional too?"

"Don't worry," he said. "It can't hurt you." He moved closer to me and held out the blade.

It seemed to be made from some kind of metallic light, blue but not a laser; there was a silver, steely quality to it as well. Slowly he moved it toward me. "Touch it. You'll see what I mean."

I reached a fingertip to the blade and my finger passed right through it, like it was a hologram. There was a cold tickle where it had connected, but no pain. "How does it work?"

"By intention. It can't hurt humans, but it's fatal to demons." To illustrate his point, he ran the blade through his own arm. There was a rippling of light, but no damage. Raising his sword, he readjusted his grip. "Try it again."

I reached for the blade expecting nothing to be there, and this time it was a cold steel, icy beneath my fingers, but not sharp. The blue light buzzed and arced around them.

"My intention can make it into a blunt instrument, but that's as much damage as it can do. We're meant to protect humanity, not harm them." There was something in his tone—guilt perhaps—that made me wonder what he'd done.

He transferred the blade to his left hand and rotated his wrist, the weapon a silent extension of his arm. So that was how he'd managed to dispatch Damiel without hurting his vessel, Giulio.

"What happened between you and Damiel?" I asked, wanting to know what Michael was talking about before he'd changed the subject. It was an area I had no memory of. "How is trusting him your fault?"

"He saw my obsession back then and tried to keep me away from you, but I wouldn't listen. His sin was envy. That envy made him competitive, so he wanted everything I had. My rank and position..." He glanced at me and I could tell it still shook him to speak of it. "You.

He wanted you because you loved me. It became a compulsion."

Envy. I thought about how Damiel had sent hellhounds to look for me but only appeared in person after I was hung up on Michael, and it made me shudder.

"He fell quickly," Michael continued. "Since we were close once, fighting him was especially hard. But I managed to keep him away from you."

"You protected me from him."

He stopped moving the sword but didn't retract it. "For purely selfish reasons."

"Are you worried about fighting him again?"

"I'm used to dealing with monsters. I've been one." He retracted his sword and sheathed it, and his face held all the weariness of someone who had lived a long life of pain and war. Although his body had healed, these were different scars and they haunted him still. "But I can't be everywhere all the time, and if he's after you—"

"You've protected me before."

"If it weren't for me, Damiel would never have come after you. We wouldn't be in this mess if I'd stayed away. I should have left when I saw you again."

His words sliced through me. Was that how he felt? That his life would be better without me in it? "Fine," I said bitterly. I was used to being alone. "Why don't you leave, then?" *Everyone else does!*

He crouched before me, his expression filled with regret. "I can't."

"Why, because Damiel's coming? Because you *have* to protect me?"

"It's what I do, Mia." He took both of my hands in his and bowed his head as though in prayer. "Let me do that, at least. Let me do it right this time and protect you because you deserve it. Because it's the right thing to do."

I pulled my hands away and got up. "I don't want you to stay with me because it's *your job* as an angel or because you feel *obligated* to get it right this time."

His face flooded with what looked like thousands of years of self-loathing and punishment. "Is that what you think?"

"Isn't that what you're saying?" I said, realizing that I didn't know what I thought. I didn't even know where I stood with him from one day to the next. "You stay because you have to."

"No, I stay with you because…" He took a deep breath, but when he spoke it was barely a whisper. "I can't stand being away from you."

"You can't?"

Hardly able to believe what I was hearing, I fought the urge to cry. I'd never known anyone who *wanted* to be around me before. Since my parents' divorce, I'd been alone. The family I'd come to rely on had all but fallen apart. Mom worked all the time to look after us. Dad had no time for me. I'd moved, made new friends, but it wasn't the same. I may have been used to being alone, but being used to something wasn't the same thing as being okay with it.

Michael had focused only on the danger, made it explicitly clear that it was real, not only from Damiel and an army of demons, but even from himself if he enthralled me or lost his way. I thought he had to protect me from all of it, that I was just something from his past he had to resolve. I accepted it, because being near him made the pain and loneliness of my life go away. But it was more than that. I couldn't bear being away from him either, and I'd never stop loving or wanting him.

Standing before me, he inched closer, and the pull to be near him tugged at my skin and tightened my lungs until I was short of breath. Then, as though he could read my mind, Michael drew me to him, wrapping his arms around me as though I were on fire and he was extinguishing the flames.

"I thought you knew," he whispered.

His arms tightened around me, and with the warmth and strength of his body pressed against mine, his heartbeat pulsing against my cheek, I felt completely safe. I crushed myself into him, matching my breathing with his.

He stroked my hair, and I raised my hands from around his waist and slid them up his back, between his shoulder blades. Sinewy muscles vibrated under his shirt, scalding my hands. They tingled and burned from touching him.

He let out his breath softly. "Your hands are cold."

"Is this…?"

"Where my wings join? Yes."

"Does it hurt when they come out?"

"No." I could hear his smile. "But I've never carried another person before."

"Really? Not even way back when?"

"Especially not then." As he said it, an image flashed in my mind of his wings, white and beautiful, outstretched behind him. Same as the wings in the dream I'd had years ago. They were *his* wings that someone was trying to take—not mine. Why did I dream it, then? Had I *actually* been there when it happened?

The next thing I saw were bloody wounds on what must have been his back, the skin dark red and puckered as it healed. "You had scars," I said, wincing, unable to think about what had caused them.

Hearing my pained expression, he backed away from me, his hands gripping my elbows. "You remember that?"

"How could anyone do that to you?"

"I chose to fall," he said harshly. "I deserved it."

"Nobody deserves that!"

"You don't know the whole story…" Crossing his arms, he leaned against the mantel, his eyes downcast, as though he couldn't face what he was about to say. "The Grigori were terrible when they—when *we* fell. Without remorse. We *took* whatever we wanted."

I wasn't sure what he was saying. Had he *attacked* me? Is that what had happened? "And you wanted me?"

"Beyond all reason. The creature you gave birth to was my fault." His gaze shot through me like he was waiting for me to hate him; clearly, he hated himself. "Something that horrible could only be conceived through coercion…or worse."

Or worse? What had he done?

I felt the room spin for a moment like I was on that ride at the amusement park, the one that twirls so fast it holds you to the sides with centrifugal force—right before the floor drops out from under you. I'd trusted him. How could he?

Focusing, I tried to recall the past, wracking my brain for any sign of what he might be talking about. I couldn't remember violence or being forced in any way.

All I could remember was the joy we felt when we were together and then his pain as he stood at my bedside, watching my life slip away. "You said we didn't know what it would be. Did you know?"

This was the past, ancient history in fact, and yet Michael's expression showed a grief so raw it might as well have happened yesterday.

"No. I didn't think it would happen to us," he muttered. "Enthrallment is a type of coercion. For all I know, I—"

I cut him off. "What do you mean, *for all you know*? Don't you even remember what you did?"

"I've done terrible things." Taking a deep breath, he let it out slowly. "I don't remember everything." His eyes shone in hollowed sockets pulled so tight, it made him look ancient. "Part of me doesn't want to... If you knew how far I fell, you'd hate me."

As he struggled to control his emotions, I wondered if this was all he thought of himself. I may not know what he did back then, but I knew what he was like now: carrying me out of the woods, saving me from hellhounds, fighting Damiel and Azazel. He'd done everything in his power to keep me safe. "I could never hate you."

"Never's a long time," he said, his voice wavering. Before I could reach for him, he backed away and motioned toward the door. "It's getting late. I'll take you home."

LISA VOISIN

Chapter Twenty-Two

From the front walk, my house seemed gloomy in the darkness, as old houses do when nobody's home. I'd been so preoccupied before we went flying that I forgot to turn on the porch light. The solar-powered lanterns lining the front walk hadn't seen enough sunlight to charge them today, so they gave off only a dim glow. Although Michael was silent on the drive home, he walked me to my front door. But when I invited him in he declined, saying he was going to check the area and keep watch.

Still shaky from everything I'd been through, I decided to take a shower—nothing like almost being demon food to make me feel I needed one. I hadn't realized how much fear Michael's presence kept at bay until I was alone. It didn't help that every time I closed my eyes I recalled Azazel's red ones watching me—and that horrible laugh. Once I got in the shower, a chill ran to the core of me, made my knees shake. Washing my hair and conditioning the tangles gave me something else to focus on, but as far as distractions went they were short-lived. I showered longer than I'd planned to and turned up the hot water more and more until it almost burned my skin, but the cold feeling didn't leave.

Realizing that having clean hair and skin was about as comfortable as I was going to get, I got out of the shower and into plaid flannel pajama bottoms and a long-sleeved T-shirt. I was exhausted, my bed more comfortable than I expected. Once my head hit the pillow, it didn't take long to fall asleep. Dreams came quickly, too.

***

I was at the beach again at night; the tide rolled in lazily and moonlight glimmered on the water's surface. The cold, damp night air cut right through my skin. I was waiting for Michael, and it seemed I'd been waiting a long time but there was no sign of him. Then the sky blackened and Azazel crawled from the sea. I could smell that horrible stench of its breath as it loomed its many heads over me, waiting to strike. I screamed, but no sound came out of my mouth, so I gasped and screamed again, hoping Michael would hear me and come to the beach, but he didn't. The third time I screamed, I broke into a run, but something gripped my wrist. At first I thought it was Azazel and I tried to pull free. Then I heard a voice say my name, a calm, musical voice. My arm shook gently.

"You're having a bad dream," Michael said. As my eyes adjusted to the darkness, I could see how concerned he was. "You were screaming."

Pulse racing, I sat up and mumbled unintelligibly, "Azazel…beach…"

"You're safe now," he reassured me, straightening my tangled duvet.

"How did you get in?"

"You left your door unlocked." He frowned. "Anyone could have come in."

Looking at him, I could see golden-orange flames inside the huge black circles of his irises. There was nothing in my room that could have made that light except for him. It was beautiful, inhumanly so.

"Stay with me?" I asked.

"You know I can't."

"Until I fall asleep. It won't take me long. Please?" Maybe I couldn't face the thought that he had hurt me. If he had, he was doing everything in his power to make sure it didn't happen again.

His body drew tight. I must have asked for too much. But slowly he relaxed, and the strain in the air was released. "Let me lock the door."

He was gone only a minute, and yet as soon as I shut my eyes, the horrifying dream about Azazel returned. It pulled me in quickly and was so disturbing that when Michael touched my hand on his return, I screamed again and practically jumped out of bed.

"Sorry," he said. "I forget how terror can be sometimes."

Taking a deep breath to calm myself, I squeezed his hand. "I'm glad you're here. My nightmares will go away now."

"Oh, so you just want someone to keep the monsters at bay," he joked, but he sounded nervous. "What makes you so sure I'm not one of them?"

"Because I can see."

His long body was all angles and limbs as he eased himself onto the bed beside me, outside the covers, and tension pulsed through him like a live wire. But eventually he settled, as though through a great act of will, and stretched out to hang his legs over the end of my double bed, his arms tight to his sides.

His cotton shirt was soft against my cheek as I leaned my head against his shoulder, afraid to breathe in case I frightened him away. It seemed he wasn't breathing either. The electric hum of my alarm clock blared even louder than normal, and I marveled at how I could ever sleep through it. A faucet had been opened inside me, the current flowing. I buzzed with it. Now wide awake, I struggled to stay still. At least the horrifying images of Azazel were gone, replaced by other memories of the night, like kissing Michael. And while lying in his arms, unable to sleep, seemed to be the perfect place to think about *that*, believe me, it wasn't. I needed to distract myself.

"You know, there's this sound your wings make when the wind hits them," I babbled. "It's a beautiful sound."

He touched my hand, intertwined his warm fingers with mine. Even that touch was electric between us. "Really?"

I swallowed. My throat was dry and tight, but I wasn't about to get out of bed for water. "Then there's the sound of your voice."

"My voice?"

I held my breath, hoping to regain control. "Sometimes it takes on a completely different sound. Like a choir."

"You can hear that?" He broke into a laugh. "I should have known."

"Is that when you're working?"

Nodding, he said, "It's the Host."

"The host?"

He squeezed my hand and brought it close to his heart. The light in his eyes glowed faintly orange in the dim of my room. "When any one of us acts on behalf of Heaven, all the angels in the network are with us. So if one of us speaks, all of our voices are heard."

I took a deep breath and let that sink in. Closing my eyes, I saw an explosion of light erupt through darkness, forging galaxies and filling the sky with stars. Planets formed from colored light. The sound it made was incredible, comprised of many notes and harmonies all playing together at once. It was as though all life stemmed from that one eruption, like a spark that started a fire. Startled by it, I gasped.

"What did you just see?" Michael asked.

I described what I saw as best I could, but I couldn't begin to explain what I'd heard. "What was it?" I asked.

"You've heard 'In the beginning was the Word,'" he said, "but what people don't know is that the Word was sung."

"Were you there?" I asked. I'd never thought how far back his life actually went; it was staggering.

When he answered, his voice was sad. "Everything that lives now, that ever lived, was there. It's just that nobody remembers it anymore."

A shiver ran through me and I didn't know what to say. As we lay there in silence, I realized then that there were so many things I didn't know. There was an entire lifetime I hardly remembered and it was affecting my present life. I was in a world beyond my imagining, a world of angels and demons, with rules and consequences I hardly understood. But beneath all of it was love, as though it were the basis of everything.

Michael broke the silence first. "The others don't like what I'm doing—with you."

"They can see?" *Of course they could.* Arielle had said as much, but I'd convinced myself she was the only one who saw us.

"All of it. As long as I'm connected, I'm never alone. Which is why sometimes I disconnect so I don't piss them off." The shadows cast on his face from the dim light of my room made him look sad. He sighed. "I can't lose them."

I squeezed his hands. "I don't want you to."

"I can't lose you either."

I couldn't tell if he meant now or if he was thinking of the past, but there was something in his voice that made my heart ache. It hung in the air between us. "You won't. Even if...I mean, even *though* we're just friends, I'll be there for you. Always. I promise."

He sucked in his breath and let it out slowly. "I'm tired of kidding myself. You and I could never be *just* friends, Mia."

He paused. Could he feel my heart racing as I struggled to figure out what he meant? Surely he wasn't going to give everything up. He couldn't!

"But if I lose the others, I'd be useless against Damiel or any of the demons after us. And if you think they'll just forget about me because I've walked away from the fight, you're wrong. They'd hunt me down."

"What about Arielle? She's your friend. Wouldn't she help?"

"She's my *sponsor*. She can't break our laws either, because she has to answer to them too. But the way I feel is my business, not theirs..." Still holding my hand, he took a deep breath and leaned closer to me, our sides touching. "What I do, on the other hand…"

A tremble ran down the length of his whole body right through me. Both of us froze. "I know," I said. "I know."

As I lay there in stillness, listening to his breathing and the quick, steady beat of his heart, I couldn't help but wonder if the others could see us now. Couldn't they see how hard he struggled to be what they expected? Didn't that count for something?

***

I woke to the foreign sensation of movement as Michael gently slid out from under me, replacing himself with pillows. It was still dark out, but the sounds of life outside told me it was morning. Michael hardly looked rumpled.

"Good morning," I said.

"Your mother will be home soon," he said. "I should go."

Stifling a yawn, I smiled at him. "I'm glad you stayed."

"You should be. You drooled all over my shirt."

I gasped, my hand covering my mouth, and he grinned at me, pulling on his shoes. I reached a hand up to smack him but was so tired I missed.

Chuckling softly, he kissed my forehead to bid me goodbye. The warmth from his lips shot all the way down to my toes.

"Thanks," I said.

"Whatever for?" There was a ring of humor in his voice.

"You only stayed 'cos I asked you to."

"That's not the only reason. I just…" He hesitated.

"Just what?" I pressed.

"Didn't know if I could trust myself."

"What about now?"

He laughed under his breath as if to say *Not at all*. But his eyes had a different look in them than I'd seen before, as though he were less haunted, more present.

"I trust you," I said.

"I know," he whispered. "You wouldn't have asked me to be here if you didn't."

He was right. I didn't trust easily. But no matter what had happened in our past, I trusted him, and not just because it was so long ago that I didn't care what he did. There was nothing he could do that I wouldn't forgive or accept, and the idea of being in love with someone that much freaked me out—mostly because it didn't feel wrong. It may have been against the rules, but nothing about loving or being with him felt wrong.

He removed his shirt and tucked it around his waist. Golden light glimmered behind the muscles of his shoulders as they prepared for his wings to connect. And then, with incredible grace, he leapt out my window.

Chapter Twenty-Three

When Michael picked me up for school I could still see something different in his eyes. He seemed more relaxed, like some war inside him was finally over. When I looked in the mirror, I noticed that my own eyes had changed, too. They shone wildly with a light that hadn't been there before. We'd spent the whole night together, we hadn't had sex, and the world didn't end.

Walking around that morning, I was really clumsy, as though my feet were floating above the ground. When Michael was with me, he managed to steer me away from obstacles and even kept a straight face. On my own, though, I bumped into a garbage can, someone's locker, and a boy with stringy red hair who gave me a dirty look before telling me to watch my step.

After lunch, Michael told me he had to leave for the rest of the day because Arielle needed backup on a tricky assignment she was working. I found it odd that he called them "assignments." He didn't look worried, but I couldn't stop thinking about the demon he'd fought the night before. Michael was strong, but his opponents were horrifying. He walked on a battleground that I was grateful to have no part in. I didn't want to know what evil was out there. I'd seen enough for several lifetimes.

I had a free period in the afternoon that I was going to use to study for an upcoming history quiz. I went to the library but found I had forgotten my notes, so I had to trudge down the empty halls to my locker.

When I opened it, a folded piece of lined yellow note paper fell out. I picked it up, unfolded it and read:

Dear Mia,

It's too bad we couldn't get together the other night. I was looking forward to getting to know you better.

Perhaps you want to reconsider?

Sincerely,

Damiel

My hands shook as I read the note a second time. Was this for real? I'd never seen Damiel's handwriting before, so I didn't know. It could have been written by anyone, Elaine even, or he could have written it any time since I'd first refused to date him. Why, then, would it only show up now? I had been at my locker not ten minutes earlier and there was no sign of it then. I scanned the still-empty halls for a clue as to who could have put it there. Could Damiel be back? I'd heard Michael mention it was possible, but so soon?

Relax. It's probably an old note.

Something didn't feel right. Without Michael around, there was nobody I could talk to who knew what a threat Damiel was. If I mentioned anything to Heather about *that*, she'd only think I was insane.

I spent the rest of my study period in the library, reading the same page over and over again because I couldn't focus. As soon as the school day ended, I rushed outside to catch the bus. I was cutting through the parking lot when I ran into Farouk and Fatima heading toward their car.

"Need a lift?" Farouk asked cheerfully.

"That would be great," I said, still shaken.

Fatima observed me curiously. "Is everything okay?" she asked.

Seeing her gave me an idea. Farouk had told me how she could see things. She could even sense something different about Michael and seemed to know Damiel meant me some kind of harm. Maybe I could talk to her.

"Yeah," I replied a little hesitantly. "Can I…uh…*talk* to you about something?"

"Of course," she said, motioning to the car as she started walking again. I followed.

I couldn't believe I was going to ask for her help with a demon. How much could I tell her? How much could she see by merely looking at me? I only hoped that because the subject was otherworldly that her psychic experience would help. Besides, she was the only person I knew who might not think I was nuts. Without Michael or Arielle around, I didn't know where else to go.

As soon as we arrived at the car, she said, "You're not wearing the necklace."

I touched my throat self-consciously. "Something happened to it; it buzzed like crazy, then broke and fell off. I'm sorry."

"When?" It had just begun to drizzle, so she climbed into the back seat of Farouk's car.

"Last night."

Farouk got into the driver's seat and suggested, "Let's go somewhere warm and dry so you two can talk."

Shaking droplets of rain out of her thick curly hair, Fatima said, "Let's go to our place. Everyone's at the store tonight. Farouk, would you take Mia home afterwards?"

"Of course."

Fatima was remarkably calm and composed. "I've never heard of a Hamsa breaking before. You must have been in real danger."

"I think I was."

"At least you're still alive."

Did she know I was dealing with a demon? I tried to follow what she might have meant. "It's just meant to block bad energy, right? That wouldn't actually kill me?"

"You tell me," she replied.

I sighed. *Why can't people give me straight answers?*

"I know you can see things too. Farouk told me. People who aren't really there."

He'd *told* her about that? I glanced sideways at Farouk. He focused on the road as though he was trying to avoid the conversation. His face flushed slightly under my scrutiny, but he didn't speak.

"It's all really new," I said finally. "I don't understand it yet. I need your help."

"I'll do what I can."

They lived in a big old-fashioned wood frame house with a large porch overlooking the bay. I followed them inside to the kitchen. Fatima excused herself for a moment to take her things to her room, and Farouk disappeared, muttering something about leaving us alone to talk.

Like the house itself, the kitchen was quite old-fashioned and tastefully decorated with white painted cupboards and a blue-tiled backsplash. In the corner by the windows was an antique oak dining table. A blue vase filled with sunflowers sat at its center.

Dark wooden furniture and a comfortable-looking sofa over a red Persian rug filled the living room. At one end of the room hung an ornate wood-framed mirror, and at the other stood a dresser. Resting on velvet cloth sat a book bound in red leather covered with ornate gold scrollwork. It looked so important I was almost afraid to touch it.

"It's the *Qu'ran*," Fatima said from behind, startling me. I was more nervous that I thought. "It's the Muslim Bible."

Not knowing what to say, I nodded. I did know that much.

"My parents are kind of religious," she said, leading me back to the kitchen, "but Farouk and I are far more liberal in our practice."

Under her right arm she carried a small wooden box, which she placed on the kitchen table. I took a seat across from her.

"Now, what did you want to know?" she asked, her face calm, impassive.

Unsure where to begin, I pulled out the note from Damiel and showed it to her. When she read it, her forehead crinkled with concern.

"When did you get this?"

"Today."

"And he hasn't been at school all week?"

I shook my head. "Do you think he put it in my locker before last week and I just found it now?"

"Let's see, shall we?" She opened the box on the table. Inside was an object wrapped in blue silk. She carefully unfolded it to reveal a deck of ornately designed tarot cards.

"How long have you been doing this?" I asked.

"Since I was twelve," she replied. "Don't tell people, okay? My parents don't even know about it. Tarot isn't very Muslim of me. Farouk doesn't even approve. He's been turning a blind eye to it for years."

Admiring how she'd managed to keep her gift a secret, I raised my hand as though I was making an oath. "Your secret's safe with me." *As I hope mine is safe with you.*

She smiled, holding the cards up to me. "Shuffle," she said, then demonstrated what she meant, "keeping your question in mind."

I took the large cards in my hands. They were cool to the touch and slightly worn around the edges. I shuffled and thought about the note from Damiel, but thoughts of Michael quickly interfered. I struggled to focus. When I had finished shuffling, I handed them back to her.

She pulled the top card and placed it on the table facing me.

"Seven of swords," she said plainly. Her eyes glazed over, unfocused—or focused somewhere I couldn't see. "It usually means someone with cunning and confidence: things are not as they appear, some kind of trickery. Someone is taking from you."

Cunning and confidence—that was most certainly Damiel. And Michael had said once that Damiel was taking from me. "How does this relate to the note?"

"It means he only seems to be away. He will be back, and he wants more than he's asking for."

A prickle ran across my skin. It was the truth. "What can I do about it?"

She pulled the next card and put it on the table. On it was a naked couple with an angel in the clouds above them, its arms outstretched.

"The Lovers," she said.

Heat rose to my face in spite of myself. If only Michael and I could be lovers! When Fatima looked past me again, her brow furrowed. I wondered what she was seeing.

"You have been given a gift of love, and for it you must love beyond anything you've ever imagined before," she said.

Well, that seemed easy enough. I had never loved anyone or anything as much as I loved Michael. But how could love possibly be the answer? In some ways it was the problem.

She pulled another card and frowned. "The Devil."

Before I could stop myself, I shivered. "What's that about?"

"It's the outcome card," she said plainly.

"The Devil is the outcome?" My heart caught in my throat. "What does that mean?"

She picked up the card thoughtfully. "It's one of the most difficult cards to read. It can mean someone you're bound to. Someone who has power over you in some way, who has enslaved you. It can also mean someone who is caught or enslaved by a belief."

"*That's* the outcome?"

"As far as I can tell."

My mind whirled with all the possible ways this could go wrong. Suddenly, all concerns about Damiel's note left me. This reading was about me and Michael. Things not being as they seemed: that was about how happy I was with him. How in spite of everything, all his warnings, I held onto the belief that we could be together somehow. Fatima didn't know Michael's history, that our being lovers in the first place had had disastrous results.

She didn't know how much I longed to be with him again. Even if it meant we could never be physical with each other.

I tried to hide how depressed I was. From the looks of the cards, it would happen again. Michael would be faced with temptation and if he caved, he would fall again.

I stood up. "Thanks."

"It doesn't have to be bad," she said, her eyes becoming more focused, clear.

I fought the urge to cry. "How can it not be bad?"

"The Devil challenges where we're caught. If we can surpass the blocks, it can lead to true transformation, or even ascension."

I thanked her again. Even though she was optimistic, I felt hopeless. There was nothing about surpassing blocks that meant I could be with Michael. I would love him forever; being with him meant everything to me. But if one thing came out of this reading, it was that I couldn't tempt him again. I wouldn't be responsible for his fall. Not this time.

Chapter Twenty-Four

I was cleaning up the dinner dishes when Michael arrived on my doorstep. Underneath his gray button-down shirt, which transformed his eyes into jewels, was the signature white tank top he wore for flying. With his hair still damp, drying in curls around his face, he looked more angelic than ever.

My hands soapy, I waved him in through the window and he joined me in the kitchen.

"I'm just finishing up," I said. "It'll only take a minute."

"I'll dry," he offered and held out his hand for the towel. There was a gash on his arm; it had to be fresh.

"You're hurt." I grabbed his hand to examine it, but he pulled it away.

"It's not that bad."

Instantly everything that had happened in my day vanished. I was lost in concern for him. "What happened?"

He leaned on the kitchen counter across from me. "We were trying to prevent a rape," he explained. "Arielle was working with the girl, trying to guide her to what she would need to do to get away or at least survive. She brought me in to work with her attacker because...well...I know the voices that he has to fight inside himself."

He paced from the kitchen into the living room. I followed him, drying my hands. "How did it go?"

"We were swarmed. They were lesser demons, but all working together, like Azazel. There were hundreds this time. Arielle and I tried to call to the others for help but they landed so fast... At first we tried to stay focused on the assignment. The girl...she was..."

He rubbed his eyes. Was he tired, or trying to wipe away what he'd seen? I couldn't tell. I wanted to hold him, give him some comfort, but his body was so wiry and tense I wasn't sure if he'd let me in.

"You did all you could."

"By the time we were done…" He didn't finish his sentence, but the look of devastation on his face said it all.

"You did your best," I said soothingly.

"Arielle said the same thing." He sighed heavily. "The girl was attacked, but she lived. When we'd dispatched the demons, it was easy enough to pry the beast off of her. Not so easy to let him live." His anger filled the room as he strained to pull himself together, his expression both haunted and sad. "It could have been you."

I took a step closer, touching his face, and he leaned his cheek into my hand. "I'm right here," I said reassuringly.

"What if it happens again?"

"You'll be more prepared," I said. "You're one of the smartest people I know. If anyone can learn from this, it's you."

LISA VOISIN

He sighed, accepting that. A smile tugged at the corners of his mouth and he opened his arms so I could lean into him. As he rested the side of his face gently on the top of my head, I listened to the steady beat of his heart, knowing I needed to mention the note from Damiel but I couldn't bring myself to do it. Not yet—not when he'd had such a rough night.

Within a few moments, he tensed and backed away. Bright light flared around him. Squinting, he shifted his focus as though he was listening to something far away. A look of resignation crossed his face.

"What is it?"

"I'm still on duty tonight." He ran a hand through his wavy bangs, pushing them out of his face. "I'm being called," he said flatly. "To Portland. Another major attack."

"Portland?" I asked, shocked. "Portland's a three-hour drive away."

"It's way faster by air," he said, and it took me a moment to realize he planned to fly.

I knew that he would at some point have an assignment and be called elsewhere; he had a larger purpose. But knowing that didn't make it any easier. He'd already been on one call that night and it seemed to have deeply affected him. Clearly, he needed time to process.

His expression hardened with determination. "I'm not going."

"Wha—?"

"I'm not going. They can send someone else."

"People's lives depend on you." I thought of the attack he'd just prevented. However badly it went, his being there had made a difference. "That girl probably wouldn't be alive if it weren't for you."

He took my hands in his. "*Your* life depends on me, too. *Your* life is the one that matters to me. Don't you get that? I've waited thousands of years to see *you* again—"

"Michael, you can't disobey."

"What if all of this is a ruse? It all picked up since Damiel left. What if it's a trick to keep me busy and away from you?" He linked my fingers through his and pulled me closer. This didn't sound anything like him. The Michael I knew was bound to his sense of duty, obedient to God, and determined to ascend. Something was wrong.

"Michael, you sound paranoid," I said, trying to keep myself calm. Seeing him this worried made me think things were a lot worse than he was letting on.

"Or maybe I'm the only one who sees this clearly." He bent his forehead to mine, almost touching. I wanted to lean in, to soothe him, but I had to talk some sense into him.

Unlinking my hands from his, I held the sides of his face. "You have to go. You can't—"

The rest of what I was going to say was cut off by his lips pressing against mine. His kisses were intense, angry, restless, as he leaned into me, filling a need within him and awakening a need inside me, too. I was swept away by it. I knew it was wrong, that we should stop, but I didn't care. In no time at all I had reclined on the couch, his body pressed into mine, and I didn't want him going anywhere.

Still on top of me, he pulled back and placed one of my hands on his chest. His heart hammered against it—as fast as my own. The look he gave me was fierce and yet gentle too, as if he saw so much more of me than I even knew existed. He stayed that way for a long time and said nothing. He didn't have to; his look said so much. I met his stare, matching his quickened breathing, my heart pacing with his.

When he finally spoke, his voice was deep, husky. "Mia, I—"

"Can't. I know. It's okay." I touched his arm lightly with my other hand. I wasn't going to stop touching his chest. His heartbeat was steady but fast. "We should stop."

"I love you," he confessed. His eyes captured mine with a dazzling blue light. "I always have."

I'd suspected he felt something for me, but hearing him say it meant more than I'd ever imagined. "I love you, too," I whispered.

He nodded. "I can feel it."

"You *can*?"

"Yes. It makes it so much harder to stop when I know your feelings, not just my own." I couldn't keep the look of amazement off my face. He brushed a stray hair out of my eyes and continued, "All the angels can feel, but for so long I couldn't. I forgot how amazing it was… It's why enthrallment is so dangerous; it reverberates. So if I make you feel something, I feel it too."

"Michael, you haven't *made* me feel anything."

He kissed me again with a dizzying intensity and swept me up into his arms until I was on top of him, kissing his face, his neck, as he let out the softest of sighs. His hands, warm and strong, gently caressed my sides, the skin just under my shirt, and the next thing I knew my shirt was off. My soft blue lace bra was pretty, and if I didn't know it looked good on me I would have from the look on his face: he regarded me as though I was the most beautiful thing in the world.

Saying my name softly under his breath, he kissed me again and again and again. It was what I'd always wanted, but something was wrong. There was something *else* he was *supposed* to be doing—not this. He turned us again until he was on top, and removed his shirt and then the white singlet. His skin was beautiful, glowing a soft gold in the incandescent lighting of my living room like he was bathed in candlelight. His chest warm and smooth, I had to touch it, feel it against my own skin.

"Michael?" a female chorus said, the voice so familiar to me now. She had entered so silently neither of us had heard her.

Of course. *If an angel is on duty and disconnects from the network,* Arielle had said, *we have to check in.* It was creepy to even think about how visible we were.

Michael's shoulders tensed but he kept kissing me, ignoring her, and the intensity shot up between us. I tried to stop but couldn't. I was drawn into him, as though we were one being separated only by skin.

"Michael," she said again more insistently.

"Go away," he replied, his voice surprisingly cold, a stark contrast to the warmth from his kiss. He didn't stop.

"Are you insane?" she asked. "You've been called. You *must* go."

He kissed my throat, the side of my neck, as one of his hands stroked the side of my waist. I didn't want him to stop. But he had to. "Michael," I whispered between labored breaths. "She's right."

I started to sit up, but he held me down. His voice with me was soft, soothing, his breath hot on my skin. "It's okay. She'll leave soon."

"Michael!" she bellowed, her voice a trumpet blast.

He stopped kissing me and sighed impatiently. "I've got to stay with her."

With her arms folded over her chest, Arielle looked furious. I sure wouldn't want to cross her. "Disobeying a direct order? Tell me I didn't get brought into this so you could fall again."

"It's just another peripheral attack. Can't you see? It's a ruse. Damiel will be back, and who's going to watch over her?"

"Can't *you* see? You can't do it." She motioned to his position on the couch. "Not like this." Her voice, still a chorus, was steady and calm, a contrast to Michael's agitation.

"Why not?"

"You know why not." She moved into him and, with inhuman force, pulled him off of me.

His temper exploded with the force of an air gun. He shook himself free of her grasp and raised a hand instinctively, like he was going to strike. I held my breath.

Fearless and ferocious, she continued, "You're weak. You're not in the network. There's no power without your connection. Without it, Damiel will eat you alive! What will happen to Mia then?"

The golden glow of her halo flamed brightly even in my well-lit living room. It burst from her in a ripple of light that rushed Michael, igniting his own halo. His hand fell and he blinked at her as though waking from being drugged.

"You've been called. You must go. You're needed."

He motioned to me. "Who will watch Mia?"

"I will. She'll be safe, I promise," Arielle said.

He nodded slowly, accepting his task. "If anything happens to her…"

"It won't."

I sat up and pulled on my shirt, flattered by the fact that he looked a little sad to see me cover myself up. "I'll be fine. Arielle knows what she's doing."

"Been at it a while now," she added and threw his singlet at him.

He put it on. "I'll be back as soon as I can."

"I know."

I hugged him goodbye, my body aching to be with him. Knowing he felt it too, that he could feel me, I pulled away. He hesitated a moment, gazing at my lips, compelling me to kiss him, but if I started again we wouldn't stop. So I turned away and he left.

"He'll be okay, won't he?" I said to Arielle, who was standing in the living room calming herself.

"He should be."

"I mean he won't fall again because of tonight?"

Her clear golden eyes revealed nothing. "I've got to go straighten out another mess. I'll be back to check on you in a little while. If you need me, call, okay?"

"I'm sorry," I said.

She didn't say anything, but her look acknowledged me before she left.

Standing up, I noticed that my legs were wobbly and my body still pulsed with desire. It had never been this intense before—like a drug—not even that first time we'd kissed. After being so close to him just moments before, Michael's absence now almost hurt. I was cold and lonely in a whole new way. Was this the enthrallment I'd been warned about? Or was it just love?

Beneath it all, I was agitated from my afternoon: Damiel's note, and then the Tarot reading—that Devil card plagued me. It seemed the longer Michael and I were together, the more likely it was that I would cause him to fall—or at least stray from what he was here to do. Knowing he could feel my feelings meant he would know how much I wanted him—which in itself was too strange to even consider. How long could I be close to him without causing a disaster? I couldn't bear to be with him and not be close, and I couldn't bear to be without him.

Grabbing my iPod from my purse, I found the loudest, angriest song I could. I didn't care that it was after ten, that the neighbors were likely asleep. I hooked it into the stereo and put it on repeat with the volume loud enough for the bass to pound against my chest. Retrieving Michael's jacket from my room, I used it as a pillow and lay on the living room floor as close as I could get to the speakers, the heavy pulsing beat filling the lonely hole in my chest. Tears flooded down my face.

I don't know how long I lay there or how many times the same song repeated. Vibrating through the floorboards of the old house, the music was so loud I didn't notice Arielle standing there until the music shut off.

"Hey! Put it back on!" I said, getting up.

Her halo blazed around her as she approached me with the grace of a cat. "I didn't need to even try to sneak up on you…"

"So?"

"Dear one," she said, her voice a musical and soothing balm, "I bring you a message."

"From Michael?" I stood up. "Is he okay?"

"No. Think higher up than that."

"Oh, so now God's going to order me to stay away from one of His angels?"

"Not at all." Arielle's smile was kind. "Will you hear it?"

Her halo had grown so bright it was hard to look at her. I nodded, my chest tightening. I realized I was afraid to know what God had to say to me. What could He possibly want from me other than for me to get lost? No wonder. I had obviously messed things up for Michael before.

"You know Damiel is coming back."

"Yes."

"And you know he wants you for some reason."

"I know."

"Sure enough. But what you do not know is *how* Damiel will hurt Michael."

"How?"

"He's going to exploit Michael's weaknesses. He's going to use his past and make him believe he's unforgivable. That's Michael's ultimate weakness. He can't forgive himself for his past, and it started with what he did to you."

"What did he do to me that was so horrible?" I said, reaching back in my memory for some kind of glimpse of what happened.

"We'd hoped that by spending time with you, Michael's memories would return on their own. The only other witnesses are on the wrong side to be of any help."

"Which leaves me as the only witness." I sat on the couch.

"Exactly. We were wrong about Damiel. If you're the only witness, it makes no sense for him to force your memories back...*unless* he was trying to short-circuit you and destroy those memories altogether."

It took me a moment to process all she had said. "My memories are that important?"

"Yes. Very. We need you to remember what happened so that Michael can forgive himself before it's too late."

"How do I do that?"

"I have an idea." She came over to sit beside me on the couch and her halo tingled beside me. It blazed much stronger than Michael's.

"Does it involve going through that network again?"

"No, we need to tap into your memories," she said, rolling up the sleeves of her beige jacket. "It'll be different this time. Hold still and, no matter what, keep breathing, okay?"

Chapter Twenty-Five

When she placed her scorching hands on my head, a brilliant white light erupted through my brain like sheet lightning. I couldn't help but gasp.

"I know it's warm, but it won't do any damage. Just keep breathing."

"As if I'm going to stop," I said, but I focused on my breath anyway.

My mind blanked as though it were rebooting, obliterating any thoughts I had about what we were doing or what would happen next. An exploding fireworks display of colors and images followed, pictures that came so fast I couldn't make sense of them. I winced, inhaling sharply as a piercing pain shot between my eyes. "What are you doing?"

"Nice, deep breaths. This will pass too." The resonant tones of her voice echoed right through me.

I closed my eyes, the sound of her voice guiding me until the pain subsided, and a tunnel of brilliant golden light presented itself. I followed it until I saw Michael. Sitting on a roughly-carved wooden stool, he watched as I took wildflowers from my hair and placed them in a bowl of water, their silken petals limp between my fingers. We were inside the same house I'd had visions of before, and through its small round holes for windows, stars sparkled in the night sky. Next to us stood a table covered with dried fruits and cheeses left over from a feast, from some kind of celebration—our wedding.

Michael stood, his full height almost to the ceiling, and held out his hand to me. He spoke a different language, but somehow I understood it.

"Come to bed—wife." The corners of his lips curled into a smile filled with desire and the promise of such pleasure that my skin flushed even remembering it.

Was this it? Was this what he was forbidden to do? Marry me?

But in that life, I smiled and danced, twirling around him and humming a tune from that time as I meandered toward our bed. Light from the fire flickered in the blackness of his eyes. He was different then. Even though his face held all the signs of his beauty, it was shadowed by a sadness that I hadn't seen in him before, as if his glory had dimmed somehow. But in that moment I didn't notice. I was focused on him, fueled as much by his desire as by my own. When I was close to the bed, he grabbed my arms, raising them above my head, and kissed me hungrily, without restraint, and a rush of passion flowed through me.

From what Michael had suggested about our past, I would have expected a wild disrobing or something forced at this part, but this was gentle, beautiful. It was strange to have a full memory of something I hadn't done in this lifetime. I couldn't see myself but saw it through my own eyes, as though it were happening to me, which it did. Even back then, the chemistry between us was incredible, and though it was only a memory my body responded.

Grappling for self-control, knowing that it wasn't actually happening in the moment, that I wasn't alone, I nervously pushed the memory aside, hoping Arielle couldn't see it. At least Michael wasn't with me. I would have jumped him for sure.

Next, I saw us waking with the sunrise, naked on a bed of furs, Michael peaceful as he slept. Scars ran down the length of his back where his wings had once been.

Like being startled awake, I snapped out of the memory with a pounding heart, a dry mouth, and sweaty palms. Arielle's hands rested on my shoulders as she searched my face for an answer.

"Could you see what I saw?" I said.

She shook her head. "I could only see you were getting memories and feel your feelings."

"*All* my feelings?" I cringed, thinking that some things should be private.

"You were so in love."

"Still am," I muttered under my breath.

Arielle hugged me. "Human love is frightening and tempestuous, but it can be beautiful, I'll give it that."

"I don't understand what Michael did that was so wrong."

"What did you see?"

"Our wedding night," I began, then explained the image as clearly as I could, leaving out the personal, embarrassing details. Arielle asked me if I was forced or in pain at any point, but I wasn't. There was nothing in that memory that I didn't want to hold onto. It was beautiful and I would cherish it. "He slept. He told me that angels never slept."

"That's because he'd fallen," she explained. "Angels were forbidden to mate with humans. Breaking our laws would drain him—make him mortal—so he had to be careful. Those who continued to fall would steal people's life force in order to survive."

"You mean Damiel?"

She nodded pensively. "Would you be willing to look again? Perhaps a different memory?"

"Yes. But I'm thirsty," I said, and got up to pour myself a glass of orange juice. The muscles all over my body were strained and achy. My legs wobbled, so on my way back from the kitchen I stopped to stretch them out. As I bent forward and clasped my hands behind my back, one of my ribs popped back into place at least, but the pain in my muscles frustrated me.

"What you're remembering isn't coming from your mind in this life. It's coming from your soul. I'm taking you so far into your soul's past that your mind can't process it, so it resists with physical pain. You may also experience fatigue or anger," Arielle said, smiling kindly at me. "You're doing really well."

"How will this ever help Michael?"

"Are you ready to try again?" she asked. "You'll be perfectly safe. I'll be right here."

"Yes." I tried to not betray the sense of anticipation that welled inside me.

When she placed her hands on my head again, the heat was less intense than before. The images came as soon as I closed my eyes.

This time, I saw more of the ancient city where we used to live. It was near the sea. A huge sandstone wall surrounded it like a fortress, and in the center of the city was a great sandstone ziggurat. The house I lived in was on a farm near the edge of the city. It belonged to my family. Not sure where to go next, I thought about Michael.

Next thing I knew, I was in the woods outside the city walls. Michael stood before me wearing a long robe, and his downy white wings glowed behind him in the shade of the trees. Physically, he was huge. The top arc of his wings reached a good two feet above his own head, compounding his size as he towered over me. Seeing him filled me with a mixture of dread and awe that drove me to my knees. My breath came in gasps and I was dizzyingly afraid, astounded by this wondrous creature.

He caught me and lifted me back to my feet, shaking his head. Kneeling before me, he bowed his head and stayed there, motionless, until my fear subsided.

From a pouch on his belt, he presented me with a small ornate jar, carved from a clear crystal. Each incision captured the light, refracting into colored spectrums—like the light from his wings. When I opened the jar, the oil inside smelled of flowers and amber from the trees. He motioned for me to put some on my wrist, so I did.

"What are you seeing now?" It was Arielle's voice, interrupting my memory.

"A meadow. He's giving me perfume," I said. The image wobbled slightly as I spoke. It was difficult to talk and focus on it at the same time.

"Try to see what happens next," she offered.

"Okay." I strained to concentrate. The images flickered slightly and faded out.

"Relax a bit more. You can't force it."

I tried to relax, but a flash of light erupted between my eyes again, followed by that short, stabbing pain. Instinctively, my hand gripped the bridge of my nose. Then the image flickered and shorted out, giving way to darkness.

I let out a groan of frustration. "It's gone now."

"It's late," Arielle said. "You're tired. We should take a break."

"What about the other memories?"

"The soul's memories are delicate. They're between a person and God. As an angel, I can take you to them but we can't force it. If we do, we could damage them, which is what Damiel tried to do," she said firmly, "and I won't do that."

"When can we start again?"

"A few hours. I'll be right here." Leaning forward on the couch, she tilted her head sideways and closed her eyes, listening. I imagined it was the way she tuned in to the others. "Michael's fine." She waved me off. "Get some rest."

As strange as it was to have Arielle babysitting me, it would be pointless to argue about it, and when I lay down exhaustion took over. As soon as I closed my eyes, my dreams came in heatedly, almost too numerous to track. One of them was the dream about the birds I'd had the first day of school. This time, they were angels—Michael and Damiel destroying each other—and I still wasn't able to stop it.

I woke up with the sunrise on Saturday morning, filled with panic. Heart racing, I got out of bed, my muscles complaining as though I'd overdone it in gym class. The coppery metallic tang of adrenaline filled my mouth, so I went to brush my teeth. Splashing cold water on my face to wake up, I caught my reflection in the mirror, surprised to see that the eyes staring back at me belonged to a stranger. They were mine but not mine, like I was looking at myself from a different life—*that* life. Brown skin, long black hair, a slightly more streamlined nose, higher cheekbones, and a smaller mouth. I was me but not me, the face unfamiliar and yet strangely so.

As soon as it appeared, it faded, and my own face stared back at me again.

Trying to shake it off, I jumped into the shower, hoping the hot water would soothe my sore body and frazzled nerves. It did. When I got out and got dressed, I realized Mom was already home and in bed. I had nothing planned for the weekend. I'd been keeping the day open to spend with Michael, and his absence left an enormous hole. I didn't think about Arielle until I went into the living room and found her sitting on the couch. I nearly jumped when I saw her.

"Good. You've rested," she said. "Are you ready to try again?"

I nodded, seating myself beside her.

"I want you to go back to the memory you were having last night, about the perfume," she said. "We can use it as a marker and move forward from there."

"How do I do that?"

"Just think about the memory. I'll do the rest." She placed her hands on my head as she had the night before. This time they seemed to burn even less. The images returned instantly.

"Got it." I could see Michael in the forest, the perfume bottle, Michael encouraging me to try some. In the vision, he smiled at me and left.

"Try going forward now."

I focused again, trying to both relax and concentrate at the same time. The image advanced quickly, as though I were chasing a dream.

I was in the woods, collecting ingredients to make dyes for the cloth I was weaving. The sky grew increasingly darker and it was time to head back. As I gathered the last few red flowers and placed them in my basket, Michael stepped onto the path. Darkness surrounded him. His once-white wings were gray and tattered, as though they'd been singed, and his eyes, usually clear and blue, took on strange red hues. They were rimmed with shadows. He looked stricken with— what was it? Anger? Need?

"What's the matter?" I asked.

A haunted smile touched his lips. "I fell."

Not fully understanding, I shook my head.

"It was the only way," he said. Tears filled my eyes, shocked by the realization of what he'd done. Brushing my cheek, he leaned into me until his face was inches away. "I've wanted to do this for so long."

Then he kissed me, and the feelings I'd been trying to hide around him flooded through me. They were met by an even stronger force: him. I let myself be taken by that force like a storm. It wasn't right to want an angel this way. The tribal elders had warned all of us, but I didn't care what anyone else thought. In that moment, none of those barriers existed. We flowed smoothly together, and when he swept me up into his arms, I was no longer afraid of anything.

My memory jumped forward a few minutes. This time, I was partially disrobed under the shadow of the trees, cool in the moonlight. His warm hands—strong and rough from working the fields—held me back as I strained to reach for him. The more he hesitated, the more I wanted him closer to me, mesmerized by the darkness. In him, it was beautiful. He stopped and gazed at me as the blue returned to his eyes. They were still mostly black, and something urgent and inhuman flickered behind them, something he was holding back.

I kissed him again as he slid out of his robes. His body was lean and incredibly strong. It both frightened and excited me. His skin burned against mine as I traced the muscles of his chest, down the tight ridges of his abdomen to the corded muscles above his hips, and he moaned softly, his lips pressing against the side of my neck.

The next thing I heard was a deep, musical voice—several of them. A bright light shone above us.

"They're over here."

I tried to see who was there, whose voices made the chord of music that spoke, but I couldn't see over the cover of Michael's wings. Whoever they were, their approach had been as silent and stealthy as hunters.

Michael didn't pay attention to the voices. Exploring the length of my body, he held me, locked in some kind of trance.

A few things happened at once. Two sets of huge, strong hands grabbed him by the chest and lifted him off of me as he let out a snarl of frustration, trying to struggle from their grasp. Another set of hands grabbed the skirt of my dress, covering my body before the others could see it. I turned to the person who covered me. It was Arielle. She glowed the same as she did now, but back then was the first time I'd ever seen it, and it frightened me.

"You were there!" I spoke out loud to the Arielle in the room with me. As I did, the memory shook like a glitch in worn filmstrip.

"Stay with it," Arielle said. "Stay with the memory."

I returned my full focus to the vision playing in my mind's eye and saw the two larger angels hold Michael back. They were also huge. Though he looked different, one of them was Damiel.

"Leave now, Arielle," Damiel said. "You do not need to witness this."

She bowed her head obediently and turned to walk away; the forest dimmed as she left. My attention returned to the two other angels who held Michael captive. Though Damiel was slightly smaller than Michael, the other angel with them was huge. He towered over both of them, his hair the color of wheat, his eyes a golden fire. His wings were white and clean, with the slightest graying around the edges. The light around him shone brilliantly, not as bright as Arielle, but brighter than either Michael or Damiel.

Damiel slapped Michael's face. "I warned you about this."

The other angel touched Damiel's arm, restraining him. He spoke directly to Michael, his voice stern, condemning. "Do you know what your crime is?"

Michael nodded, his head bowed.

"Speak it."

"Lust." His voice was hoarse, barely above a whisper.

"You admit it freely?"

"Yes."

"Are you aware of the punishment?" the angel asked, walking around to face him.

"Banishment," Michael answered, bracing himself.

"So be it," he said firmly, not seeming to take the slightest pleasure in his work. "Michael, third rank in the Order of Grigori, in the name of God, I banish you. You are no longer welcome in the Kingdom of Heaven." The blond Grigori's words hit Michael like a blow to the chest. He exhaled sharply and his shoulders slumped in defeat.

Damiel's face shone with satisfaction. "My Lord Raguel, what if he tries to come back?"

"He won't," said Raguel.

"We've seen others try before. We must prevent him. Make an example of him... We must take his wings."

Raguel was contemplative, and Michael's eyes widened in terror. The thought that someone so fearless could know such fear horrified me. I wanted to comfort him. Even if he had broken their rules, he didn't deserve this. Nobody did.

"We will use them for good," said Damiel. "They can be used to warn the others so that no more of us will fall."

"No!" I cried out.

Damiel turned to me fiercely. "You tempted him with your body. You made him do it. Don't think I don't know your guilt in this." He moved closer to me, staring me down as though he could see right through my clothes. Even then, his harshness with me was covering something. *Was it my fault? I did want Michael. What if he could feel it then, too?*

"Enough," said Raguel.

"What if she tempts another?"

"We will take his wings—as an example—but do not torment the girl. God created women for a reason." His expression shifted to one of disdain. For an angel he was a pompous ass, but he terrified me nonetheless. "If a woman tempts an angel, it is the angel's weakness... She has Eve's curse upon her. That is enough."

ISA VOISIN

Damiel bowed his head obsequiously. "As you wish, My Lord. Do you want to perform the excision, or shall I?"

I looked at Michael, horrified, unable to move or run away, as shame draped itself around him like a tattered cloak. I was his only witness. The punishment didn't fit the crime. He'd chosen to fall, but what if I had tempted him? I had loved him, admired him, yearned for his presence.

There was a part of my memory that was blocked, too terrible to witness—too challenging to remember. All I could see was darkness. All I could hear were Michael's screams and Damiel's voice, cold and chilling, calling Michael a rapist, telling him over and over again that it was fit punishment for assaulting me.

Rapist? Assaulting me? Is that what Michael believed? It wasn't like that at all! My chest ached as the light around him went out, fading to a blackened memory.

Chapter Twenty-Six

Not wanting to see any more, I pulled myself out of the vision. Tears streamed down my face.

Arielle placed her hands on my shoulders as she had before. They were warm and reassuring, like her voice. "Just breathe," she said. "You'll be okay."

The sound of Michael's tortured screaming echoed in my ears.

"They were angels," I said, trembling. "How could they…" I couldn't finish my thought. I was sobbing too much.

Bathed in a shimmering golden light, Arielle said nothing but her silence spoke volumes. Her presence soothed me as I steadied myself.

"He called Michael a rapist," I gasped. "It's a lie."

A look of astonishment crossed her face. "Tell me what happened."

I told her everything, from being caught with Michael in the woods to the things Damiel said when he cut off Michael's wings. When I was done, she didn't speak, but inclined her head as though she were listening to something that only she could hear.

"You were there," I accused, angrier than I expected. "Didn't you know?"

"I was naïve."

"The other angel," I said, thinking of the golden-haired one in charge. "He let it happen. It wasn't just Damiel."

"Raguel was very powerful. He had already started to turn." She leaned forward and rested her hands on her knees. The gesture made her seem uncomfortable, anxious, when she was normally so calm. "I didn't see it coming. None of us did."

I searched for more memories of what she was telling me, but my mind was too tired to focus. "How come I can remember this and Michael can't?"

"That's the trauma. It twisted his memory. The only way Michael's mind could make sense of…what happened…" She avoided repeating what I told her, as if she were unable to speak of such torture. "…was to believe what Damiel told him. He believes he deserved it."

"When will he remember the truth?"

Her back tensed and she rubbed her hands along the tops of her thighs, her gaze shooting around the room. "He may never."

I sucked in my breath, fighting the urge to cry again. It was almost too much to absorb at once. "You made me remember all this. Why, if there's nothing I can do?"

She got up and crossed the living room to the kitchen, where she found a clean glass in the cupboard and turned on the tap. "You're probably the only one who can reach him. We had to try." She returned with a glass of water and handed it to me. I didn't think I was thirsty until I gulped it down. "You should rest now."

I was too wired to rest, so I got myself another glass of water, trying to make sense of everything. I only remembered my life with him, but his life extended way beyond mine. Arielle hadn't told me everything, and she'd had an uneasiness when she spoke of Damiel, one I couldn't quite place. "What happened to Michael after I…?"

I didn't say "died," but she knew what I meant. "He didn't tell you?"

"No."

A heavy sadness came over her, sharpening her features and darkening the hollows of her eyes. "After you died, Damiel came back and killed him."

A huge tidal wave of panic crashed through my thoughts. It rumbled and swept all the way down my legs. Damiel had killed him? And Michael was going to fight him *again*?

Seeing how shaken I was, she led me to the couch to sit down. "It was different then. Michael was alone, and he felt responsible for your death. He wasn't evil, but he rejected the light and thought he should be punished. Damiel convinced Michael that he was unforgivable, so when he died he agreed to let Damiel take his soul to Hell."

Hell? Michael chose Hell?

"He was broken, Mia. Tortured for a long time." Her eyes blazed with a fierce and inhuman beauty as they blinked back tears. "Taking his wings was nothing compared to what he endured there. They made him think he had no free will, and then they gave him orders to hurt people."

"What did he do?" I asked, remembering Michael had said that demons could come and go so they could hurt people. I'd thought he'd meant Damiel. "Was he a demon?"

Frowning, she flicked her cloaked wings with the same kind of irritation that a cat flicks its tail. "He was a slave."

"But he *did* hurt people."

"He took no pleasure in it, if that's any consolation."

I was no longer listening. I knew Michael had done terrible things but never wanted to believe it. I remembered his shame. how he'd feared what I'd think of him. A quake of sadness reverberated all the way to my toes.

It was all happening again. Michael had come back to face me, and Damiel was still in the picture, trying to ruin everything. waiting for the opportunity to enslave him again. If Michael felt unforgivable for what happened to me, Damiel would always have a way to hurt him. "Damiel plans to do it all over again," I said, thinking aloud. "After everything Michael's done to get better."

She nodded. "I know."

"Can Michael die this time?"

A gritty determination came over her. "Michael won't be alone this time."

"That's not what I asked."

Arielle eyed me cautiously as I tried to process. Michael had never hurt me but had spent the last nine thousand years believing he had. Damiel had messed with his head, convinced Michael to join him in Hell, and even killed him. Michael having done some of Damiel's dirty work could only make it worse. Now Damiel was on his way back, with an army this time. The fact that Michael wouldn't be alone gave me little comfort.

There was a knock at the front door. It made me jump.

"It's okay," Arielle said, touching my wrist. "It's Michael."

When I opened the door, the first thing I noticed was that his hair was messy and the white singlet he normally wore when flying was torn and stained with blood. But at least he was visibly unharmed. When he stepped inside, I could see the stubble on his chin. His eyes shone wildly, circled by dark rings of fatigue. He hadn't slept.

"Hi," I said. Though I was happy to see him, I wondered what kind of night he must have had.

"Mia, we need to talk."

He and Arielle exchanged a look that made me wish I could still hear their thoughts.

"What happened?" I asked, alarmed.

Michael took both my hands in his and gave me a thin smile. "Nothing for you to worry about."

Arielle extended her fiery halo toward Michael in an eruption of light, which erased the lines of fatigue from his face. Brightening, he gave her a nod.

She stretched—the gossamer blue of her cloaked wings shimmering as they extended behind her—and headed for the door. "I'll put myself back on watch. You could use some rest."

"I won't be on duty tonight. Please don't look for me," Michael said as she passed.

"Your choice," Arielle said, then nodded at me. "Goodbye for now, Mia."

"Bye, and uh…thanks," I said. Still a little shaken, I led Michael to the living room to sit down. I had to talk him out of fighting Damiel. Knowing Michael, it wouldn't be easy. "What do you mean you won't be on duty tonight?"

He squeezed my hands. "I'm watching you instead."

"You're exhausted. You need to rest."

"I need to be here with you."

"Michael," I began, wishing I could tell him all that I'd seen, but I couldn't find the words.

Too agitated to sit, he got up and paced the room. "You don't know what it did to me, losing you…"

I didn't want to know what it would be like to lose *him*. Now that Damiel had the time to regroup, it would be too dangerous to fight him again. Michael couldn't win against an army. Having just relived him losing his wings was painful enough. His death was unthinkable.

"Falling was the only way I could be with you. I chose it," he said, half-wincing at the memory. "Nothing could stop the burning except being near you."

I held my breath. If he was going to tell me what happened, I didn't want him to stop.

"Falling from Grace, I went from being connected to everything to…nothing. The other angels were my family." Grief emanated from him as he spoke. I knew what it meant to lose a sense of family, but not like this. "For the first time in my long life, I was truly alone, and I never knew how cold that was." He took a deep, jagged breath, letting it out as he folded his arms across his chest. "After you died, though, I couldn't do it. I couldn't fight anymore."

He seemed much too far away, so I got up and wrapped my arms around his waist. He took another labored breath before he let me in, and I stayed there until his breathing smoothed out. I only had pieces of what he went through. He'd told me before that falling didn't stop, that he had to constantly fight to not continue to fall. Was that how Damiel was able to convince him to choose Hell?

"I know," I said. "Arielle told me."

"You're not the only person I hurt. You were the first, and the fact that I could hurt someone I loved so much…" Wiping his eyes roughly with the back of his hand, he choked out a sob. "How can that ever be okay?"

"Arielle said you'd been tortured."

He pulled away. "That's no excuse. I was selfish."

Now he was torturing himself. It was hard to watch. I needed to let him know the truth.

"You didn't hurt me. You may have done other things, but you never hurt me."

"I did," he insisted.

"No." I grabbed his elbows, wanting to shake him. "Michael, listen. You *think* you hurt me, but you didn't. It's a lie. That's why you don't remember..." My voice trailed off as his eyes became glassy, far away. "Because it didn't happen."

"What didn't?"

"When you first fell, you never hurt me. It wasn't like that. It was...beautiful."

He shook his head as though what I'd *said* had hurt him. "That's because I enthralled you, Mia. I could have made you do anything." Taking a step back, he raked both his hands through his hair and let out an exasperated sound. "Don't you see? Your will wasn't involved. It was coercion, the same as if I'd drugged you."

"You didn't," I said. Our actions had been motivated by love, but there was no way to prove what I was saying. It was my memory against his.

He took a step closer and backed me against the wall. Pressing himself into me, he caged me there with his arms. I could smell his skin, feel the heat of his body through my clothes, and I wasn't sure what I wanted to do, push him away or wrap my arms around him. When his eyes softened and gazed into mine, everything else around me became quiet and still. A pulse of golden light brushed my skin, and it was like a flame ignited, searing me from the inside.

He slid one of his hands down the wall to touch the curve of my lower back, and my legs trembled. I forgot everything I was thinking. All I could see, all that I wanted, was *him*. I was dizzy from it. Snaking my arms around his neck, I curled my fingers in his hair. He leaned in, his breath sweet on my tongue, and I tilted my mouth up to his, closing my eyes, expecting his kiss.

The look on his face was a challenge. "You still think I didn't enthrall you?" he whispered.

I pushed him away angrily, unable to speak. My pulse hammered in my throat and my body shivered from his sudden absence. I tried to think, but my mind reeled. Was it the truth? Had he been enthralling me all along?

He sighed, taking another step back. His eyes were soft, full of love—not the eyes of someone who wanted to hurt me. His breathing was quick, as though I'd affected him, too.

My knees weak, I leaned into the wall for support as I fought to recall my senses. All the times that we'd kissed. They were *real*. Not like this. He didn't toy with me. He didn't have to. "I saw what happened. All of it."

He shook his head. "I didn't expect denial."

I knew what I saw. How could I get him to believe me if he wouldn't see? "Can't you just *trust* me?"

"It's not like—"

But it was exactly like that. He could trust Damiel's lies about him, believe the worst about himself, but he couldn't trust me—that what I felt for him was real. It *always* was. "Why are you here?" I snapped.

He took a step toward me. "To be with you."

"Why?" I inched myself along the wall, trying to put distance between us. I still wanted to kiss him. "Why would you want to be with me if you don't trust me?"

"Look. I know I've been pushing you away…"

"I trust *you*."

"Last night I lost control, and I know I can't go there again, but I'll do everything in my power to be with you. If you'll have me."

Of all the times I'd wanted to be near him, they were nothing compared to that moment. He *loved* me, *wanted* to be with me. A flush ran all the way up my spine, and it called me toward him. I'd backed up, but he stood less than a foot away; all I had to do was lean into him, show him I accepted him. Everything in me wanted to.

As though he sensed my hesitation, he inched forward, his hands at his sides. "Once Damiel is defeated, it'll be a lot easier. You'll see."

Damiel. He would still have to fight Damiel. The one who killed him, took him to Hell. He'd never win. Not with a guilty conscience over something he didn't do. If Damiel could use Fiona's insecurity against her, he could certainly use Michael's guilt. He'd done it before. I pushed Michael away. "No."

"No?"

"I can't be with you if you won't listen to me."

"I am listening. You believe—"

"No, I *know* you didn't hurt me." I took another step away. If he couldn't hear that he hadn't hurt me, there was no way he could defeat Damiel. It was too dangerous. If Damiel used me as a weapon, Michael didn't have a chance. "Not unless you can tell me truthfully that you believe you're innocent." *Otherwise Damiel will defeat you again. He'll kill you.*

I refused to back down. A war of restraint and emotion waged across Michael's face. Before he spoke, he looked at the fireplace, the mantel, the window. Anywhere but at me. "I do trust you. I just…"

"Don't trust yourself."

A hard, brittle feeling settled in my chest. If he didn't trust himself, he'd be duped by Damiel again, even killed, and I couldn't let that happen. I loved him too much. I would rather break my own heart than risk his life—not to mention his soul. Nothing I could say would change his mind. So I took a deep breath and said what needed to be said. "Michael. It's over between us."

He let out his breath as though I'd punched him. "Over?"

Even in pain, he was beautiful. Tilting his chin back, he gazed at me with eyes that were as clear and blue as a cloudless summer sky, and from that angle he seemed more angelic than ever.

I couldn't believe what I was doing, but I needed to keep him safe. If Damiel was after me because of how I felt for Michael, I'd have to remove myself from the equation, show Damiel I didn't care. I would run away, catch a flight to Oakland, and stay with Bill in Berkeley. I had enough in my savings to do it. Damiel wouldn't expect that. Even if he did, if he got me, that was one thing. I'd be far away and Michael wouldn't be anywhere near us. He wouldn't have to feel responsible for what happened this time. He wouldn't have to die.

I turned toward the fireplace and mustered up the courage to speak. "You should go now."

"Mia."

"Leave!" I yelled at him.

He touched my shoulder gently, and the warmth and strength of his hand seeped through the thin fabric of my shirt. "At least let me protect you."

Despite how cruel I was being, he was still trying to help, which only made it worse. The effervescent fire of his halo enveloped me, bathing us both in golden light. I shook it off and faced him again. I had to be strong. "I don't want you near me."

The light dimmed. "You don't know what danger you're in."

I wanted to say *I don't care! Just stay safe yourself.* But he didn't seem to care how much danger *he* was in. "Let Arielle do it. I don't want you around."

He paled and took a step back. "You don't want this. I can feel it."

He could tell I was lying. Damn him for feeling what I felt! Since I couldn't change that, I had to use his own laws against him to end it now. I crossed my arms in front of my chest, attempting to block him out. Even if pushing him away made me cold and empty inside, it was nothing compared to how I'd feel if he were dead. *If anything happened to him because of me.*

"Aren't you supposed to respect a person's free will—no matter what?"

He watched me as though I was dealing him a death blow.

Unable to look at him and do what I needed to do next, I turned away. "Then respect mine."

At that, he didn't argue, and I didn't turn back to see if my daggers hit. I was sure they did. I could feel them as though they had pierced my own heart.

"Fine," he muttered.

Then the coldness inside me took over as I listened to the sound of his footsteps walking out the door.

***

I went through the rest of the day like a robot, or some other creature without a heart. Knowing I'd cut it out myself only made it worse. Cold and spent, I had a scalding hot shower that didn't touch the icicles that had formed inside my chest. When Mom woke up, I put on a brave face and made dinner for both of us, holding back tears. I didn't deserve to cry. It was my choice. I'd pushed him away and it worked. He was gone.

I kept the TV on so we wouldn't have to talk. I didn't want her to guess anything was wrong, that I was planning to leave. She was groggy from switching her sleep patterns from day to night shift and didn't say much herself. I vowed to myself that I would call her when I arrived safely at Bill's apartment.

Even though everything was dulled by my grief, there was no way things could work between Michael and me. Before, all the obstacles we had between us didn't seem real, as though we could be okay if we played it safe. Being together felt right. But now, my feelings for him couldn't be reason enough, not when his life was at stake. I had to do whatever I could to keep him away from Damiel. Leaving Michael. Leaving town. They were the right things to do. I *had* to do them. I was sure of it.

When dinner was ready, Mom and I ate in front of the TV, watching the early news. A lot of crazy things were happening in the city: three big fires, a high-speed car chase, and several muggings. What had caused them? Was it Damiel's army? The time for believing in coincidences was over. I couldn't afford to be naïve. People I cared about would get hurt.

Then the news announced a freak ten-car pileup on the freeway Mom usually took to work, which meant she had to leave earlier than usual to take an alternate route. Sadder than I expected, not knowing when I'd see her again, I almost choked up when I kissed her goodbye.

Anxious to get going, I pulled my suitcase out of the closet and laid it open on my bed. I was folding my favorite pair of jeans when the doorbell rang. I froze, thinking that if it was Michael, there was no way I could say no to him again. But it wasn't.

"I know you're in there." The cruel, familiar voice sent icicles down my spine. "Let me in."

Chapter Twenty-Seven

I didn't open the door, for all the good it did me. Even though it was locked and bolted, it blasted open like it had been hit by a hurricane. Standing in front of me was someone I hoped I'd never see again. He looked exactly the same as the last time I'd seen him, which meant he'd re-possessed Giulio.

Damiel pressed his hand through the open doorway, and a faint blue arcing light flared and fizzled around it. "Sigils," he said. "Useless."

Instinctively, I stepped back. He laughed, and the sound was colder than I remembered, more sinister. He crossed the threshold slowly, purposefully, as though he knew there was nothing I could do to get away. Unfortunately I knew it too.

"What kind of welcome is that for a friend?" he chided, "especially one you've known as long as me?"

"You're hardly a friend!"

"Now, now. We had a date." He moved in closer to take my arm in his.

I pulled my arm away, trying not to freak out. "Leave me alone!"

"I don't know why you won't give me a chance."

"Because you're evil." I backed away from him and hit the coffee table. It hurt, but I didn't want to let on. Damiel grabbed me before I lost my balance.

"Evil," he said. "I don't think you get me at all."

"Well, if you're not evil, then leave."

His mouth twisted into a sneer and he came in so close I had to crane my neck to look up at him. Not wanting to fall into the coffee table, I held my ground.

"Why would I do that, sweetness?" he said. "We're old friends. We go way back."

When he called me *sweetness*, my skin crawled a little. "Friends? You hurt Michael, cut off his wings!"

"That was punishment for his crime. But, while we're pointing fingers, you're the one who seduced him. He fell because of you. No one can hurt him the way *you* can, Mia."

When I was seven, I fell off my bicycle and broke my arm. I screamed so much on the way to the hospital that Mom gave me half a Valium to calm me down. I felt that way now. Something inside me was screaming, but the intensity wasn't there. My reasoning was muddied now, my mind fuzzy. "You killed him."

The doubt must have shown on my face because he continued, "That was too easy. Not only had he given up Heaven to be with you, but when you died you took away everything he cared about. He was willing to do anything to forget you—anything we told him to do—and a few things of his own that were far from angelic." Damiel smiled in recollection, actually *smiled*. "Falling took most of his soul, but you destroyed the rest."

Knowing he had me hooked now, he wandered toward the fireplace. Picking up the fire poker, his hands caressed the brass handle meditatively. I held my breath. So easily, it could be used as a weapon—one well-landed blow and I'd be dead. Without a word, he turned his attention back to me and casually waved his free hand in my direction. A strange dark smoke filled the air as he put the poker down, and the room began to spin. Instinctively I closed my eyes, trying to steady myself.

"Like I said, nobody can hurt him the way you can. You're his weakness. Leaving him now, you've hurt him all over again." Damiel ran his hand lightly up my arm, sending a shiver from my neck to my ankles, heady and strong, a force that pulled in waves at my mind and stomach. "I wanted to thank you for making this so easy for me. Nothing destroys us the way love does. You've hurt him more than falling ever did."

There was a truth to Damiel's words that cut me to the bone. It left me woozy and tired, like something was being taken away. I remembered the look of hurt on Michael's face, hurt I'd put there, and I knew Damiel was telling the truth. Whatever I thought I was doing to save Michael had only made it worse. *How could I be so stupid?*

"It's for the best," Damiel continued with a mock sympathy that jarred me out of my reverie. "He's got too many rules to follow. He can't be with you, not really." A slow, sultry smile touched his lips. "But I can."

Leaning in a bit closer, he stroked my arm again. His touch sent a pulse through me, followed by a staggering wave of dizziness and nausea that lasted only a moment. Then everything in the room shifted to soft-focus. He was the old Damiel again, not a demon, just another guy at school. It was as though I was seeing him through someone else's eyes, and I noticed how attractive he was. Black leather jacket, white shirt, tendrils of hair curved at the nape of his neck, touching his collar. He even smelled good, cologne and leather. Up close, he glimmered and shone. I wasn't afraid anymore.

When he kissed me, it was deceptively soft, as his touch had been. A current of energy rushed through me with a dizzying intensity, and suddenly I found myself kissing him back. Not like it was with Michael. Nothing at all like that. But this eerily soothing voice in my head told me that Michael was too good for me, that I'd never be with him again.

"Come with me," he said. "There's something I want to show you."

"No, I love Michael—"

"Forget about him," he said. Another wave of dizziness hit me and I forgot what I was thinking about.

I followed Damiel to his Maserati. Its heated leather seats were already warm, but I was experiencing everything as if through a fog. Damiel sped the Maserati down the main road, weaving through traffic, and took the freeway at racing speed, but it didn't faze me. Something was wrong. It was like forgetting something important, something you swore you'd remember. In that moment all I could think about was Damiel: his mouth, his touch, his skin.

We drove in silence through a hilly, wooded area outside of town. I had no idea where I was. I just knew we were going uphill, and I caught glimpses of lights from houses below as we turned hairpin corners toward some kind of summit.

He steered the car onto a gravel road and took us into a clearing in the trees, where he parked the car. Even in my stupor, I couldn't imagine anyone wanting to take a six-figure sports car onto a logging road, but perhaps Damiel was edgy like that. He helped me out of the car before I could figure out the locks, and I stepped out into the cold without a coat. Above us the stars glistened, and the night air smelled of damp pine.

"This way," Damiel said, motioning ahead of him. Since I could hardly see more than a few feet in the darkness, I faltered. He put an arm around my waist to move me along, and I noticed how warm it was.

Strange images flashed in my mind, too fast for me to understand, and I was dizzy again, queasily so. Something was wrong. But what?

The dizziness continued as I walked with Damiel. Surrounded by trees, we no longer had the sky to guide us, but Damiel seemed to know the way. I followed.

We had been walking a long time before I asked, "Where are we going?" My voice sounded distant and slurred.

"Almost there."

In the woods ahead of us, a tiny log cabin came into view. It looked warm and inviting; light from the windows streamed along the ground, illuminating the path to the door. Inside, the walls were rough, exposed wood, as were the tables and chairs. The room itself was lit only by candles covering every surface—shelves, tables, floor—casting a flickering, golden glow, one I normally associated with Michael.

Michael. Something was wrong. *I should not be here. Not with Damiel.* Michael had warned me how persuasive he could be. Scattered images flashed in my mind again, images of Michael after everything he'd been through. The look of happiness from our wedding night so long ago, and the look of devastation on his face earlier tonight when I sent him away. Damiel was right. I was Michael's weakness.

Damiel led me through the rustic living room to the cabin's only bedroom. A shrine of candles lined the floor, dressers, and windowsill. Despite their heat, I could smell the damp wood from the walls. Like the rest of the furniture, the bed was wooden, too, and had a huge, rough-hewn headboard. It was covered in a soft-looking, blood-red duvet and overstuffed gold pillows, reminding me of a hotel suite.

Was *this* what he wanted to show me?

Two large, hooded figures entered through the front door. With midnight-black shiny skin, they had the faces of gargoyles. Their blood-red eyes glowed embers as they nodded obediently at Damiel, clinging to his every word.

"Kill anyone that gets near us." Motioning to the outside, he sent them away.

The bones in my legs melted. I staggered, and the fog in my brain started to lift. *Surely Michael wouldn't come. Not after everything I said to make him go away.*

"Steady now," Damiel said, gripping my arm so hard I thought it might bruise. "We don't want you to panic."

A montage of dreamlike images bombarded my mind—of Damiel and me in that lifetime so long ago. We were naked, having sex. It was harsh and wrong. Painful. I had been terrified, overpowered, unable to escape, but then a haze came over me, and my body hungered for Damiel. What I remembered of being with Michael had been fueled by desire. It was nothing like this. Damiel was the one who had enthralled me. This was rape.

My stomach turned to ice as I realized that this was what he was planning to do. It was going to happen again. I had to get myself out of there and fast. *But how?*

"Wow, this place is great." I scanned the room for something to use as a weapon while I pretended to still be under his spell. Where was a fire poker when you needed one?

On the dresser was an ornate silver tray with a bottle of wine and two glasses. The fact that he'd thought of getting me drunk to seduce me, given all the other things he could do to my mind, seemed completely absurd. The bottle was full, heavy, and if I hit him just right, I might have a chance to escape, providing I made it past his minions.

One of the candles by the bed sparked and caught his attention. As swiftly as I could, I grabbed the bottle and swung it at the side of his head as though it were a baseball bat, aiming for the temple. I wasn't even sure it would break. I must have gotten the angle right, because the glass shattered in my hands and red wine spilled everywhere, covering the bed, the floor, his shirt.

He was surprised, but uninjured. I had heard once that the purpose of breaking a bottle on someone's head was to keep hitting them with the broken glass. So I swung again, but with bullet-fast reflexes, he caught my wrist.

His face twisted into a cruel expression of rage and he backhanded me. The force of it threw me into the dresser. I fought for breath, my face throbbing. Blood trickled down my cheek.

"Such a shame that you can't see how I feel about you." He was maniacally calm. "How I've always felt."

He reached up to touch my face; I turned away from him.

"Please don't."

His fingers hovered above my skin and heat came off of them in cascading waves. Waves that would soon overcome and persuade me to do his will. "Don't what?"

"Tamper with my mind."

"Will you behave?"

I nodded, blinking back tears. I would not cry in front of him.

"I have wanted you for a long time. Ever since that day I found you and Michael in the woods, I had to have you. Even though we had banished him, he still got to be with you. He wouldn't let you out of his sight, so we had to be careful, keep what we did secret so he would never know."

"I didn't want you—"

"You did," he insisted, his dark eyes gleaming at me in the candlelight. "You just didn't know it."

"No, I loved Michael. I still do."

"You were my lover. You gave birth to *my* son."

"*Your* son." Images of the birth came back to me then as I struggled to breathe. The child was huge, far too big for my human frame. I remembered there had been the agony of my flesh tearing inside, but the pain itself I could not remember. It had killed me. All this time, Michael thought the monster he felt so responsible for had been his child, a result of his sins. *Something that horrible could only be conceived one way...through coercion or worse.*

It was *never* his!

"Michael killed him," Damiel snarled. "Not this time. I want that chance again. A chance to be a father...and I want you to be its mother."

The pain in my head throbbing, I struggled to get up, glancing around the room. There had to be a way out of here. Damiel's hand gripped my arm and he lifted me up to my feet as though I were weightless.

"Did you hear me? You're going to have my child." His mouth turned into a crooked smile as he petted my forehead.

Across the room, a candle flickered. It had almost burned out. I pushed his hand away. "Giving birth to that…that monster killed me!"

"That was unfortunate. I don't expect it to be easy, but medicine has advanced significantly over the last thousand years. You might even survive it. If you're good."

I don't know why that last statement affected me so much, but I freaked out, screaming and pounding his chest with my fists, trying to get my fingers into his eyes. "You enthralled me, you bastard! I never wanted you!"

He swiftly grabbed both my hands in one of his. I scarcely saw him move. "Now, now, none of that. If you're not good to me, I won't be good to you."

I froze, and my breath caught in my chest.

"Holding your breath won't work either." He threw me onto the bed, and my head hit the headboard with a sharp crack. I actually saw stars.

In spite of the pain, I scrambled to sit up, but he lunged on top of me and held me down with one strong arm as I tried to wriggle free. His body weight pinned the rest of me down, and his free hand reached for my face.

"Hold still," he warned. I squirmed and resisted with all my might, for all the good it did me. He laughed, and when he touched my face the muscles in my arms and legs went limp. I struggled, concentrating with everything I had to move even one finger, but it was futile. Each one could have weighed a hundred pounds.

"That should do it," he said, half to himself, and backed away.

The horror of what he planned to do with me started to set in and I screamed.

"No one can hear you." His voice was an eerily calm contrast to mine. "I only did what I did because you wouldn't hold still. Don't make me silence you as well."

I stopped yelling and refused to look at him.

Damiel sat beside me on the bed, taking my limp, frozen hand in his. "I only wanted you to look at me the way you'd look at him. Just once."

A hard, bitter lump formed in my throat. I didn't want this to be my first sexual experience. It was supposed to be special, with *Michael* (if that were even possible), not some crazy act of violence and revenge. What if I did get pregnant? Then what? Michael could never know about it. It was for the best that I'd broken things off. He couldn't see me now, not like this.

Was that how I handled it when it happened before? Did I want to believe the child was Michael's so much that I convinced both of us it was? Back then, it would have been a possibility. It would have destroyed Michael to know what Damiel had done to me. I must have lied to save him then, but it didn't work. Instead, I took the secret to my grave, and Michael died thinking that birthing his offspring had killed me, that he had killed his own son, when all along it was Damiel's.

Damiel spoke, pulling me out of my reverie. "I chose this body because I thought you might prefer someone closer to your own age. I think I chose well."

"Fuck off!" I shouted. "I won't have your offspring. I'll abort. This is the twenty-first century!"

He threw back his head and laughed. "Impossible. First of all, do you think I couldn't stop anyone who tried to kill my child? There's nothing they could do in the womb to destroy it, not that wouldn't destroy you first."

A shudder ran through me. I had almost preferred my mind being taken over to this. At least I wouldn't have to feel it as much. With luck, I'd never remember it.

"Now," he said, "I can do this nicely or not so nicely. You decide."

"Uh...nicely?"

"What are you going to give me in exchange, then?" He was touching the backs of my arms with his fingers, giving me shivers again. Even though I couldn't move, I could feel everything—perhaps more so. I wished I could bite his fingers off.

I wanted to ask what the hell I could give him that he wasn't already taking, but I refrained. "Your son?"

"That is inevitable. I mean other than that?"

His hands wandered over my chest now, cupping my breasts through my clothes. I tried to squirm, without luck. I had to resort to internal flinching instead. The same dark smoke that had filled the air around us earlier returned, along with the spinning sensation, and suddenly his touch was no longer repulsive. In fact, it felt good. But I was tired, as if my own energy, my will to fight, was being taken from me.

"Tell me how much you want me."

I swallowed, afraid to say anything to encourage him. "Stop that," I said.

"Stop what?" he asked, like a cat playing with a terrified bird.

"Making me feel this way."

"Your choice." With a quick movement, he lifted his hands away and the glamour of his energy subsided. All the fear and revulsion returned. Instead of boyish and handsome, he looked harsh and cruel. "It would have been easier for you the other way. I thought you'd want to enjoy your first time."

"I might have if I were with someone *else*." I put as much venom as I could into my voice. It was bad enough being forced to have sex with a demon, but actually *enjoying it* would be too much to endure. Was that what he'd done to me before?

"Would you prefer my real form?" He laughed at that. Not a warm laugh—it was cold, fiendish.

I didn't want to think about what his *real* form was, probably something black and slimy like his minions outside, or worse, Azazel. "Well, since you went to all the trouble of getting this one," I said, hoping he wasn't bluffing, that he hadn't planned to show me his true form anyway. Maybe I couldn't cope after all.

"Fair enough. But if you give me the least bit of trouble…"

He was touching me again and this time his hands were cold. Instead of shivers of pleasure, I shuddered with horror.

He had just unbuttoned my blouse when I heard a piercing, inhuman cry come from outside. Damiel cocked his head to listen.

"Well, well, it seems we have company," he said with an expression of delight. "This pillow talk has been lovely, but it's time to get down to business now."

I strained to move my head, trying to see something, anything, in the darkness, hoping against hope that Michael didn't try to come. Swiftly, Damiel undid my jeans and straddled me. I squirmed and resisted with all my might and one of my legs moved ever so slightly. It was a small improvement, but not enough.

"You're getting some movement back," he said darkly, like he might just immobilize me again.

One of the black-skinned minions came to the doorway, so tall he had to tilt his head. "There's an intruder. We've taken care of it. He's dead."

Dead. What if it was Michael and he'd been killed again? A new wave of terror ran through me. I couldn't deal with that.

Damiel jumped off the bed. "Bring him to me!"

It couldn't be Michael. *Please, not him. Anyone but him.*

LISA VOISIN

Chapter Twenty-Eight

The body the two cloaked creatures dragged in lay slumped on the wood floor like a statue of defeat. His broken, immobile wings furled crookedly behind him, and his head lolled to the side. His dark, wavy hair was damp and matted with blood—a head wound. Though I'd tried to stop him from having to face Damiel, deep down I should have known Michael would come. It was his nature, and he was dead because of it.

Nothing mattered now. There was nothing Damiel could do to me that was worse than this. Not his gleeful laughter nor his gloating. Bile burned in my throat at the sight of Michael's limp, lifeless body, a body that I had been so close to only a few hours earlier. Now his once-white singlet was tattered, covered in grime, his muscular form covered in claw marks, bloody scratches, and bites. It wasn't a clean death. He'd been hurt first. A lot.

Tears stained my vision, blurring the room, so I didn't see Damiel walk toward Michael's body, but I could hear his footsteps and the dreadful thudding sound of flesh being hit.

"That's for not letting me kill you again myself," Damiel growled.

In that moment, the last vestige of hope locked itself away as the reality of my situation seeped in. No one else would come for me. Nobody knew I was here, which left me as good as dead. I didn't have a plan for surviving this. My plans ended at trying to leave town. Now Michael was gone too, and all I had left were memories. I hadn't deserved his love, but he gave it to me selflessly, despite the trouble it caused him, to the point of fighting to the death to try to save me.

It was up to me to get myself out of this alive and preferably not pregnant. All I had to do was outsmart Damiel and get past his minions. *But how?* There *had* to be a way.

Damiel turned back to me, a gleeful expression on his face, as though seeing Michael dead had excited him even more. I turned my face away to hide my tears. The heat and demand of his attention pressed upon me. I tried to think fast. Since I couldn't move, all I had left to trick him with was my mind. But a fog returned to my thoughts.

"Look at me."

"No!"

Roughly, he grabbed my face and turned it. Seeing my tears, he said mockingly, "Aw, you're grieving him."

This time, his kiss was hungry and repulsive. His hands grabbed me like I was meat, making my flesh crawl. It made me sick. How could I have gotten myself into this? Turning my face away, I gazed idly in Michael's direction, grasping for any memory of him I could to comfort me.

With all his attention on me, Damiel was no longer paying attention to Michael's body. Nobody had noticed that his wounds were healing or that there was a golden glow coming off his skin. I did. I held my breath, hoping against hope that Michael was still alive.

When his body first moved, I hardly believed it. But then he moved again. In one swift and precise motion, he was standing, with his sword out. Then he crossed the room with incredible speed, grabbed Damiel, and pulled him off me. He'd feigned his death. It was only a bluff. Relief coursed through me as Michael took up the battle with Damiel, slashing at him with his sword.

From the other room, I heard the door burst open and a woman, or rather a female chorus, said, "Hello, boys."

I recognized Arielle's voice and heard her attack the two henchmen, making quick work of them. But she kept her distance from Damiel and Michael. It was their fight.

They moved so quickly I could hardly see them. Yet Michael and Damiel were desperately well matched in strength and skill. Because Michael was strong and graceful, Damiel had to be cunning. He fought hard and dirty, taunting Michael mercilessly.

"That sweet little girl of yours sure looks good. I'm surprised you can resist her," Damiel said.

"That's because you're you," Michael replied, lunging at Damiel with his sword and missing by an inch. Damiel used a different weapon; his hands were heated. Red flames licked off of them. He threw the blaze at Michael, searing his flesh.

"I'm going to enjoy her," Damiel persisted, "and she'll enjoy it, too."

"You've incapacitated her. She can't even move," Michael said through clenched teeth. His sword landed on Damiel's right shoulder, disabling the demon's next blow. Hellfire sputtered to the floor and fizzled, leaving no mark. "You're pathetic."

"Your memory's selective, old friend," he sneered, hurling flames from his left hand. Michael dodged, and the flames missed but Damiel's words didn't. "Have you forgotten where you've been?"

Michael paled and his concentration faltered. Lunging, Damiel grasped the handle of Michael's fiery blue sword and threw it to the ground.

"There was this one girl. It was twelfth-century Portofino, I believe. She looked just like you, Mia—well, how you used to look," Damiel said, positioning himself between Michael and the now-extinguished sword. "Her father wouldn't let him near her, but Michael was determined. He killed him."

I wished I could cover my ears. As much as I wanted to know more about Michael and what he'd done, I didn't want to hear about it from Damiel. Not like this. He would only twist things.

Michael didn't even try to deny what was said, as though Damiel's words had a narcotic effect. Damiel quickly gained the upper hand, lunging and thrusting at Michael with fiery fists, and I couldn't do anything to stop it. All I could do was watch as Damiel hurt him all over again.

"If you could only see the things he used to do…" Damiel said.

Michael had been hurt. What he had done in Hell was probably worse than I could imagine, but it was as though I was hearing about someone else. It didn't fit with the guy I knew. Michael wasn't like that anymore.

Right? Holding him to blame for something that happened after he was tortured was as unfair as blaming a prisoner of war for doing what he had to do to survive.

"It's for the best that you left him, Mia," Damiel sneered and swung at Michael, his left fist connecting with Michael's ribs. "Why would you want to be with someone so ruthless and bloodthirsty?"

Someone like you, you mean. Damiel was trying to stop me from loving Michael, but I couldn't let anything change the way I felt. Michael had been disarmed. Knowing he could feel everything I did, even doubt, I had to trust him more now than ever. Or Damiel would kill both of us.

I focused on my feelings of love, the way Michael had told me to do around Azazel. This time, I refused to fail.

Staggering from one of Damiel's blows, Michael glanced at me, and to my relief something changed. A white rage came over him and, seeming to regain his senses, he caught Damiel's next punch and threw one of his own.

LISA VOISIN

Seeing the change in Michael, Damiel hissed. "Do you think I'm back just for her?"

Without a word, Michael lunged for his sword. The blade shot out immediately in a flash of blue light, slicing Damiel's waist. It left no mark. "I think you came back for me."

"You flatter yourself." Visibly weakened, Damiel spat on the floor. But when Michael kept his attention on the fight and didn't respond, he continued, "I'm back for another chance at having my offspring. You *killed* him last time."

Michael stopped fighting as a look of recognition and horror crossed his face. Every candle in the room flickered as though they'd been hit by a gust of wind. Seizing the moment, Damiel persisted. "That's right. Your precious Sajani was unfaithful to you." Hearing him use my ancient name felt obscene.

What he said must have affected Michael too, because Damiel was able to knock him down, driving a thunderous blow between the wings that brought him to his knees. "I was always better. Even better at satisfying her."

Michael looked at me and there was pain in his eyes. More pain I'd put there. The memory of being enthralled and overpowered by Damiel millennia ago came back to me. I didn't have a chance to fight him off. And now, unable to move or speak, I still couldn't fight. I couldn't even explain what happened. There was no way to tell Michael the truth.

The room chilled, and hoarfrost formed on the windows as hundreds of black, shadowy creatures— hellhounds—stormed the cabin like a massive infestation of cockroaches—that is, if cockroaches were the size of wolves. Although I knew a lone hellhound could hardly get past an angel's halo, a group of them was another matter. These had already materialized, and soon, after several had fallen to the strength of Michael and Arielle's halos, others managed to get through. Within a minute, they were swarmed. The two of them fought well, their swords blazing blue light with speed and deadly accuracy, but they were quickly overcome. Black smoke, slime, and blood spattered everywhere. As fast as Michael could heal, the creatures tore at his flesh. His breathing labored, he even cried out. Arielle lost her balance and fell.

Certain that the hellhounds would finish the angels off, Damiel walked away from the fight with a smug look on his face and turned to me. "Now, where were we?"

I fought the urge to scream, knowing I wouldn't make a sound. It would just make me feel pathetic. I could wiggle my toes now and move my hands with great effort. I had to outsmart him, to buy myself time, so I gave Damiel what I hoped was a sultry smile and said nothing. It seemed to work. He walked toward me, unbuttoning and removing his shirt.

Could deceit work on the deceiver? I was about to find out.

"Right. You were going to tell me how much you wanted me." He waved his hand and something released in my throat.

"How do you see this playing out?" I asked him. He glared at me seductively. I swallowed the bile that rose to my mouth. "I mean, once we do this, what about the child? What about me?"

"What do you mean?"

"You keep saying you want me. But what if you got me?"

"Oh, I will." He gave me a menacing look.

"What if I *wanted* to be with you?"

He looked dubious, so I lied more. I could only hear the fighting in the other room, Michael's increased breathing, the wet, thudding sounds of flesh being hit, the cracking of bones. I had to focus, keep my attention on Damiel and remember that his sin was, above all else, envy. I had to use it to my advantage.

"You were right, you know. I could never be satisfied with half a relationship. That's why I ended it. Wanting but never having—this whole celibacy thing gets tired after a while," I said, hoping he'd buy it.

To my relief, he did. He rushed me then and kissed me. It was animalistic and passionate, and very human. Hardly demonic at all. The heady flood of his energetic glamour poured into me, making the experience less horrible than I expected. Not that it was pleasant or exciting by any means, but my body seemed to know what it needed to do to survive, and I responded to him.

Just close your eyes and think of Michael, a voice inside me said. *Tell him what you'd tell Michael.*

"I wish I could touch you," I heard myself say, motioning to my hands with my eyes.

Damiel stopped kissing me and placed his hand on my face. The gesture freed me from my bondage so I could move again. As promised, I touched his chest, pretending it belonged to someone else, someone I loved. His skin was smooth and warm to the touch. It was Giulio's skin, but Damiel seemed to enjoy it.

"What if…" I began, then paused, waiting for him to want to hear what I had to say.

"What if what?" he asked, kissing my neck. I held my breath so I would be forced to gasp, to elevate my own breathing.

"What if I wanted you more than him?"

His eyes glowed red. "I can make that possible for you." He then lifted his hand to my forehead again and I could see the dark swirls coming off his fingers. All I had to do was let him touch me and I would want to be with him. All of this would be easy.

I shook my head. "It won't be real if you force me."

He stared at me a long time, as though trying to figure me out. I did my best to give him a smoldering look. I still heard fighting in the next room, but couldn't move to watch what was going on. I just prayed that Michael was safe. Arielle, too. At the very least, I needed to keep Damiel distracted.

"Why wouldn't I want you just for you?" I put on a smile, stroking his chest. "Have you *seen* you?"

He let out a deep laugh that sounded even more inhuman than before and kissed my neck, his teeth grazing my throat. I gasped involuntarily with fear but pretended to enjoy it.

"If you want the love that should be Michael's," I said, "you can have it."

He hesitated. Envy is the act of wanting what another person has. Once something was given freely, would it mean the same? He said he wanted me to look at him the way I looked at Michael. Would it work? Would he still want my heart if it didn't belong to another? I remembered how I felt with Michael, the breathless need to connect, and I tried to show that in my eyes. I could only hope he bought it. Then he kissed me again, hungrily, without gentleness, as his hands explored my body. I squirmed involuntarily; luckily he took it for pleasure.

I kept talking and, not sure what exactly to say, I ad-libbed. "Yes, you can have me…and I will have your son, as I did so long ago." He let out a grunt of pleasure hearing that, which told me I was on the right track. "Let Michael keep his goodness…"

Hearing that, he stopped kissing me. A snarl formed on his face.

Ignoring the threat of his rage, I continued, "And his redemption."

Damiel sat up abruptly, his eyes flashing red. For a moment, I thought he might hit me. "I don't want that!"

"Good. Everyone leaves me. Even Michael. I can never be with him. All he cares about is seeing Heaven again, his home. He misses it. There was never a day in our past that he didn't, and I wouldn't want the same from you. I need a guy who knows what he wants."

The fighting sounds in the background slowed. I held my breath in the eerie quiet, waiting to see who won.

"I did miss it," Michael's voice echoed from the doorway. I bit my lip, trying not to show my relief at seeing him alive. Even with dark rings under his eyes and blood and black fluid matted in his hair, covering his clothes, he was a glorious sight. Light seemed to emanate from him. "Every day on earth, as beautiful as it is, can never touch the beauty of Heaven."

Rage exploded through Damiel like a firecracker and he was on his feet. "Why won't you die already?" Turning to his opponent, he poised himself to attack. Michael tilted his head to one side and swung out his sword, ready.

"No. Wait. Damiel. Please hear me!"

He backed up, a step out of Michael's reach. Not letting Michael out of his sight, Damiel wouldn't turn to look at me, not even for a second. "What is it, sweetness? Don't you think your charade is over now?"

"No. I don't want him to hurt *you*."

Damiel gave me a triumphant grin. Michael looked defeated. All I could do was pray he'd understand what I was doing and count on the fact that he could feel my feelings and know the truth.

"You're not going to leave me, are you? Go back?"

This time Damiel did look, and Michael could have taken a shot but didn't. Instead, he watched me with curiosity as the demon asked, "Back where?"

"To Heaven," I explained. "If Michael had a shot at redemption after all *his* sins, why wouldn't you?"

My words hit Damiel like a blow, visibly shaking him.

"It's only fair." Arielle stepped through the doorway, covered in grime and dusting black soot off herself. "She's right, you know," she said, her face perfectly neutral. "You could always come back…if you wanted to."

"It would be work," Michael said. He glanced at Arielle, and a look of understanding shot between them. "A lot of work."

I had no idea if what we were saying was true, but it seemed to have an effect. Energy swarmed around Damiel like black angry wasps, as though he were being stung by his own greed. He rushed Michael, and in turn Michael raised his sword and dug it into Damiel's—or, rather, Giulio's—body. As I had seen before, the body went limp, undamaged. Only this time it was different. Michael stood fiercely, watching the body, or rather the energy *around* it, form into a dense black swirl.

Accompanied by a loud electrical cracking sound, the swirl grew and began to take on a skeletal shape, growing taller and taller until it almost touched the ceiling. Then it fleshed out, literally, as black sinews and muscles grew over the bones. The body resembled the hooded creatures Arielle had been fighting—only much larger. Strong and completely hairless, it towered at least six inches above Michael. Tattered, leathery wings sprang from its huge, spiny back, but they remained tucked to fit in the small room. The demon turned sideways and its face was pointed, angular. I didn't need to look into the eyes to know they were red.

It spoke in a deep hiss. "What makes you think I would want to go to Heaven?"

Michael stepped in toward the creature that was Damiel and let down his sword. His eyes ablaze and his halo flaring, he too was something to behold. I'm not sure if it was the sight of him or the danger he put himself in, but I had to remind my heart to beat.

"Because," he said, "I remember who you are."

Damiel stood transfixed, and Michael leaned in to place a hand on his opponent's heart.

A golden fire blazed between them, engulfing and searing the demon. Screaming, Damiel writhed and squirmed in the heat of the flames, while Michael stayed cool. When the flames burned out, replaced by a golden light, Damiel's skin turned a light bronze, as though an image had been superimposed over him. His features softened, hair returned to his head, his wings became feathery and light. This was who Damiel was. We were seeing his angelic self.

Then Damiel's screams of pain turned to ones of anguish. His body shook as the grief consumed him, driving him to his knees. Underneath, the black being that he had become writhed in agony, but Michael held his ground, as though holding in place the image of who Damiel used to be.

"You can choose to be that again," Michael offered. Beside him, Arielle stood impartial as a judge, her face a mask of calm scrutiny.

I sat up on the bed and closed my blouse, awed by the sight of them. The light shining from the two of them brought tears to my eyes. This was what Michael was, his purpose, and no matter how much I wanted him, my feelings couldn't matter more than this. Nothing could.

The choice was Damiel's now, as the demon part of him bucked and roiled like an angry tide. Yet there was another side of him that seemed at peace. As the demon stood again, these two halves seemed to battle each other in a struggle for dominance. The cabin's small windows rattled, extinguishing candles from the force of it. Michael stood in the center of a beam of golden light, as though he were in the eye of a tornado.

"Has he chosen yet?" he asked Arielle.

She shook her head. "He's without remorse."

For some reason, Fatima's reading from the day before came to me. I remembered her words in my head: *You have been given a gift of love, and for it you must love, beyond anything you'd ever imagined before.*

Love. In order for Damiel to have remorse, he needed to feel love. I needed to remind him what it was. Michael wasn't the only one who needed to remember. Damiel needed to remember, too. Realizing this, I connected with a force I'd never felt before. It filled me, thrumming through my body like a huge river that connected me to all of life.

Everything I'd ever done, every mistake I'd ever made was seen, and it was strange, like having your life flash before your eyes. I recalled the anger toward my dad, the judgment I sometimes had for no good reason, the secrets I kept from my friends, and even breaking up with Michael. All of it. In that moment, it had *all* been forgiven. I just had to accept that it was so, and I could do what I needed to do.

It wasn't about me anymore. I remembered my past life with Michael: how I felt because he gave up so much to be with me, how I felt I betrayed him when I didn't tell him what Damiel had done. A serene voice in my head told me to stop blaming myself, that it was never my fault—and I believed it. Taking a deep breath, I let this feeling in as tears welled in my chest.

Then I was on my feet, walking toward them like I was floating, held in a giant spotlight. Michael's eyes widened as I approached, first with concern, then with awe.

"Mia," he said. "What…"

I shook my head and Arielle touched his shoulder to silence him. She motioned to me with her eyes and I could hear her inner voice, the one she used for telepathy, say to him *Wait*.

I didn't have time to process how strange it was to hear her. Instead, I walked until I stood between him and Damiel, and I grabbed the demon's hand.

Up close, he flickered, a broken filmstrip, alternating splices of angel and demon—beatific one moment, horrific the next. Facing the demon, I stared him down. "Love, Damiel. Do you remember it?"

I should have been terrified as the demon glowered at me, while the angel part cast his eyes down in shame. But I wasn't. Not only was Michael there, and Arielle, but I was protected by something much bigger. I felt connected to them, as though I had been given a chance to do an angel's work, even in human form.

Images of Damiel from millennia ago came to mind. He had once been gentle and fair—a being of love. I saw faces of the other Grigori who mattered to him, friends. "You loved God...and your brothers..." Then I saw my own face in that lifetime so long ago. "You even loved me, once."

The demon snarled and raised a hand to silence me. Michael instinctively raised his sword, but Arielle held him back.

"You hurt those you loved, and those who loved you... And I know that it hurt you to do it. On some level, it hurt." I squeezed his hand as the angelic part of him winced. Still furious, the demon glared at me— malicious but visibly weakened. Its weakness gave me strength. "Because you turned your back on what you are, and you have lived for so long now without love that you forgot what it's like... But deep down you remember. I know you do. Deep down, I know you feel bad about what you did. Don't you?"

I had the angel's complete attention. Its eyes, full of tears, blazed at me through a golden light, while the demon turned away, and a voice unlike any I'd heard Damiel speak with before said a quiet yet resounding, "Yes."

I knew exactly what I needed to say. I didn't question it, and the words I'd heard Michael use before rolled out of me like music. "You are loved. You are forgiven. Everything you've done is forgiven."

The angelic part of Damiel shook, slowly at first and then violently, as the demon struggled to be freed. Arielle said one word.

"Now."

Faster than sound, Michael raised his sword and thrust it into Damiel's heart, and the sword that did no damage to human flesh burned and seared the demon, leaving the angel's image behind. The image itself faded quickly, having only been held in place by Michael's focus. The demon let out loud, horrible shrieks as steam and black, sulfuric smoke escaped its body, deflating him. To speed the process, Michael raised his sword above the demon's head and cleaved what was left of its body in two.

The entire room filled with a corrosive black smoke that stung my eyes and tasted of rotten eggs. Beneath it all was a flicker of golden light, a tiny sphere not much bigger than a firefly, but it grew brighter and stronger as it rose to the ceiling and hovered there.

Then a tear opened in the middle of the living room, as though the room itself and all the furniture in it was projected onto a curtain that was being ripped open. Behind that was a mouth to a different reality—a very dark and upsetting one. On the other side, I could hear moans of agony and roars of pain that made the hairs on my neck stand up. The tendrils of black smoke hanging in the air were sucked right into that mouth, slowly at first, and then building in speed as if the mouth were inhaling just the smoke—leaving everything else behind. It took seconds for the room to clear, and once it was done the mouth closed and the tear sealed itself. The room was ordinary again, and someplace far away I heard the clanging of an iron gate.

All that was left was the golden ball of light, which had grown to the size of a giant beach ball. It circled the room and hovered in front of Arielle, who smiled at it as though they were having an exchange I couldn't hear. A moment later, it floated toward Michael, who bowed his head. Then it came to me. Not sure what to expect, I tensed.

Arielle placed a hand on my shoulder. "It's all right."

Taking a deep breath, I looked at her and then back at the golden ball of light. It was warm and pure. As it approached, its presence tingled my skin.

Put out your hand.

I didn't know where the voice came from—so deep and melodic—but I obeyed, and the golden ball landed on me like a rare, exotic bird. With it, a sense of warmth and gratitude ran up my arm.

Thank you, it said.

And in a flash it was gone.

Chapter Twenty-Nine

The look on Michael's face was one of awe and reverence as he encircled me in his arms. "Do you know what you did? You gave a demon a chance at redemption."

The light that had filled me began to fade. It was replaced by the warmth of Michael and an incredible sense of peace.

"Is that good?"

"Very." He smiled, his gaze tender as it held mine. "That took real courage. I wish you could hear the celebration on the other side."

"Can you?"

"Yes."

I blinked back tears. His shirt was ripped, his hair messy, but he was alive. Even covered in blood and grime, he was the most beautiful thing I'd ever seen.

"Fatima told me to love, and I just remembered it." It probably didn't make any sense, but it was all I could think to say. "What will happen to him now?"

"There wasn't much of his angelic self left. We had to time it right; if you hadn't got him to feel any remorse, he would have just been sent back through the gates of Hell." He pulled me closer to him. "But you did, and he had that slightest bit of remorse that made it all possible."

I didn't say anything, waiting for Michael to continue. From his answer, I still didn't know what would happen to Damiel.

"We cleared the darkness off of what was left of him. That is really big, Mia. We seldom reclaim demons as far gone as he was. Not even I went that far."

"I'm so sorry," I blurted out, remembering that the reason Michael went to Hell in the first place had to do with my death and the belief that he'd killed his own son. "I should have known that monster was never yours. I don't know why I didn't tell you… I couldn't—"

Michael put a finger to my lips. It was rough from being cut and it tasted of blood and burnt flesh. His. "It's all right."

"You're not mad?"

He let out a soft laugh, his eyes shining brighter than I'd ever seen them before. "Mad? No."

We were so connected, his relief washed over both of us, and something else—something effervescent and warm. "What was that?" I asked.

"I'm glad you're safe," he said. His expression darkened as he glanced at the bed behind me. "You were lying there, not moving."

Touching the side of his face, I turned his face back to mine. "I thought that, too, but you were playing dead."

He grinned. "Minions are pretty easy to trick."

"I'll remember that next time."

"I hope you never have to." Carefully, he touched my cheek, avoiding where I'd been struck. Even though the bleeding had stopped, it throbbed bitterly.

A warm, tingling sensation soothed my skin as he extended his halo around me. "Hold still." He placed his fingers where I'd been hit. A hot brightness shone around that side of my face. It stung at first, but then the throbbing pain slipped away as shadows do in daylight. When he was done, I felt fine, as though I'd never been hurt. I touched my skin; other than the left-over dried blood, it was smooth, without scars.

"You healed my ankle that day in the woods," I said, putting the pieces together, surprised at myself for not recognizing it before. The pain had been agonizing right after I fell and then got better in his presence—of course he'd healed it.

"I couldn't bear to see you hurt. Not then. Not ever."

"How did you find me?" I asked. "I could have been anywhere."

"It was hard. Damiel knows how we work, so he hid you well. But I found you the same way I always have. I felt you." Then he laughed to himself and his eyes lit up. "You know, I can't explain it, really."

"Then don't." I leaned into his chest and inhaled the grassy scent of his skin. He was covered in sweat and blood and God knows what else, but I didn't care.

Behind me, Arielle placed a hand on my shoulder, and I sighed. Surely she wasn't going to split us up. Not again.

"Michael's right," she said. "You did good work tonight."

"You must have known…"

"God doesn't tell me *everything*. I knew you needed to remember, but I didn't know you would be able to get Damiel to a place of remorse, and forgiving him…" She smiled and a wave of warmth wafted off of her. "Brilliant!"

Before what she said could sink in, Giulio stirred and sat up. Groaning, he rubbed the back of his head, and I couldn't help but feel sorry for him. He probably hurt everywhere.

Arielle approached him. "Hi," she said, smiling. "I'll bet you don't know how you got here."

He nodded, and Arielle helped him up, holding his wrists. She didn't let go of them when she spoke.

"You were possessed by a demon. I know it sounds weird."

"Uh, okay." Giulio staggered a little, baffled, as though he'd just woken up. In a way, he had.

"We've dispatched the demon that did this, so now I can remove the mark it left behind and you can forget any of this ever happened. I hope you understand."

She placed her hands on his heart and her halo flared a brilliant white, enveloping both of them. Giulio's body relaxed and he smiled with relief. He looked young, and in his groggy state, kind of sweet, nothing like the brutal, malicious spirit that had possessed him.

When she was done, he said, "I couldn't possibly forget all of this."

"You will," she said, walking him to the door. "But you'll know this: that life is a great mystery, one you have yet to really discover." She stopped at the door. "Oh yeah, and on your way back, turn left on the gravel road, and then left on the main road. Drive downhill all the way back to the freeway. You should know your way home from there."

"Uh…thanks. I think," Giulio said. "I'm sure I'll remember someone as beautiful as you."

Arielle waved goodbye and closed the door, then said straight-faced, "They all say they'll remember me. They never do."

Serious, fierce Arielle had made a joke, and it took me by surprise. I laughed, and she and Michael both joined me, their spirits high from winning the battle. Then, not wanting to burn the cabin down, Arielle cased the room, snuffing out the remaining candles. Michael and I headed outside. The cold air refreshed my skin.

He had no vehicle with him, so we had to fly back. This time he took me directly home without circling the harbor first. The night sky shimmered and sparkled brilliantly above us and the city shone below. It was our time together. He was sharing an experience with me that I'd never have with anyone else. Anyone who wasn't an angel.

Michael dropped me off before he went home to clean up, and I asked him to come back later so we could talk. On the front doorstep I found a small box, and inside was another necklace from Fatima. This time, she left me a note:

> *Mia,*
>
> *I wanted to replace the necklace that got broken. This time, it's been blessed by a Muslim priest and a Catholic priest. It wasn't easy. I had to tell the Catholic priest I was thinking of converting—which I'm not. I hope God understands.*
>
> *Fatima.*
>
> *P.S. Things have been a little strange lately, so I got some for your friends Heather and Fiona too.*

I would have to thank her for both her advice and the necklaces later. She had no idea how valuable they were. The thought that my friends would also be protected filled me with relief.

As I went inside, I was glad Mom was working all night so I wouldn't have to explain where I'd been. She would never have to know how close her daughter came to being a mother herself. Having sex with a demon, even using protection, couldn't be considered "safe" by anyone's standards.

After having been through so much, I felt like a different person. Things I'd never noticed before had more meaning for me now. Even my home seemed different. I needed a shower, so I went to my room to grab my bathrobe, and once I was surrounded by all my things, a wave of gratitude flowed through me, bringing tears to my eyes. Being with Damiel was horrific, but the memory slid to the back of my mind like a bad dream. I was still *alive*.

I took a long, hot shower to wash away the blood and shock of everything that had happened. When I finished it was almost midnight, and my cell phone rang. I scrambled to find it in my room, plugged in beside the bed. Who would call this late? At least it could no longer be Damiel. He was better now—surely not in Hell again.

It was Bill.

"Where've you been?" he demanded, sounding worried. "I've been calling for hours. I even tried calling the house. Is everything okay?"

I didn't know what to say. The memories of what had happened were too new to tell anyone—if I ever could. My throat tightened. "Yeah."

Bill let out his breath. "I had this weird feeling as if something was wrong."

Bill had a *feeling*? Some kind of *premonition* feeling?

He cleared his throat. "Then I called and there was no answer."

Perhaps I wasn't the only person in my family who sensed unusual things. Maybe I did see angels, flashing lights, and demons and stuff, but maybe Bill sensed things, too.

"Stupid, isn't it?" he scoffed.

"No, not at all," I said, thinking about how much Bill had changed over the summer. How alike we were. How even though Dad was all awkward and distant with me, Bill never was. "It means a lot—that you called."

"We're family," he said simply.

I'd just had the craziest night of my life. I'd been captured by a fallen-angel-turned-demon. I'd thought I'd lost Michael for good, only to watch him get up and battle a roomful of hellhounds and minions—not to mention Damiel himself. Connected to God or whatever force the angels connected to in their network, I'd been

482

able to forgive a demon for all the horrible things he'd done. Maybe, just maybe, there was hope one day for me and my dad.

"Yeah." I grinned. "We are."

After I hung up with Bill, I checked my messages. It was a busy night. Aside from four voice messages from Bill, I had half a dozen texts from Heather trying to convince me to come to that party they were all talking about last week. Apparently it was really good. Everyone was there. Even Fiona made a brief appearance. Nothing, not even demons, could keep that girl down.

Heather also left me a voicemail. I could hear music playing and people talking in the background.

"Hey, Mia. I've been checking around and the coast is clear. There's nobody named Chloe here. She's off at school, and apparently she's not all that. So you can come, right? Call me."

I couldn't help but smile when I heard it. Heather was matchmaking again, in spite of herself, trying to fix something she saw me struggle with a few days before. She had no idea what I'd been going through, but at least she cared.

As I got into my pajamas and dried my hair, I wondered what would've happened if I'd told Heather how I felt about Michael right from the start. Would I have ever accepted that date with Damiel? Or discovered how Michael and I were connected? Maybe I couldn't bring her along with me into this part of my strange new life, but she was my friend. With all the angels—and demons—around me lately, I needed someone to bring me back to earth.

A few minutes later, Michael arrived. Standing in my doorway, with his hair still damp from the shower and his skin smelling of soap, he made me the happiest girl alive. Tears welled in my eyes and I almost couldn't speak.

His clear blue eyes softened as they searched my face. "You okay?"

Swallowing hard, I nodded and stared at him. There were tiny red lines on his skin, but they were all that was left of the huge gashes from his battle with Damiel. As he stepped inside and circled me in his arms, his energy felt warm and intoxicating. He was alive. He'd come for me, saved my life, and now he was *here*—

despite everything I'd said earlier, despite the way I'd pushed him away.

"About breaking up with you…" I said.

He stepped back, his hands grazing the sides of my waist. "Yeah?"

"I was trying to keep you away. I thought—"

"I didn't trust you?"

"That you'd get *killed*." I touched the side of his face.

He covered my hand with one of his and its warmth raced through me. "You thought you'd just tell me to leave and I'd go away? When I knew how much danger you were in?"

When he put it that way, my plan sounded foolish, considering he'd been there watching over me so many times. "Something like that."

"So you do want to…try to be with me?" Leaning closer, he gave me a hopeful look. "Given all that it means?"

"Yeah." I draped an arm around his shoulder, bringing his face even closer to mine. "Think you can handle it?"

His lips curled into the sexiest grin. "I'll do my best."

Epilogue

That night, Michael joined me in my bed. I lay fully clothed, with my head on his chest, listening to the sound of his heartbeat. As he held me, stroking my hair from the top of my head all the way down my back, a rich, electric tension built between us, pulsing through my skin. I could almost taste it in the air, as sweet as a warm summer night. The horrors from earlier that evening seemed unreal in comparison, flat and colorless. Michael's touch was real, the only thing that mattered.

His chest rose and fell under the duvet as his breathing became more quick and shallow than usual. When I glanced up at him, the heat in his eyes pierced me, drew me to him. Drew my lips to his. We kissed gently at first, but the thought of how close I'd come to losing him fueled my desire. It was so easy to roll on top of him and press my body into his, to plant kisses on his throat and listen to his soft exhales as his arms held me firmly in place. His halo tingled my skin as he let me in, and I savored the warmth of his body beneath me as his fingers brushed the back of my neck.

It took him longer than usual to stop himself. He whispered my name, almost inaudibly at first—I thought he was just enjoying himself—then firmly. The third time he said my name, he flipped us both with one arm and was suddenly on top. The heat of his desire shone in the blackness of his eyes, searing through my clothes, my skin. His desire might have scared him, but it didn't scare me. In that moment, I didn't want him to stop. I'd saved a demon—surely I'd done my good deed for the day!

I watched him struggle to control himself, to resist the pull between us. Willing myself to stay off him, I pressed my spine into the mattress. He sat up partially and closed his eyes.

When they opened again, they were an incredible glacial blue. I was expecting a scolding, more repression. Instead he leaned back on his knees, further out of arm's reach, and unbuttoned his shirt.

"All right, that's it! You've asked for it."

Oh God, was this really it? Was I ready? Were we finally going to… No, we can't! What would it do to him? Before I could finish my thought, his shirt was off and the golden light around him brightened. Mesmerized, I waited for him to kiss me.

The lights flickered and I heard an incredible silence envelop us as he pulled forth his wings. Though I had just seen them on the flight home, they were still a dazzling sight. Each time I saw them, especially now, they brought up a different set of emotions in me, emotions I didn't fully understand, but I was beginning to.

"Much better," he sighed. The air cooled slightly as he fanned them out, and sparkling prisms of light refracted off them. Even in the darkness of my room they were brilliant, luminescent.

"Now, how are we going to do this?" he asked more of himself than of me.

"Do what?" I blinked at him.

He grabbed a spare pillow. Rolling it, he laid it out lengthwise so it would support his head, neck, and mid-back. "That should do." He laid himself down on the pillow, which gave enough support to free up his wings. "This is the next best thing. I promise."

He opened his arms again for me to come back to him. I hesitated, staring at his bare chest. There was no way I could be that close to his skin and maintain any self-control.

"Oh, sorry," he said, pulling the sheet up over himself. "Better?"

I wanted to say "Not really," because there was nothing better about him covering himself up. Instead, I motioned to his wings. "Won't my lying on them hurt?"

"Not at all. You'll see."

The wing I rested on was softer, more plush than I could have imagined, and remarkably flexible, considering they kept him in the air. I leaned my head back into his chest as both his wings enveloped me.

Nothing I'd ever experienced had prepared me for the way they felt. The soft, warm, downy sensation of feathers and the cocoon of stillness felt as though they shielded me from a noise I didn't even know I'd been aware of. Then there was the sensation of light itself, of glowing, as the prismatic filaments reflected themselves. It was like being inside a rainbow of refracted starlight, our own little world. I had a sense of peace, of being so loved.

"This must be what Heaven is like," I muttered into the sheet, millimeters away from his skin.

"You in my arms?" I could hear the smile in his voice. "Yes, it's close."

Warmth rushed through me when he said that, knowing he enjoyed being close to me as much as I did him. "When was the last time you were there?"

"Physically? About nine thousand years ago."

His answer shocked me. "You mean you haven't been back since…?"

491

"Since I fell? No. I can see it in vision, which is a way of going there, but physically entering the gates?" He shook his head. There was longing in his eyes that told me his desire to go home again was at least as strong as his desire to be with me. He was conflicted. Once, he'd given up everything to be with me. I didn't want it to happen again, no matter what that meant for us.

"You'll get back there," I said. "I know you will." He ran his fingers through my hair; the light touch on my back almost burned—in a *good* way.

"You should know what Damiel said tonight, about me killing someone." Tension shot down his arm and he stopped moving, his hand frozen in place on my back. "It wasn't premeditated."

"I know. Damiel has a way of twisting things," I said, feeling his arm relax. "But you are going to tell me everything that happened, right? So I don't have to hear about it from someone else?"

His arm tensed again. "Now?"

"No. Soon, though."

He let out his breath. "I'll tell you everything I can."

"You said I've always seen you even when other people can't, and you've told me how dangerous it is to see these things, but what you haven't told me is why. Why can I see these things in the first place?"

"Hmm," he said, pondering. "I don't know exactly. But I do know there's more to you, Mia Crawford, than meets the eye." Kissing the top of my head, he tightened his arms around me. "I thought about what you said earlier tonight, about how I don't trust myself, and I realized I do. I can't change what I've done, but when you found out, you didn't judge me for it. Your faith in me, your memories... You didn't just help a demon tonight. You helped me, and I owe you for that."

"Hmm. You owe me, do you?"

I propped myself up on his chest, gazing into his eyes. They looked calm and happy, but a little worried. It seemed that, as powerful and fearless as he was, something about me frightened him, exactly the way something about him frightened me.

493

"Yes."

"Will you stay tonight, like this?" I motioned to the wing cover above me, and prisms of light danced along my skin.

"If you want me to."

Grinning, I leaned back into his chest and sighed. "Then we're even."

Acknowledgements

I owe my deep gratitude to the many hands that have guided me along the journey of writing this book.

I'll start off with heartfelt thanks to Elinor Svoboda and Cara Anderson, brilliant screenwriters and true friends, who've read this book almost as many times as I have, and gave me the encouragement I needed every step of the way.

Matthew, I don't know where I'd be without your loving support and unwavering faith in me. Thank you for every late night reading, for listening to my ramblings about these characters, and for every dinner you prepared so I could have time to write. I could not have done this without you. Dad, thanks for being there, for your support, and for teaching me to never give up.

I also want to thank all my friends who read this work and gave me their honest feedback: Anna, Bennett, Blair, Bryony, Hannah, Jen, Jessica, Josh, Laurie, Marilyn, and Steve.

Thanks to Betsy Warland and the VMI Solo program, I was mentored by two amazing authors: Nancy Richler and Alyx Dellamonica. Nancy, thank you for giving me confidence in my work. Alyx, thank you for your lessons, patience, and much-needed advice. I learned so much from both of you.

Shauna , thank you for our fabulous chats. Faye Fitzgerald, thank you for your metaphysical training and for teaching me how psychic gifts work.

A huge thank you also goes to Shilpa Mudiganti, at Inkspell Publishing, for taking a chance on me and making this book a reality. I also owe my gratitude to my editor, Rie Langdon, who polished my words and helped me clean any vestiges of Canadian dialect off these American characters. Thank you, also, to Najila Qamber for designing such a gorgeous cover.

I am grateful for you all.

ABOUT THE AUTHOR:

A Canadian-born author, Lisa Voisin spent her childhood daydreaming and making up stories, but it was her love of reading and writing in her teens that drew her to Young Adult fiction. When she's not writing, you'll find her meditating or hiking in the mountains to counter the side effects of drinking too much coffee. She lives in Vancouver, B.C. with her fiance and their two cats. Find out more at http://www.lisavoisin.com.

Enjoyed This Book?

Try Other

Fantasy and Paranormal

Romance

Novels

From Inkspell Publishing.

Buy Any Book Featured In The Following Pages at

15% Discount From Our Website.

http://www.inkspellpublishing.com

Use The Discount Code

GIFT15 At Checkout!

THE WATCHER

The world is about to be cloaked in darkness.
Only one can stop the night.

Finding a new home has never been so dangerous.

For Lily Drake, slaying vampires is easy...Dating them is the hard part.

LIFE & DEATH OF LILY DRAKE

"IN TERMS OF HEROINES TO ROOT FOR, I DARESAY LILY DRAKE GIVES POOR 'OL SOOKIE A RUN FOR HER MONEY."
- KEALAN PATRICK BURKE, BRAM STOKER AWARD-WINNING AUTHOR OF THE TURTLE BOY AND KIN

T. MICHELLE NELSON

CPSIA information can be obtained at www.ICGtesting.com
Printed in the USA
LVOW121542200313

325240LV00001B/108/P